PERFEKT MATCH

THE ÆRE SAGA: BOOK FOUR

S.T. BENDE

To my family and friend-family—my absolute, hands down,
unconditional perfekt matches.
And to everyone who brings love and ære to our world.
Tusen takk.

"I love you with so much of my heart that none is left
to protest."
–Beatrice, *Much Ado About Nothing*

CHAPTER 1

BRYNN

"FIRE IT UP, *SÖTNOS.* If our estimations are right, soldering red-one to blue-three should get things moving." Henrik clicked a key on his laptop before crossing the man cave that doubled as our laboratory. He stepped into place behind me, leaning over my shoulder to tap the wires with the tip of his pencil. "These two."

Instead of focusing on the object of his direction, my attention pinged to the stubbled cheek scratching lightly against my jaw. And the smell of sunshine filling my head. And the battalion of butterflies running Olympic-level sprints across my heart. Good gods, Henrik Andersson was hot. And by the grace of Freya, Goddess of Love, he was all mine.

Finally.

"Here?" I deliberately aimed the soldering iron a quarter inch too high—in the off position, of course.

"Not quite." Henrik's muscular chest pressed against my back. *Yes.*

"How about here?" I over-corrected, earning a chuckle from my longtime lab partner.

"*Sötnos,* if you need me to show you, just ask." Henrik placed his hand over mine and guided the soldering iron into position. "Here."

His cool breath tickled my earlobe, sending a shiver dancing down my spine and a heatwave rocketing through my hips. A light pressure at my fingertip shot a burst of flame from the iron just as Henrik slid his palm across my stomach. *Double yes.*

It took every ounce of my concentration to *not* melt the entire interior of the closer together, but after an endless moment of extremely tense soldering, the red and blue wires fused. My boyfriend celebrated by running his thumb along the ridges of my upper abs, and murmuring an appraising, "Nicely done."

It took all of two seconds for me to turn off the tool, lay it on the smooth surface of the worktop, and spin around in Henrik's arms. He slid his hand down to palm my butt, upping the heat in my belly to an all-out inferno that rivaled the flame from the iron a moment before.

"Stage two's complete." I reached up to run my fingertips through Henrik's wavy hair. "And since it took us all morning, we probably deserve a break."

"Probably." Henrik dropped his head, running his lips along my jawline and sending a fresh surge of shivers traipsing along my spine.

"Definitely," I agreed. My head tipped back and Henrik moved his mouth to the spot just behind my ear—the one that drove me completely and totally crazy, and made me want to wrap my arms around him and beg him to blur me down the hall and back to—

"Oh. There you are." The flat voice of the Goddess of Love doused my hormones like a fire hose. *Skit. We're caught.* I dropped my hands to Henrik's chest and pushed, attempting to put distance between us. He wrapped one muscular arm around my back and held tight.

"She signed off on our being together over a year ago," he murmured. "We don't have anything to hide."

"Right." I exhaled. "Forgot. Again."

Henrik's chest rumbled with gentle laughter. He planted one more kiss on my neck before shifting me so we could face my boss. "*Hei* Freya. What's up?"

The Goddess of Love—and head of Odin's High Order of the Battle Goddesses, the Valkyries—stood in the doorway. Her waist-length, strawberry-blonde hair hung in uncharacteristic disarray over her slumped shoulders, and her once warm eyes bore their now telltale look of glazed confusion. "I'm...uh..."

"Freya," I said. My friend wrung her fingers together. "How are you feeling?"

"Fine." Freya raised her chin and pulled her shoulders back. "I'm just fine."

"Okay." I kept my voice soft. Henrik squeezed my shoulder, and I angled my gaze to look up at him. When he tilted his head toward the hall, I understood.

Get Freya de-stressed. She's not herself. Again.

It was a message we exchanged daily. Sometimes twice.

"We just finished up in here, and we're heading downstairs for tea." I offered a too-bright smile. "Want to come? I think Mia's meemaw sent her more cookies yesterday. The red velvet kind."

"What is it with those people and red velvet?" Henrik muttered. I threw a swift elbow to his ribcage.

"Freya likes the red velvet," I hissed.

"My snickerdoodles are better. Just saying."

"So, what do you think?" I spoke over my boyfriend. "Join us for tea?"

"Oh. I suppose…" Freya's gaze swept the room. She lingered over the closer, still smoking lightly on the countertop. "What's that?"

Henrik shot me a worried glance. "It's the closer—the portal-sealing device we've been working on all month. We talked about it over breakfast. Remember?"

The corners of Freya's mouth turned down. "No. I don't." My breath caught in my chest as Freya's bottom lip quivered lightly. "I can't remember much anymore."

Oh, gods. If the toughest *flicka* I knew was crying, this day was definitely going downhill.

"Hey, it's okay." I crossed the room in hurried strides, and clasped Freya's hands in my own. "You're doing great. Let's just get that cup of tea. Maybe Elsa can come over and spend some time with us. Watch a movie, maybe check in on you to see how—"

Freya ripped her hands from mine. "I do not want

another healing." Her eyes shot silent daggers. "I just want my life back."

"We all want that for you." Henrik stepped forward to place his hand on my lower back. "And we're all here to help you. Brynn more than anyone. You know that."

The anger in Freya's eyes dimmed a notch before snuffing out. Mortification pooled in its place. "Sorry," she whispered.

"It's all right." What else could I say? Freya had been...*off* since we'd rescued her from Helheim more than a year ago. She never spoke openly about what she'd endured during her time as Hel's prisoner, but it was painfully obvious that whatever she'd been through had been harrowing at best.

I raked my bottom lip between my teeth and met Henrik's gaze. *Help.*

"Okay, ladies, follow me to the kitchen. Meemaw's cookies aside, Mia was baking me some 'thanks for being such a great math tutor' cupcakes. They should be ready now." He nudged Freya with a playful elbow and she turned to wander down the hallway.

Henrik wrapped his large hand around mine, tugging me gently out of the lab. I followed him into the hall and down the stairs, studying Freya's downtrodden shuffle for any hint of her once-confident gait.

Nothing.

"Henrik," I murmured as we hit the bottom of the stairs. "She's not getting better. We knew it would be rough after she came back from Helheim, but I thought between taking the spring off to focus on healing, and slowly easing back into her high commander duties, that maybe…"

"She just needs time."

"It's been over a year, and it's starting to affect more than just Asgard. You've seen the uprising of hate crimes on Midgard—and the string of civil uprisings on Vanaheim. Fear's taking over the realms. And since fear is the absence of love, it's pretty clear Freya's energy isn't reaching its target audience."

Or anyone.

Henrik rubbed the back of my hand with his thumb. "That's why Odin appointed Nanna as interim love goddess, and ordered Freya to move in here—to give her time."

Nanna was our Goddess of Warmth, and our friend Forse's mom. Her heart was so full of love and kindness, she was the logical choice to hold the realms while Freya was out of commission. But after months of living with us—and undergoing twice-daily healings with Elsa—Freya still wasn't fully herself. Elsa couldn't even pin down a diagnosis. Whatever ailed our friend, it had never been treated in the history of Asgard.

And occasionally, like today, Freya regressed. Big time.

"What if time's not enough? What if…" I dropped my voice to a whisper. "What if she never gets better?"

Henrik's anxious eyes betrayed his concern, but he pulled me to his chest and cradled my head in his hand. "We'll figure it out, *sötnos*. We always do."

He wasn't being arrogant. In the years we'd spent as

bodyguards for our friend Tyr, there hadn't been a problem we couldn't tase, engineer, or coerce into submission. Henrik and I were so finely attuned as both warriors and lab partners, that very little got past us. We were the *perfekt* problem-solving force, and we were steely in our determination to protect everything —and everyone—we loved.

Failure had never been a part of our vocabulary. And failing Freya was most definitely not an option. The realms needed love to survive. And our unconventional family needed Love, period. We weren't complete without her. For this reason alone, we *would* find a way to bring Freya back, both to the realms and to our family.

Even if we had no idea how.

"Say it, Mia." Henrik's deep tenor rang through the kitchen. "It doesn't count if you don't say it."

"Seriously? The cupcakes aren't enough?" Our adorably sweet mortal raked slender fingers through her glossy brown waves.

"Nope." Henrik leaned back in his chair with a grin. "I'm waiting."

"Fine." Mia huffed a long-suffering sigh before reading from the paper Henrik slid across the table. "Henrik Andersson, you are the greatest math tutor in the history of ever. I am so lucky to have been graced with your wisdom, genius, and—you're kidding, right?"

"Say it, Ahlström," Henrik warned. "Or you're on your own next semester. And junior year math is extraordinarily difficult…or so I hear."

"Ugh. Okay." Mia picked up the paper. "I am so lucky to have been graced with your wisdom, genius, and…and penultimate hotness. There. Are you happy?"

Henrik sank his teeth into a heavily iced cupcake. "Very," he mumbled through a mouth full of red velvet crumbs.

A bubble of laughter burst from my throat. "Henrik! You're so mean!"

"No, I'm not. I'm just making sure due appreciation is paid to the awesomeness that is me." He finished the cupcake in a second bite, and treated me to an icing-lipped grin. Elsa and Forse chuckled as they settled into their chairs, and even Freya gave a small smile.

Tyr carried the tea kettle from the stove with a hearty eye roll. He poured hot water into our waiting cups, placed the kettle on a trivet, and dropped his six-and-a-half-foot frame into the chair next to Mia's. "You'll be more awesome when you finish the closer. How's it coming?"

"It's coming. We're a few days away from being ready to test it, but once we hit beta phase it should be pretty smooth sailing." Henrik snatched another cupcake from the platter in the center of the table while I added honey to my tea.

"I don't know why we couldn't have coffee with our cupcakes." I shot Elsa a pointed look.

"Because, Brynn." Her sky blue eyes danced with

amusement as she raised her mug. "We are *all* working on purifying our physical beings."

"Then why are we eating cupcakes?" I challenged.

"Whoa!" Henrik raised his hands. "Just because Elsa cut off your happy juice, don't take away mine."

"I didn't cut her off." Elsa shook her head, sending her golden curls tumbling over one shoulder. "I just *suggested* that Brynn enjoy her morning coffee—or three—and switch to tea after that."

I added another shot of honey to the lavender tea that *so* did not taste as good as the double espresso Henrik snuck into the lab for me earlier, and selected a cupcake from the pile. "Just don't take away the morning coffee, and we'll get through."

Somehow.

Elsa's delicate laugh filled the kitchen. She reached over to slip her fingers through Forse's, her engagement diamond sparkling beneath the lights. "Morning coffee is now, and ever shall be, permitted."

"Thank gods," Tyr muttered.

I shared a pained look with the God of War. The coffee thing was part of an overall household purification. In her ongoing quest to heal Freya, Elsa had decided to reduce the availability of anxiety-inducing stimulants—like caffeine—from our Arcata cabin, and introduce calming agents some of us could have done without. Since Freya had come to stay, we'd been subjected to aromatherapy (green mandarin made Henrik crazy hyper, but doubly productive), a gluten-free diet that gave me and Tyr level-seven cookie withdrawals and level-ten irritation fits, the vegan diet that had ended the day Henrik threatened to permanently move back to Asgard, and floral essences (upping Mia's elm intake right before exams made *all* of our lives easier). Nothing had fixed Freya's condition, but we'd keep trying until something stuck.

And if we all went crazy in the process, well, it was a price we'd have to pay. The cosmos needed Freya. Desperately.

"How were your exams, Mia?" Forse wrapped the hand not holding Elsa's around his mug. He studied our mortal from across the table. "Nothing too taxing for you, I presume?"

"My math tests were fine, but creative writing was a nightmare." Mia shuddered. "Thank God it was my last non-core course."

"You have a tremendously creative spirit, Mia," Elsa said gently. "Why was that subject difficult for you?"

"It wasn't difficult for her," I said. "She aced it. She just doesn't believe it should affect her GPA."

"A professor's opinion shouldn't impact a student's grade. Math is either right or wrong. Writing is...well, it's too subjective to be quantifiable." Mia frowned at her cupcake.

"Please. Professor Carter loved you." I rolled my eyes. Mia had gotten an A on every paper she'd turned in.

"Either way, we're done with exams. Now we can enjoy summer vacation." Mia took a delicate bite of her cupcake.

"Although apparently by 'enjoy summer vacation,' you mean spend six hours a day studying Unifying with my sister and another four working on the closer with Brynn and Henrik." Tyr shook his head. "You know you *can* take a break. Don't you, *prinsessa*?"

"Can *you* take a break?" Mia countered.

"Depends on what kind of break you have in mind." Tyr lowered his head to whisper something in Mia's ear. Her cheeks pinked.

"Stop it." She giggled.

"You're not going to spend six hours a day with Elsa. She and Forse are busy with wedding prep." I tried to ignore the way Tyr's hand moved possessively behind Mia's chair. He had a thing for his girlfriend's butt, big-time. Instead, I turned my attention to Elsa. "Speaking of, the big day's only two months away, and you still haven't given me any jobs. Come on, you have to need something."

"We're keeping things really simple," Elsa repeated for the umpteenth time. "Just a quiet ceremony with immediate family and you guys. No pageantry. No frills."

"In other words, no fun." The corners of Mia's mouth turned down. She objected to Forse and Elsa's low-key celebration every bit as much as I did. "Y'all have to need us to do *something*. Flowers? Decorations? Will you *please* let me bake a cake?"

"Hey, I called dibs on the cake." Henrik stared Mia down.

"See? That's why we're keeping it simple." Forse

chuckled. "We want to be married. Everything else is just details."

"The details are the fun part!" Mia threw her hands in the air. "Mama would have *words* with the two of you if she knew you weren't letting us throw you a shower."

"I know. And I appreciate you wanting to make a fuss. But like Forse said, we just want to be married." Elsa sounded wistful, and I shot a quick glance at Freya to see if she'd picked up on the undertone. Since the love goddess was staring blankly out the kitchen window, I figured we were good.

When Forse had proposed to Elsa, they'd hoped to be married right away. But Freya's illness, Forse's mom taking on Freya's role, and a string of unseasonable storms that bore an uncanny resemblance to the prophesied markers of Ragnarok—the Norse end of days—had set things back. After a while, Elsa and Forse decided to forego the traditional Asgardian pageantry in favor of a quiet ceremony here on Midgard. Their genuine desire to start their life together was beyond sweet.

Their refusal to let us make a big deal out of this, however, was *so not cool.*

"We'll sneak something fun in," I vowed. I mouthed the words *"bachelorette party"* to Mia, who nodded enthusiastically.

"*Yes,*" she mouthed back.

"*No,*" Elsa mouthed from my side.

I burst into laughter.

Henrik ignored us all. "When does your brother get here, Mia? Saturday?" He and Jason had hit it off when they'd realized that teaming up enabled them to crush Tyr at pool. Since then, my boyfriend had looked forward to Jason's summertime visit with green mandarin-level enthusiasm. Our basement rec room would never know what had hit it.

"Yes." Mia beamed. "That gives me two days to bake all his favorite cookies. Want to help?"

"That's right, *prinsessa*." Tyr leaned back in his chair. "Weigh him down with sugar so it's easier for me to destroy him at pool."

I blinked innocently. "Isn't he, like, his fraternity's best pool player, um, ever?"

The vein in Tyr's jaw bulged. Gods, he was so easy to rile.

Elsa giggled softly. Tyr's bulge morphed into an angry pulse, and Elsa quickly schooled her face into one of studied calm. "I heard they just gave Jason a special award," she offered. "All-time greatest pool master."

"Pool master?" Henrik snorted beside me. I elbowed him in the ribs. "Uh, right! Yes, he is the official pool master. Mia showed me the e-mail."

Mia's violet–blue eyes executed a perfect roll. "You guys."

"Oh, it's on," Tyr growled. "This weekend. Tournament of champions. Me. Jason. Whichever of you lot think you can keep up."

"No cheating," Forse warned Tyr. "I remember what happened last time."

"I never cheat." Tyr drew his shoulders back.

"So that wasn't you I saw blur around the table last summer? You know, right before you sank the winning shot?" The God of Justice raised one eyebrow.

"Oh. That. Well, Elsa was going to fall. And she was still frail from being trapped with Runa so—"

"I was never frail," Elsa objected.

"Else." I frowned. We all knew that was a lie.

"I was sore, yes. Limping, sure. But never frail." She raised her chin in defiance.

Tyr stared at his sister, no doubt doing that weird head-communication thing Odin had gifted them with. After a seemingly intense moment, and what must have been one Helheim of a silent apology, Elsa shrugged. "Fine. I forgive you."

"Right. Hey, speaking of Runa, remember Jason still doesn't know anything about all of this." Mia waved her hands in front of her, gesturing to the six Norse gods sitting around the table. "He thinks you're Swedish exchange students and that I just spend some weekends here, so remember (a) Brynn and I live in town, (b) none of you are immortal battle deities or justice deities or love deities"—Freya finally looked up, the flicker of recognition earning her a smile from Mia —"or bodyguards or any of it, okay? I don't want to blow your cover. And I don't want to freak him out."

"Your brother won't know a thing." Freya spoke for

the first time since we'd gathered at the table. "We've kept this secret for a long time."

Mia smiled gratefully. "I'm so happy you're *finally* going to get to meet him, Freya." Her eyes shone with the enthusiasm she always embodied when she talked about her family. "He's smart, kind, and funny, and he's *really* looking forward to spending two weeks with us. Senior exams wiped him out, and he's ready to blow off some steam."

"And nobody blows off steam like a house full of Asgardians, some of whom have been stuck going through Midgard's version of torture this semester—bodyguarding a mortal who chose organic chemistry for her sophomore science requirement." I finished off my cupcake with a decisive chomp.

"And waiting for their girlfriend to stop stressing over exams so she could *relax* already." Tyr gave Mia a lingering look. Her cheeks flushed.

"And who are *finally* just a few weeks away from marrying the love of their existence." Elsa batted her crystal blue eyes at her fiancé.

"Finally." Forse kissed the top of Elsa's head. She nestled into his chest with a contented sigh.

"So, it's agreed. Mum's the word about all of this." Mia gestured around the table again. "We're just going to rest, and relax, and have the best start of the summer ever. I can't wait for my brother to get here." Mia turned to Freya and shot her a brilliant smile. "He's the best. Oh, Freya. You're going to love him!"

CHAPTER 2

FREYA

LOVE WAS NOT WHAT I felt for Mia's brother. *Disdain. Disgust. Intense dislike.* But definitely not *love.*

When Tyr got serious about our mortal, my duty as Goddess of Love required I thoroughly vet her family. Most members had demonstrated exemplary moral character and the appropriate level of respect for humanity, but Jason had attempted to seduce the valkyrie I'd sent to assess his character. Rayn Vindahl was one of my top spies—one who was smart enough not to breach protocol by dallying with a subject. And when she'd rejected Jason's advances, she found herself abandoned in a bar at midnight. As a member of my elite fighting team, she'd ably deflected the aggressive advances of drunken males. But had she been the mortal she'd pretended to be, she would have been horribly compromised…all because Jason Ahlström was far from the angel his sister believed him to be.

The realms would darken Mia enough. I'd never tell her the truth.

My head nestled deeper into my pillows as I studied the hail now pelting my bedroom window. A new storm had just kicked in, the latest in a series of unusual weather patterns wreaking havoc on our coastal California town. The winter's snowfalls were clear markers of Ragnarok—the not-so-mythological end of days. According to Asgardian prophesies, a string of winters coupled with cosmos-wide unrest would culminate in the death of Forse's dad—Asgard's God of Light—and trigger the sequence of Ragnarok. The fact that Balder's wife, Nanna, had abandoned her position as Goddess of Warmth to cover my job made me sick. All of Nanna's attention should have been focused on surrounding her husband with love, compassion, and hope—the positive energies that deflected the fear, hatred, and anger that would be the light god's undoing. But Balder was more exposed than ever.

All because of me.

I'd have given anything to god up—to seize control of my own mind the way I'd commanded my legion of valkyries since the day I'd been gifted that honor. But I couldn't claw my way out of whatever darkness Hel had created in me. The deep, aching void that drained joy from my heart and left my head in a near-constant fog would not be eradicated by crystals or flower essences or meditation or prayer or, bless, the absence of caffeine. I'd explained this to Elsa—and quietly advised Henrik sneak espresso to Brynn in the interim —but our High Healer couldn't accept what *was*.

I was sick. Maybe terminally so. And nothing we'd tried was helping.

Tap. Tap. Tap.

The light rapping pulled me from the bleak landscape of my thoughts. My gaze shifted from the window to the door.

"Freya?" Brynn's tentative call from the other side crushed my heart. Her fear reminded me of exactly how weak I was. How was I supposed to pull myself together if everyone kept acting as if I was already half dead?

"Freya?" Brynn hemmed. "You in there?"

"*Ja.* Come in."

I tried not to break down at the way Brynn carefully opened the door and sidestepped into my room, as if one wrong move would terrorize me. The strong-willed captain had been one of my favorite charges since the day she arrived at the valkyrie compound, shiny-eyed and ready to conquer the cosmos. I'd foreseen the brightness of her star when we were still in school, but when she submitted herself to the order I knew that Brynn would rule the realms one day. Possibly in my place.

"How are you feeling?" she hedged.

"I'm okay. Cupcakes were fun." I injected as much cheer as I could into the words, but they still sounded flat. My cool tone was foreign to me, even after all these months. When had I stopped being warm, and compassionate, and…loving? The wall between me and my friends grew thicker by the day.

I hated it.

"Yeah…" Brynn's teeth raked her bottom lip. This was more than just nerves—something was wrong.

"What's going on?"

"Well, I don't want to worry you, but…" Brynn wrung her fingers together.

"Spit it out, valkyrie."

Brynn sucked in a deep breath before blurting, "Frigga just called, and she's super freaked out. She made all the beings in the realms take an oath not to hurt Balder, thinking that would just be an additional layer of security. But once word got out, the council lifted its protections and the guards Odin had protecting Balder stepped down, and everyone in Asgard's celebrating by taking their best shot. *At Balder.*"

I leapt from my bed so quickly, the grey–blue walls spun. Brynn blurred to my side, her steady hands holding me upright. "We have to stop them. An oath's not going to keep Balder alive. And it's not going to stop Ragnarok."

"I know." Brynn's fingers tightened around my shoulders. "Tyr's on his way to catch the Bifrost—he's going alone. He asked Elsa to take Forse on a hike for a few hours—distract him while she sends her Unifying energy to Asgard. He's afraid of what Forse might do if he sees…well, what's going on. Henrik's staying here to run communications. I figured you'd want to know."

"Know?" I grabbed my jacket from my closet, and shoved my arms through the holes as I barreled down the hall. "I'm going with him."

"That's a bad idea." Footsteps pounded behind me on the stairs. "You need your rest."

"I do nothing but rest." I flung the front door open. Tiny balls of ice pelted my face as I charged toward the clearing between Tyr's cabin and Elsa's. "Stay here and look after Mia. Let Elsa know where I am when you make contact with her. And if Forse finds out…tell him I'm doing everything in my power to help his dad."

"Freya! Please!" Brynn cried.

I ignored her, closing the distance between me and the Bifrost site in a display of sheer Asgardian speed.

Tyr's brow furrowed as he registered my sudden appearance. "Freya?"

"I'm coming with you." My tone left no room for argument.

"But—"

"No buts, War. Heimdall!" I raised my head to the sky. "Bifrost!"

The immediate burst of wind and flash of light caught me off guard. Tyr reached out as I stumbled, pulling me against his chest. I steadied myself before taking a step back.

"You should be resting," he said. "Doing this together is not a good idea."

"Then don't come." I moved out of the hailstorm, entering the rainbow with crossed arms. My heart tripped over the chill in my voice, but I didn't bother lamenting the goddess I'd become post-Helheim. It wouldn't do me any good.

And it sure as *skit* wouldn't help us save Balder.

"Fine." Tyr sighed. "Brynn, keep my girl safe. Tell her I'll help her with the baking when I get home."

"Not sure that's a prize in her world." Brynn rubbed her arms against the cold. "Just protect Balder—stop this madness, reinstitute the guards, Helheim, bring him here—we'll take care of him. Do what you have to do to keep him safe."

Tyr and I exchanged a loaded look. We understood what was at stake. The God of Light wasn't just the last thing standing between us and Ragnarok; he was also Forse's dad. If Balder fell, Forse would be devastated. Nanna would be heartbroken. Their souls would be shattered beyond repair, and the fabric of our unconventional little family would be forever altered.

We couldn't let that happen.

Tyr gripped my hand and looked to the sky. "To Asgard," he ordered.

And just like that we were sucked into the sky, pushed through Midgard's atmosphere, and rocketed toward the realm of the gods.

I hope we're not too late.

"Tyr, thank gods you have arrived. Odin is away managing a conflict with the fire giants, and I did not know where to turn." Frigga, Odin's wife and the queen of Asgard, threw herself at my friend. Her petite frame trembled in his sturdy arms, their faces a masterpiece of grief and worry, set against the pristine backdrop of Asgard's central lake and silver willow tree. Frigga's handmaiden, Yande, stood off to the side.

"I came as soon as I heard." Tyr tapped Frigga's shaking shoulders. Mia had brought out a softer side of War, but his stiff back and wide eyes made it clear he still wasn't comfortable around female tears. Bless.

"Oh, Tyr. I did everything I could to talk them out of this, but they would not listen to me. They are in the meadow adjacent to the dark forest, whipped up into a frenzy. They must be under a spell to be so intent on playing a game that can only end in…in…" Frigga's voice cracked, and she burst into a fresh wave of tears. She threw her head back and wailed at the heavy grey clouds. "Nanna will never forgive me!"

"Where is Nanna?" I asked.

Frigga lifted her head from Tyr's chest. His cream-colored Henley bore two tear-laden patches. *Oh, Frigga.*

"Freya." Frigga wiped the moisture from her eyes. "You should not be here. You need to rest, regain your strength."

Frigga, too? "I'm fine." The words were aural ice. "Does Nanna know what's happening?"

"No." Frigga sniffled. "Before he left, Odin made it clear that she was not to be disturbed."

"While a group of crazy gods try to kill her husband?" It took all of my self-control not to stamp my foot in the flower-dotted grass. "Is Odin insane?"

"Freya," Frigga chastised. "You must not speak against our ruler."

I'd spoken against our ruler plenty of times; I'd called him out every time one of Odin's decisions put my valkyries at undue risk. Balder may not have been under my charge, but he was my friend's father, and Asgard's Ragnarok trigger. If somebody needed to say harsh words to save our realm, I had no problem being the whistleblower.

"Nanna must be informed," I reiterated. "Immediately."

"Freya's right." Tyr offered a nod of solidarity. Also, of sanity. "Nanna needs to know what's going on. The whole of Asgard is aware of the consequences inherent in putting Balder at risk. If its members are knowingly endangering his life, they cannot be acting of their own volition—dark magic must be at play. And the strongest available countermeasure to darkness is our Goddess of Warmth. Contact Nanna at once."

"That is not possible." Frigga shook her head. "She is in Odin's personal meditation chamber, attempting to rectify a pressing matter."

"What? What could she be doing that is more important than saving her husband's *förbaskat* life?" Tyr growled.

Frigga's eyes darted to me, then back to Tyr. "A situation in Jotunheim requires the attention of the acting Goddess of Love."

Silence descended on the three of us, Frigga's unspoken words a dagger in my gut. Nanna was doing my job when her realm—and her husband—needed her. Whatever happened to Balder fell squarely on me.

Skit.

I drew my shoulders back and forced my gut to still. Calling up a strength I hadn't felt in a long time, I narrowed my eyes and barked my orders. "Go to Nanna and tell her the jotuns can fend for themselves. Tyr, you and I will put a stop to this nonsense. Now."

"Freya, I already attempted to—"

"I said *now*, Frigga." Then, because Frigga was my queen, and not a valkyrie under my command, I added, "Sorry. Please."

"Yande, inform Nanna she is to report to me at once," Frigga instructed. With a sharp nod, the handmaiden scurried back to the castle. When she'd gone, Frigga turned her attention back to me. "I will return to the gathering with you. Perhaps the three of us will have more power than I alone."

I didn't wait for her to finish before turning on one heel and charging across the meadow. When I didn't hear footsteps behind me, I shouted over my shoulder, "War! Move it!"

Tyr instantly appeared beside me. Frigga must have been somewhere behind him. We raced away from the pond, charging past the willow tree and heading for the thick cluster of evergreens that marked the portion of the woods we referred to as the dark forest. Nothing good ever happened there—it was the lone section of Asgard within which our enemies managed to open portals, and it was the site of more Asgardian casualties than any other in the realm. My feet pounded damp dirt as I lowered my head and picked up speed. How had Odin left the realm without knowing dark magic was afoot? Even if the rest of Asgard had been spelled, our leader—and those under his immediate command —should have been impervious. Odin's guards were more vigilant than any other in the corps, and he had a full-time energy master assigned to his detail, specifically tasked with deflecting dark entities—including spells. Unless Michalio had been compromised, there was no way that anyone could get past—

"Stop," Tyr commanded. He planted his feet in the mossy earth, crouching behind a pine tree. Frigga blurred right past us, apparently too intent on reaching Balder to process Tyr's order.

I dropped into a ready position beside him. "What is it?"

"The gathering is at my ten o'clock, but look fifty meters into the forest, at your one-thirty. What do you see?"

I narrowed my eyes and drew on my Asgardian sight. Sure enough, a cloaked figure in the exact location Tyr specified drew a hood over his head. His back was to me, and he was blurring between the trees too quickly for me to lock in on his face, but his shifty movements and heavy energy reeked of darkness. Whatever he was up to, it wasn't good.

But we had bigger problems to deal with than a creepy lurker. Stopping our people from killing Forse's dad was priority one.

Especially since Thor's wife, Sif, was about to hurtle a massive stone at the god whose death could mean the end of us all.

"Sif!" My hand flew to my face. "What is she doing?"

Tyr shifted his gaze to where a cluster of Asgardians circled the God of Light. Balder's arms were outstretched, and his warm voice carried across the meadow.

"Come now, Sif," Balder said kindly. "You know what my mother said. She had every being in the realm take an oath to protect me. Even the Norns cannot challenge that."

A sharp inhale burned my chest as Balder gestured for Sif to proceed. She unleashed the stone and it barreled at Balder, veering off course at the last possible second. Sif's golden hair tumbled over her shoulder as she threw her head back in laughter. The joyful sound echoed off the trunks of the evergreens, bouncing back at us in delighted peals.

"What the Helheim is wrong with them?" Tyr narrowed his eyes. "Move it, Freya. We have to stop this before somebody—"

"*Skit*," I swore. Balder's brother stepped forward, a bow and arrow in his hands. Hod was lining up to take his shot.

"*Förbaskat*," Tyr chimed in. His eyes met mine for one horrified moment, and we both took off, charging like twin raging bulls. Blood pulsed so heavily in my ears I was barely able to discern Hod's declaration as he drew back his bow.

"It's only mistletoe."

The world shifted into slow motion. Frigga launched herself forward, her hair fanning out as she tried to stop the arrow. "No!" she cried. "Wait! Do not shoot!"

The words were high-pitched shrieks, but the pounding of my heart dulled their terror. Fear coursed through my veins, the *whoosh* of adrenaline filling my ears so the cries of the onlookers were almost completely muted as the arrow left Hod's bow, soared toward Balder, and pierced his left wrist. *Oh, gods. No!* Hod's face slackened, his once joyful grin dropping into a mask of horror while his brother clutched his arm in confusion.

"But Mother said…" Balder withdrew the shaft, his hand shaking as red liquid dripped down to his palm.

Balder's blood undid me. My toe caught on a rock, and I face-planted into a bed of mossy dirt. The taste of copper filled my mouth, but I didn't have time to assess my own injuries. With a spit, I pushed myself up to my knees. Tyr was already back at my side, his expression unreadable.

"You okay?" He pulled me to my feet.

"Let's move. It might not be too late to save—"

"It is." His voice cracked. "Balder has fallen."

Moisture filled my eyes, and I blinked hard as Balder dropped to his knees. Frigga descended with him. A thick, red film covered them both, dripping from their bodies to coat the green tapestry of the meadow at their feet.

We were too late.

My heart seized, and I gripped Tyr's forearms for support. He steadied me as Hod's voice carried across the air. "I—I had no idea," he stammered. "That man gave me the arrow…"

Creepy lurker.

Sure enough, when I managed to raise my head, Hod pointed to the spot in the forest where the cloaked figure had stood. He was gone now; no trace of his traitorous form lingered in the dark forest.

Frigga wailed. My attention returned to the circle of gods, some of whom had dropped to their knees. "No!"

The color drained from Balder's once joyful face. As his body withered in Frigga's arms, he drew his final breath. The gods wept.

"Find the perp," I barked. Action was the only thing that might keep me from falling apart. I ran into the dark forest, scanning the trees for the monster who had caused this. He was going to pay with his life.

"Freya, wait." Fear colored Tyr's voice. "I can't lose you again!"

But I couldn't stop moving. I darted from tree to tree, scanning the woods for any sight of the hooded demon who had murdered Balder—who'd signed the death warrant for us all.

He was nowhere to be seen. He must have fled the forest right after…after…*oh, gods.*

"Freya." Tyr finally caught up to me. He wrapped

me in his thick arms, pulling me so close I struggled to breathe.

"Too tight," I gasped. Tyr's grip loosened, and as I sucked in air he gently pulled my head to his chest.

"It's going to be okay," he offered. But I knew the words were a lie. We hadn't been fast enough. We hadn't stopped the worst from happening.

And it was all my fault.

Forse's dad was gone. And unless Frigga's hand-maiden had the speed of a caffeinated *älva*, Nanna didn't know any of this was happening. She was locked in some meditation room, covering for me because I couldn't get it together enough to do my own job. Her husband—my friend's father—was dead because of me. Ragnarok was upon us because of me. We were all going to die *because of me*.

A darkness filled my head, thicker and more cloying than any I'd known before. The weight was unbearable, and for the first time since I'd returned from Helheim, I gave in to the overwhelming feelings of solitude and despair. They overtook my consciousness, choking out the light as I folded over in Tyr's arms. And with two words, I allowed myself to escape.

"I'm sorry."

I closed my eyes, and surrendered.

CHAPTER 3

THEY MADE ME DELIVER the news to Nanna. Freya was in no state—she'd been in and out of what Elsa deemed a "self-preservation coma" since her return from Asgard. Her spirit kept shutting her body down to keep it from experiencing an overload of grief.

Forse, obviously, couldn't be the one to do it—he'd dropped to his knees when Tyr had delivered the news, and wept onto Elsa's chest with a desolation I'd never seen in the normally even-keeled justice god. Elsa had held him until his tears ran dry before helping him to his feet and gently guiding him away from the Arcata cabin. He'd sequestered himself within Elsa's cottage to mourn privately, and refused to see anyone since.

Tyr had returned to Asgard, where he'd locked himself in the cabinet room with the rest of Odin's Council, and began strategizing for the now-imminent unleashing of Ragnarok. Mia, as a mortal, still couldn't legally enter the realm, so she'd busied herself making comfort food for Elsa to deliver to Forse.

Which left me and Henrik to rock-paper-scissors it out to determine who got the mother of all bad jobs.

"Paper covers rock." Henrik gently placed his open hand over my fisted one. "Sorry, Brynnie."

I swore. Loudly. How had I forgotten Henrik *always* chose paper? Must have been the eleventy billion other things on my mind…like my comatose friend, my grieving friend, and my friend who was, literally, on a warpath as we spoke.

Awesome.

"I'll go if you want me to," Henrik offered. "You can stay here and protect Mia."

"No, I'll do it." I sighed. "Mia needs some semblance of normalcy right now, and you can cook together. I'd be of no use—I'm this close to losing it."

Henrik closed his hand around mine and pulled me to him. "I know you are, *sötnos*. How can I help?"

"I don't know." I closed my eyes, breathing in the scent of sunshine emanating from Henrik's chest. "When Tyr gets back, he'll have some kind of ballpark on our enemies' trajectories. If doomsday's not imminent, maybe we can go on one last date before all Helheim breaks loose."

My gut churned, and I immediately relegated the thought to the banished bin. *Don't go there. Do not think about Ragnarok, and the end of days, and the fact that you and Henrik are in all likelihood about to die. Be like Elsa and think about the now. The moment. The mind-blowingly amazing date Henrik will take you on. Right after you go to Asgard and tell Nanna that...that her husband's dead.*

"I'll do you one better than that," Henrik offered. "How about you and I take a mini break? A few days, just you and me, away from all the crazy before the crazy..."

"Deal." I stood on tiptoes to kiss Henrik's stubbly chin. "Walk me to the Bifrost?"

My boyfriend angled his head down so his lips brushed against mine when he murmured, "Always."

Three toe-curling minutes later, I stood in my warmest jacket at the drop site. Balder's death had brought on another summertime sleet storm. The mortals *had* to be noticing this. They could be unobservant to things they didn't want to recognize, but nobody was this dense. *Right?*

"Love you," I called to Henrik as I stepped into the blinding rainbow bridge.

"*Jeg elsker deg.*" He waved morosely. "See you in a few."

"See you." I clutched my stomach as the Bifrost sucked me upward, hurtled me across the cosmos, and deposited me in a nauseous heap entirely too close to the dark forest for my liking. *Wait. The dark forest is where...oh gods.* A coppery tang filled my nose, and I stumbled backward, stopping at the squelch of gooey liquid beneath my boot. *Oh, oh gods. Please don't let me be at...*

Mia's cupcake threatened to make an unsightly return as I registered the thick pool of red coating the mossy earth at my feet. Balder had only been gone for a few minutes; it made sense that his blood would still be fresh. But why in the name of Odin would Heimdall have dropped the Bifrost into the spot where Light had died? What could possibly make him be so cruel as to—

"Brynn?" Nanna's soft voice came from behind my shoulder. "Frigga's handmaiden told me to come to the meadow, but she wouldn't give a reason. What's going on?"

That was why. Because Heimdall knew Nanna was on her way, and he wanted someone there to support her when she stumbled onto the spot where her husband had just been murdered.

Sorry, Heimdall. My bad.

I pushed my nausea down and hastened to Forse's mom. "Oh, Nanna." I hurriedly slung my arm around her shoulders and steered her away from the clearing. Odin had cultivated a rose garden not far from here. We would talk amidst beauty, not horror. She deserved that much.

"Brynn?" Worry lined Nanna's brow. "Why aren't you saying anything? And why was Yande crying?"

"Because something has happened," I said honestly. "Come with me. I have something to tell you."

All things considered, Nanna took the news better than I'd expected. She wept. And screamed. And she showed a lot more anger toward Hod than I'd imagined the Goddess of Warmth would be capable of exhibiting, especially after I explained Hod was probably under the influence of dark magic. But when she calmed down, her primary concern was for her sons. I assured her we were taking good care of Forse—omitting the tiny detail about him locking himself away and refusing to talk to any of us—and I promised we'd send him to see her once he was fit for travel. Then I escorted her to her other son Nils's house. The two of them could grieve together. And, Odin willing, offer one another a modicum of comfort.

The entire trip took less than two hours, and I returned to the Arcata compound just as Mia was serving a *delicious*-smelling roast to a party of one. Henrik was the sole god in his usual seat at the kitchen table.

"Comfort food," Mia insisted as she placed a platter of au gratins on a trivet. "Brynn, pull up a chair. It's best when it's hot."

She didn't have to ask me twice.

Henrik and I waited until Mia took her seat. We heaped servings onto her plate before turning our attention to the piles of roast, potatoes, and carrots we'd piled onto ours. We ate in silence for a good two minutes, but even after Henrik made a substantial dent in his dinner, his chalk-hued face hadn't regained any of its normal color.

I nudged him with my foot under the table. "You okay, big guy?"

"I've been better," he admitted. "Still no word from Forse?"

"Elsa texted that he's going to stay in for the night," Mia said. "He's not ready to see any of us."

Henrik's curse echoed my thoughts exactly.

"And Tyr?" I ventured. All of Asgard was on edge knowing the council was locked in Odin's war room. That space was reserved for plotting during *extremely* dire circumstances. Like the end of the worlds as we knew them.

Yikes.

"Tyr texted too—I guess he'll be home sometime tomorrow." Mia picked at her meat with her fork.

"Did he give you any updates?" I already knew what the answer would be. Tyr was beyond protective when it came to Mia; he never wanted to scare her.

"He said to pack an emergency bag." Mia raised her chin bravely. "And to be ready to evacuate with Henrik the minute he sent word."

"With Henrik?" I lowered my au gratin-ladled fork, mid-bite. "What about me? I'm supposed to be your bodyguard."

"You were in Asgard when he sent the message," Mia offered.

Oh. Right.

"I packed a bag for you too, *sötnos*," Henrik said. "I got your back."

"Thanks." I resumed shoving potatoes into my mouth. "So, I guess we just wait for news?"

"I guess." Mia raked her bottom lip between her

teeth. She set her utensils diagonally across her mostly full plate and refolded her unsoiled napkin.

"You're done?" If Ragnarok really was upon us, I intended to enjoy every bite of what could well be my last decent meal. Battle rations majorly sucked.

"I can't eat," she admitted. "Oh, Brynn, what if he doesn't come home? What if the fighting begins while he's still in Asgard, and he can't get back to us? What if—"

"Stop right there." Henrik reached across the table to save Mia from shredding her cuticles to bits. "Balder's death marks the *beginning* of Ragnarok, but it could be months before the actual fighting starts. Did Tyr ever explain the prophesy to you? Or are you going off what you learned in your textbooks?"

"Textbook," Mia admitted. "Tyr never wanted to talk much about it."

Henrik and I exchanged a look. That was both good and bad—the humans' books painted a distorted view of a Ragnarok that, for their own peace of mind, we'd pitched to them as already having happened. Odin bless their fears of their own mortality.

According to the texts we'd gifted them—in which we'd kindly pitched Ragnarok as having happened once upon a time—the end-of-days kicked off with the death of Balder and quickly spiraled into a cosmos-wide annihilation during which the realms were demolished and a new world order rose from the ashes. A small handful of minor gods survived the apocalypse, and were tasked with rebuilding Midgard,

Asgard, and everything in between. Our stories were deliberately fuzzy on details. And right then, our order-oriented Ahlström looked like she was about to lose her over-analytical mind. I couldn't blame her. Everything about this was scary.

"Okay, here's the deal." Henrik whipped his fake eyeglasses out of his pocket and pushed them up his nose. He'd worn them a lot when we first got to Arcata and he was trying to blend in with the humans, but now he reserved them for emergencies. Like when Mia was on the verge of an all-out panic attack, and needed instant mood-lightening.

As always, his trick worked like a charm.

"You carry those things all the time?" Mia giggled delicately.

Henrik shrugged, and I squeezed his thigh under the table. He was *the best* at handling Mia. Gods, I loved him.

"Forget everything you've ever read about Ragnarok," he ordered. "The kill count, the survivor list, the destroyed realms doc—all of it."

"There's a document of *destroyed realms*?" Mia's voice reached a whole new octave.

Oops.

"Like I said, forget about it. The true prophecy of Ragnarok is short, and succinct, and tells us very little. It says—" Henrik cleared his throat and made quotation marks in the air with is fingers. Oh, gods, he wasn't going to actually *tell* her the verbatim prophesy, was he? "Ahem. 'With the death of Balder, the powers of darkness will burst from their tethers. Jotunheim shall crack open; a terrible frost shall suffocate all things good.'"

Holy Helheim, Henrik *was* telling her the prophecy. Mia's eyes were wide as saucers, and she'd resumed shredding her cuticles. I nudged Henrik under the table and sent a silent *stop talking, you idiot,* which he either didn't pick up on or chose to ignore.

"'The great beast will attack, the wicked ship sail, and the light of Asgard—'ouch! Why'd you kick me, Brynn?"

"Okay," I interrupted with a beatific smile. "That's enough prophecy quoting."

"What? What happens to the light of Asgard?" Mia's head whipped frantically between Henrik and me. "Who's the great beast? What ship? You can't just stop!"

"We can, and we will," I said, mentally rescinding my praise of Henrik's calming abilities. "Because the truth is that in centuries—millennia, really—of trying to interpret that prophecy, none of us have been able to work out a plausible interpretation. There are infinite variables that create thousands of potential outcomes. The beast could be a fire giant or a frost giant, or some creature we've never encountered. It could be Fenrir or Hymir, or even an Asgardian who turns dark. And our Midgardian followers were Vikings, for Odin's sake. The 'wicked ship' could be a vestige of one of a thousand wrecked vessels...or something one of our dark realm enemies build. We just don't know."

"Yes, but—"

"The one thing we do know," I continued, "is that Balder's death is the call to arms. But a substantial period of time could very well pass between his death and the initial battle. So yes, dark times are ahead, but the best thing we can do until then is support Tyr, try to heal Freya, and enjoy this period of peace, however short or long it may be."

"*Förbaskat.* Freya." Henrik looked down at me with big eyes. Was I going to have to kick him again?

"Freya will be fine," I asserted. She had to be.

"If she's not better by the time the fighting starts, who's going to command the valkyries? Brynnhild was removed from her post—with reason—but did Freya ever appoint a successor?"

"No. Nanna's been handling Love—though I'd imagine she'll need a replacement now too. But Freya's still guiding the valkyries, with Tyr's support." Of course, once Ragnarok went down, War's sole focus would need to be on overarching strategy. He wouldn't have time to oversee Odin's elite female fighting squad. Which meant we'd need another high commander. Where were we going to come up with anyone who had even close to Freya's level of experience? Gods, we were screwed.

No, we're not. Everything's going to be fine, Aksel. Fine. Because..."Freya will just have to be better before the battle begins. We've probably got a few weeks—maybe months. We'll get her well."

"The world's going to end in a few weeks?" Mia's

voice climbed another octave. We were seriously failing to keep her calm.

"Or months," Henrik offered.

"Or never," I corrected. "We could win, you know."

"We could?" Mia asked hopefully.

"Absolutely," I said, stomping on Henrik's foot the second he opened his mouth. He winced, but shot me a look that said, *got it.* Thank gods we were *finally* on the same page.

The truth was, the prophecy *was* clear on how Ragnarok would end. According to the Norns, fire would consume the earth, and darkness would swallow the sky. Nobody god or mortal, would survive.

Nobody.

"We could most definitely win Ragnarok." The lie slipped easily through my too wide smile. "And the best thing you can do to help us is keep holding down the home front with your seriously epic dinners and cookies. And continue working on your Unifying with Elsa."

"Unifying is hard." Mia paled. "What if I don't have it mastered by the time the fighting starts?"

"Just do your best." Henrik shrugged. "Elsa's got the skill down, though she'll be pretty busy healing the wounded—"

Was I going to have to kick him *again*? "What Henrik's *trying* to say," I interrupted, "is that two Unifiers—even one who's only halfway trained up—are better than one Unifier. You'll help as best you're able."

I'd thought my words would pacify Mia, but her

nostrils flared as if I'd lit a fire under her. "I don't do anything *by halves*." She spat the words out, as if they'd left a bad taste in her mouth. "I will learn this. And I will help you. And I will fight at your side and defend our realms with every ability I have, so help me, God."

"That's our girl." Henrik cuffed Mia on the shoulder across the table.

My smile didn't quite reach my eyes. "Absolutely. We've got this. Now eat up, and when we're done, I'll check on Freya."

"She's been asleep since right after breakfast," Mia said anxiously. "Elsa's supposed to come over later on —bring Freya some flower essences, and pick up the roast I made for her and Forse. I offered to drop it off, but I think they need some space."

"I'll call Elsa. Why don't you and Henrik finish that…pie?" I eyed the pastry cloth covering something on the countertop. "What are you working on for Jason?"

"Meemaw's red velvet torte," Henrik said. Of course. Because it was red velvet *everything* when an Ahlström came to visit.

Not that I was complaining.

"Right. You guys bake. Elsa and I will get Freya in fighting shape—er," I amended, when Mia's face paled, "in tip-top condition. Then it's early to bed for everybody."

Because the truth was, we had no idea what tomorrow would bring. And if, Odin forbid, the fighting began while Tyr really was still in Asgard, we needed Mia alert so we had the greatest likelihood of evacuating her to one of our secure locations.

And after that…Odin help us all.

"Hei hei. We're back!" Tyr's voice rang up the stairs with false cheer.

In typical overprotective fashion, he'd insisted on accompanying Mia to the airport to pick up Jason. He hadn't left her side since returning from Asgard, except during the briefing he'd given Henrik, Forse, and me while Mia trained with Elsa. Apparently, things were, in fact, as dire as they seemed. We were to review war drills, increase production of debilitating tech, and prepare for immediate relocation to wherever hostilities broke out, all while avoiding detection by the mortals. It was hardly an ideal time for Mia's brother to visit, but not only would canceling his trip at the last minute have aroused suspicion, but Mia desperately needed a dose of the normalcy her family provided.

And it could well be the last time she ever saw her brother. Alive, at least.

Stop it. Think positive.

"Hello?" Mia called out. "Anybody home?"

"Be right down," Henrik shouted. He turned off the mini blowtorch, and raised his safety goggles so they sat on his forehead. He appraised the closer with a self-satisfied smirk. "This seems like a good place to stop. We'll let the transformer cool, and finish it up tonight."

"Then we can run some tests tomorrow." I grinned at my partner. "Odin help the jotun, or fire giant, or *whatever* that thinks it can open a portal anywhere near this bad boy. They'll be shipped to the nether realm before they know what hits them."

"I hope so, Brynnie." Henrik's brow furrowed. "I know we're putting on a good face for Mia, but you do realize the odds are stacked against us?"

"When aren't they? We've been fighting impossible odds since the day I joined this team. The fact that we're still alive means somebody inside that Norn compound is on our side." My throat tightened at the memory of my sister, a junior Norn who'd died protecting Midgard during Freya's first kidnapping. I liked to think Anja looked out for me from her seat in Valhalla.

"You're right, *sötnos*. Somebody out there *is* on our side." Henrik wrapped his arm around my waist. He removed my goggles, placing them on the table before gently pressing his mouth to mine. His tongue trailed across my lower lip, then delved into my mouth, massaging mine in a dance that sent my blood pooling south. When my lips tingled and my face was thoroughly flushed, Henrik pulled back with a lazy grin. "Come on. Let's grab Jason, head down to the pool table, and kick Tyr's butt. We can resume saving the world after lunch."

"Sounds good." I hung my apron on a peg and traipsed happily from the upstairs lab.

When we passed Freya's doorway, I glanced inside

out of habit. But instead of the sleeping love goddess I'd expected to see, I was treated to a sight I hadn't dared hope for. Not for a few days, at least. "Freya, you're up! Sit tight. Let me get Elsa."

"No need for that." Excitement bubbled in Freya's eyes as she shrugged a cardigan over her V-neck tee. The pale green looked gorgeous against her long strawberry locks, and there was a flush to her cheeks I hadn't seen since she'd first awoken from her semi-coma. "I feel really good."

"You slept all morning," I said. "Maybe you should take it easy today. Read in bed, watch a movie. Henrik and I just watched *Much Ado About Nothing*–super fun. I can grab it and—"

"I said I feel good, Brynn," Freya reiterated. "Better than I have in weeks. Maybe I just needed to power down for a few days. I don't know."

"*Ja*, but you've been pretty out of it." Henrik said from behind me. "I'm with Brynn—we don't want you overtaxing yourself. How about I go get the movie, and we'll bring you up some food so—"

"For Odin's sake, I said I am fine!" Freya exploded. "What I need is for all of you to stop treating me like I'm dying!"

Henrik's chest tightened against my back. My breathing stilled as I took in Freya's balled fists, clenched jaw, and narrowed eyes. It was the first time any of us had spoken the "*D* word" out loud. We couldn't open those gates—we just couldn't. Freya was my friend; my mentor; and more than that, she was the very source of love the worlds depended on to thrive. She *had* to be okay.

For so many reasons.

"Everything okay up there?" Mia's tentative voice echoed up the stairs.

"Everything's great. Here we come." Henrik wrapped his hand around my arm and pulled me from Freya's door. His gaze softened at the end of the hall, where he reached up to wipe my damp cheeks with the pad of his thumb. Freya pushed past us, her shoulder bumping against mine as she stormed down the stairs. I blinked helplessly, then turned imploring eyes to Henrik.

"How do we fix this?" I whispered.

He pulled me to him, cradling my head so my check nestled against his strong chest. "Come here, *sötnos.*"

I soaked in the comfort he offered for a minute longer than necessary before extracting myself. With a determined sniffle, I drew my shoulders back and wiped my eyes on my sleeve. "Everything's going to be fine. Right?"

"Everything's going to be fine," Henrik confirmed. "She said she felt better than she has in weeks. Or, she did before we reminded her she's sick. Who knows? Maybe she turned a corner."

"Now? What could possibly affect her health more than the dozens of medicines, hundreds of energy healings, and the infinite number of flower essences Elsa's pushed on her over the past few months?"

"I don't know." Henrik followed me down the stairs. "Maybe she really did just need some sleep."

"Maybe," I muttered, unconvinced.

We entered the kitchen, where Mia was uncovering plates upon plates of baked goods she'd lovingly prepared for her brother. "Oh, Jase, I'm so happy you're here! Henrik and I made Meemaw's torte, and her cake, and the apple pie you liked so much two Christmases ago, and—"

But Jason Ahlström wasn't paying a lick of attention to his sister's menu itemization. Usually he doted on Mia, and spent the first few hours of their visits reconnecting with the family member he so clearly cherished. But this time, things were different. Instead of the easy energy I was used to enjoying when two Ahlströms came together, the kitchen was thick with anticipation. With tension. *Weird.* Where was it coming from?

Henrik was normal beside me, and Mia was her usual cheery self. That only left Tyr, who beamed proudly at his girlfriend, his back to the counter and his arms folded across his chest. And Jason.

Oh. *Oh.*

I zeroed in on Jason, observing the way his knuckles cracked as he tightened his grip on the island. He ran one hand through his chocolaty brown hair, studying the goddess who'd stormed into the kitchen several paces ahead of me. His violet–blue eyes roved up Freya's unfairly long, skinny jean-clad legs, along the cardigan that hugged her toned waist and strong arms, then settled on her porcelain face. One corner of his mouth turned up in approval, and he leaned forward, resting his elbows on the island in the universal male posture of interest.

Oh. This should be good.

My gaze darted casually to Freya, to see what my friend made of the mortal who was eyeing her like she was the last slice of pizza in the pie. I expected polite dismissal, or at best mild amusement. But Freya, her cheeks a rosy pink hue I hadn't seen in *ever*, was staring back at Jason with the blend of fascination and frustration I knew all too well. I'd sported it myself every day of the Midgardian years I was stationed alongside Henrik yet not allowed to act on my feelings—when I'd known the love of my existence was right under my nose, and I was bound by the valkyrie code to *not date him* until Freya promoted me to captain—a rank I'd believed I wouldn't achieve until long after Henrik was married, with babies and grandbabies.

As I wondered what Freya might possibly be considering, her mood abruptly shifted. Her gaze clouded in a mist of fury until abject loathing akin to what I'd once felt for the code shone like twin flecks of fire in Freya's blazing eyes. It was an intensity of emotion—albeit an unfriendly one—I hadn't seen from my friend in a long time. And while I appreciated that Freya seemed to have finally come alive again, the level of anger radiating from the goddess whose purpose was to fill our realms with love made my pulse quicken.

I shot Henrik a screaming *should we step in?* vibe. But Freya's fury dissipated as quickly as it had come, my friend's chest rising and falling as she seemingly struggled to regain control. And then…

No. Freaking. Way.

And then Freya, the Goddess of Love, who was forbidden by the Norns to give her heart away lest the worlds tumble into Chaos, blinked at Mia's mortal brother as if he was simultaneously the most curious and the most abominable creature who had ever walked into her life. Awareness slammed into me like an electric prod as I realized that Freya's nap had diddly squat to do with her improved health. It was Jason's arrival—and his subsequent awakening of long dormant feelings, and the dream of a possibility Freya rarely let herself hope for—that made my friend look more alive than she had in months. But if that was the case…what the Helheim were we going to do about it?

JASON AHLSTRÖM WAS CONSIDERABLY better looking than I'd expected. The strong planes of his cheeks gave way to an impressively square jaw, and his eyes held the timeless intelligence innate in older souls. Despite the frat-boy vibe radiating from his flannel shirt and strategically ripped jeans, it was clear that Jason was a man in command of both himself and his world. The easy way he settled into the room filled with some of the most alpha gods in the Norse pantheon proved he had no problem holding his own—a trait mortal girls must have found highly attractive. Helheim, *I* found it highly attractive. Not that I'd ever admit it.

Ever.

Somewhere in Arcata, Jason's *perfekt* match was registering said attractive mortal's proximity. I knew this because the quadrant of my brain dedicated to my duties as Goddess of Love was flashing like a homing beacon, indicating a matched pair was nearby. I didn't usually oversee human relationships—I'd relegated that task to the subsidiaries who served under Verdandi, the primary Norn who'd bequeathed me my matchmaking title. But Jason must have been entitled to special treatment—either because his sister was matched with War, or his union with his *perfekt* match was somehow vital to the realms—because the cue that should have gone to a subsidiary was beaming straight to me. The back of my brain was lighting up like a Midgardian Christmas tree. And it was giving me a major headache.

I threw a mental redirect at the light, sending it to the subsidiary Norn compound in Asgard. Then I shifted my focus to the mortal in front of me.

Jason leaned forward, his forearms resting lightly on the island countertop. He'd cocked his head to the side, studying me with an affected calm that only barely betrayed his interest. I supposed it was fair—I was the only member of Mia's friend-family he hadn't met yet. He was no doubt sizing me up. And apparently, he approved of what he saw.

Too bad I couldn't say the same.

Despite Jason's confident air and admittedly attractive appearance, the foremost detail in my consciousness was that he'd left my valkyrie to fend for herself in a sea of drunks. Proper gentleman, he was not. And in spite of the appreciative glance he was shooting my way, or perhaps because of it, it would serve me well to remember the kind of guy Mia's brother really was.

"Jason! Are you listening to me?" Mia placed one hand on her hip.

Jason's pale, pink lips turned up in a half smile. He offered me his hand in affable greeting. "Hey," he drawled, a hint of a southern accent in his erudite voice. "We haven't met. I'm Jason."

"Freya," I said primly. My hand shot out of its own accord, the pleasantry no doubt driven by the warmth that had ebbed back into my heart following my nap. "Tyr and I grew up together."

"In Sweden?" Jason wrapped a large hand around mine and gave it a firm squeeze. A spark shot up my arm as I processed the energy. Jason's grip radiated confidence. He was clearly comfortable in his skin, a trait I respected...even if I couldn't respect the human who possessed it. "Freya?"

"Uh." I shook my head. "*Ja.* Tyr and I were neighbors. In Sweden." I hoped I was remembering our cover story correctly.

"And now you're here. Are you a student at Redwood State, too?" Jason still hadn't released my hand.

"Um..." The flashing in my head continued with a vengeance. *Wake up, subsidiaries. I have one of yours.* "Uh..."

"Freya?" Brynn turned to Henrik. "She's swaying. Maybe she should lie down."

"No, I'm...uh..." Gods, I wished I could turn off the light show. Somewhere in Asgard, a subsidiary Norn was *not* doing her job.

The flashing intensified as Jason stepped right into my personal space. He lifted the hand not holding mine to my forehead, turning the inside of my head into a disco. "You're not warm, but you're white as a ghost. And Brynn's right, you're swaying. Lying down might not be a bad idea."

Jason's words snapped me back from the ledge. *Not him, too.*

I wrenched my hand away. "I feel fine. *Fine.*" The second *fine* came out with more force than I'd meant it to, but I was so sick of being coddled. How was I supposed to heal if everyone insisted on treating me like I was on borrowed time? Even the guy I'd known all of two minutes?

"*I'm fine,*" I said again, this time through gritted teeth.

Jason's eyes narrowed. "Sorry, love. I didn't mean to upset you. I just wanted to make sure you were feeling all right."

"Love? Why did you call her Love?" Brynn blurted.

My own eyebrows shot up in surprise. Had the infinitely discreet Mia shared our secret?

"He calls all girls 'love.'" Tyr pegged Brynn with a look that clearly signaled *take it down a notch.*

Right. Because "love" was a perfectly common human endearment.

"Well, he calls *special* girls 'love,'" Mia corrected. Her giggle earned her an eye roll from her brother. "Sorry. But it's true."

"Anyway." Henrik diffused the tension with a wave

of his hand. "Mia and I have been baking like crazy, so we hope you're hungry. Welcome, *kille*."

"Thanks, man. Good to see you again." Jason crossed the kitchen, skirting carefully around me and proving he wasn't entirely daft. He high-fived Henrik, and wrapped Brynn in a tight hug. She squealed as her feet left the ground. "Hey, Brynn."

"I missed you!" Brynn beamed up at Jason. "When's the pool tournament? I've *so* been looking forward to watching Tyr lose again."

"Hey," Tyr warned. "I've been practicing."

"Not nearly enough, I'm sure." Jason's laughter filled the kitchen. "If I recall, my record is undefeated."

"Which is why I call you for my team," Brynn declared. "Tyr, you can have Mia."

"What am I, chopped lutefisk?" Henrik frowned.

"You and Freya can be a team," Mia offered.

"Aw, man." Henrik groaned. "Freya's mean at pool."

"I am not mean," I countered. I ignored the flip in my stomach when Jason moved back to his spot at the island. It wasn't like I could *not* notice the way his jeans hugged his butt. Or the way his biceps flexed against his T-shirt.

I mean, I did have eyes.

"Freya, please. Did you or did you not bench me the last time we were paired *because I missed a shot?*" Henrik raised an eyebrow. "And did you or did you not tell me I played pool like a little baby? In front of Brynn. I was trying to impress her!"

"I—"

"And didn't you tell my sister her 'magic rocks' made better partners than I did?" Tyr raised one eyebrow.

"Well, if you'd have—"

"Now that I think about it, you did threaten me with two weeks of trash duty if I didn't carry my weight when we played boys versus girls last month." Brynn raised her shoulders in a shrug.

"You did," Mia agreed. She shot me a wink, and I realized that in their weird way, my friends were trying to make me feel better. With my attention focused on defending myself, I'd stopped swaying...and my headache had nearly gone.

Bless.

Jason's gaze moved from Henrik to Brynn before settling on his sister. He raised one eyebrow, and at Mia's tight nod, his lips curled up in a smile. "Well, this I have to see. When's the first match?"

"After lunch...and dessert. Go unpack, big brother. Tyr left your bag on your bed." Mia turned to me with an innocent smile. "Freya, why don't you show Jason to his room?"

"Me?" Wouldn't someone he'd met more than five minutes ago be a better choice?

"We've put him in the downstairs guest room," Mia offered helpfully.

I looked to Tyr for help. My best friend gave me a helpless shrug. *Jerk.*

"Fine. It's this way." I motioned for Jason to follow me out of the kitchen and down the hall.

When we were nearly to the front door, I pointed to the bedroom directly across from the living room—the one with the view of the front porch and the impressively sized *en suite* that Mia had occupied when Fenrir was on the loose, before my time in Helheim. That felt like forever ago.

"You're staying here." I jabbed my thumb at the guest room.

Jason crossed his arms and leaned against the doorjamb. "You don't like me, do you?"

"Why would you say that?" I mirrored his posture.

"Just a feeling." Jason winked. "Don't worry, love. I'll bring you around."

I raised one perfectly groomed eyebrow. "You think awfully highly of yourself."

"And you think you've got me all figured out." Jason reached out a hand to tuck an errant strand of hair behind my ear. "Careful, Freya. I might surprise you."

And with a confident smile he slipped into the bedroom, shutting me out with a soft click. My jaw dropped as I blinked at the glossy white door. Jason's ego surpassed anything I'd ever experienced—which said a lot, given I'd grown up with titled gods. But I was not letting him get under my skin. Not when, for the first time in more than a year, I *finally* felt like myself.

I was Freya Skönsten, Goddess of Love and High Commander of Odin's High Order of the Battle Goddesses, the Valkyries. And nothing, not even Midgard's most arrogant mortal, was going to bring me down.

Not when Ragnarok was upon us. Absolutely everything was on the line.

"Yellow ball, corner pocket." Mia lined up her cue and bit down on her bottom lip.

"You said that last time," Tyr muttered. He'd removed his signature Henley so when he crossed his arms, his biceps popped against his T-shirt. Mia's cheeks flushed at the movement.

"Well, I mean it *this* time," Mia declared. Her eyes narrowed in concentration, and she took her shot. The yellow ball sailed neatly toward its destination before swerving at the last minute. "Arugh! I don't understand. This defies physics."

"Does it?" Henrik raised one eyebrow.

Mia's knuckles tightened around her stick. "Henrik Andersson, is this your doing? Because so help me—"

"Henrik's not a wizard, Mees. He can't move a ball from across the room. You just got really bad at pool. California making you soft?" Jason bumped Mia out of the way to line up his own shot.

"Oh, shut up, Jason." Mia glared at her brother.

I raised a questioning eyebrow at Henrik. *Was* he throwing Mia's game? I wouldn't have put it past him —he absolutely lived for getting a rise out of her. Mia had quickly become the sister he'd never had. *Poor girl.*

"How's your brother, Henrik?" I threw out the

tension-breaking question. "Everything going well with him?"

"Gunnar's good. He and Inga are still over in Wales. Looks like they might extend their stay. Apparently, once Ull and his girl get back from—aw, man!" Henrik's face fell as Jason sank his shot.

"Woohoo!" Brynn held up her hand. Jason high-fived it.

"That's the game. Looks like my record's undefeated again…unless you and Henrik can actually beat us this time." Jason passed the cue to me while Brynn racked the balls. I tried very hard to ignore the buzz that shot up my arm when our fingertips touched. Obviously, my redirect had failed—I still hadn't closed down my link to the connection between Jason and his Midgardian match, wherever she was.

"Dream on." I snatched the stick and bent low over the table. Mia bit down on her bottom lip, and I shot her an easy grin. "Don't worry, Mia. Henrik and I will crush them. We call solids."

"Think you'll cash in on our lucky streak, eh?" Jason chuckled as he walked along the space between me and the wall. His thigh brushed against my butt as he moved. If he thought he was going to flirt me out of my A game, he had another thing coming.

"Nope." With practiced calm I broke the rack, watching several balls roll easily into pockets. "I just happen to know Brynn hates stripes. The movement of patterns throws off her orderly brain. Okay, yellow ball, corner." I lined up the cue and took my shot. "*Skit.*"

"Freya." Mia clucked her tongue as my ball bounced off the wall. "You're better than that."

I was. But I also wasn't used to playing with Mia's brother in my space. Next time, I wasn't taking a shot until I made sure Jason was on the *other* side of the pool table. *Cheater.*

"It's okay—we'll get 'em on the next one. We all know Brynn can't handle rolling stripes." Henrik gave an encouraging nod.

"*Thanks,*" I mouthed.

"They're distracting." Brynn huffed as she took the cue from me. "Okay, red ball, center pocket." She easily sank that shot, then missed her next. "Stupid stripes," she muttered.

"Let me show you how it's done, *sötnos.*" Henrik quickly cleared the table of all but two solid balls, before passing the cue to Jason. "Record's not looking so secure now, is it, *kille?*"

"I'm not worried." Jason shot me a disarming wink, his indigo–blue eyes twinkling with amusement. He sank two balls, and had just lined up to shoot a third when footsteps from the first floor made me look up.

"*Hei hei?*" Elsa's musical lilt rang down the stairs, filling the basement.

"Maybe we should just go." Forse's baritone lacked its usual ease. "I don't want to be a distraction. Now that my father's gone, we have no way of knowing what's next."

"Which is why you should let your friends be here

for you while we can all still be together. You have those two crystals I gave you?"

"In my pocket."

"Good. Hold them; they'll keep you grounded. We'll just stay for five minutes, and if it's too much, I'll make up an excuse to go home, no questions asked. Please?"

"All right." Forse's voice cracked.

No doubt it had taken unimaginable strength for him to leave the cottage—especially if he believed he had to be strong for our sake. It was so typically Forse —nobody did the "stiff upper lip" act better than Justice. But it wasn't necessary—at least, not for us.

I reached into my heart to send energy to my grief-stricken friend. My skin tingled as I discovered a small reserve of love waiting for me to share. It had been a long time since that well had been anything but dry. I channeled all I could draw to Forse, praying my ability had *finally* returned for good, even in this reduced capacity.

"Poor Forse," Brynn said. She, Henrik, Mia, and Tyr exchanged anxious looks. Nobody expected him to be up and about, much less paying a social call with Jason here. Keeping up appearances was part of the job, but a god could get a pass while mourning the loss of a parent.

"*Hei hei?*" Elsa called out. "Where are you guys?"

"They must still be at the airport. We can come back." Forse sounded slightly relieved.

"No, they're here. Look. The cookies are out. Hello?" Elsa called again.

Mia snapped to attention. "We're down here! In the basement!" She turned her attention to us and whispered, "Everybody, act normal."

"Why wouldn't we act normal?" Jason asked.

"Because Forse just lost his dad," Mia explained quietly.

"Oh. Man." Jason ran a hand through his hair. "That's rough."

He had no idea.

"I'll go get them." Mia jogged up the stairs while Jason sank another shot. She returned moments later, a plate laden with cookies in her hands, and Elsa and Forse on her heels. Elsa's long blond waves hung limply over one shoulder. She'd pulled the sleeves of her light blue cardigan over her palms, and now tugged at the hem with one hand while she guided Forse down the stairs with the other.

"*Hei* everybody. Jason, it's good to see you." Elsa's voice was steady, but as she reached the bottom of the stairs, she shot a worried look at the god who stepped into position beside her.

"Hello," Forse said soberly. He shoved his free hand into his pocket, no doubt clutching the crystals Elsa had given him. *Oh, Forse.*

I channeled the last of my love reserve at him, hoping it would be enough to get him through this interaction.

"Hey, Elsa. Forse." Jason nodded at the justice god. He furrowed his brow and parted his lips, but a subtle headshake from his sister stopped whatever sentiment he'd been about to express.

"*Normal,*" Mia mouthed.

With a nod, Jason lined up his shot, missed, and swore. He gave a mock bow as he passed the cue to me. I snatched it from his hands, careful not to let our fingers touch. "If you sink those two, the championship's yours, love."

"Why's he calling her Love?" Elsa hissed.

"It's okay; he calls girls he likes that," Brynn hissed back.

"Shut up," I gritted at everybody. "I am trying to focus."

"You can focus all you want. You'll never sink them both." Jason crossed his arms and leaned back so his denim-clad butt pressed against the table. Gods, he had an exquisite butt.

Arugh! *Subsidiaries, take this stupid connection already —mortals are not my job!*

"Freya can sink them both," Brynn said confidently. "If she can *keep her eyes on the ball.*"

Tyr's snort fanned the flames of my annoyance.

"Watch it, Fredriksen," I warned.

"She can't sink them. Stripes block all conceivable shots. Unless Henrik really *is* a wizard, it looks like I'll remain the all-time Arcata pool champion." Jason shot me a wink. "But by all means, give it your best."

"Oh, I will," I promised. My brows knitted together as I studied the table.

Jason laughed.

"What?" I snapped.

"You're too tense to pull this off." He chuckled. "Are you always this uptight?"

"Excuse me?" I balked at the same time as Brynn piped up, "She totally is."

"Shut up, Brynn," I snapped.

Brynn shrugged. "See?"

"I am not uptight." I glared first at Brynn, then at Jason. "And I don't see what that has to do with me making these shots."

"Are you serious? It has everything to do with you making these shots." Jason took a step closer, so only the corner of the table separated us. "Your shoulders are rigid, your jaw's locked, and your knuckles are white. Tension like that's bound to lead to a pull—no way can you hold your aim without some kind of slip. Now, if you need somebody to help you release some of that tension…"

I didn't realize I was leaning forward until my elbow buckled. My torso bent over the corner of the table, and I face-planted into Jason's chest. *Seriously?*

"Sorry," I muttered, scrambling to right myself. Jason's hands wrapped around my biceps, steadying me.

The minute I regained my balance, I wrenched myself free. From the corner of my eye, I saw Tyr and Henrik double over in silent laughter. Brynn's distinctive snort was even more obnoxious. And when I dared meet Jason's eyes, his smile deepened and a dimple appeared on his right cheek. *A dimple.*

Now the Norns—and their stupid, lazy subsidiaries—were just screwing with me.

I snatched up the cue, shoved my thoughts into a deep pocket of mortification, and refocused on the game. Jason hadn't been wrong about stripes blocking solids, but the added difficulty made my job harder—not impossible. I quickly worked out the best angle, and lined up my cue.

"Blue ball, center," I declared.

"That's what she sai—ouch!" Henrik winced at Brynn's swift elbow.

"Not a chance," Jason countered.

"Freya's made more difficult shots," Elsa offered helpfully.

"Thank you, Elsa," I said.

I tuned all of them out, and zeroed in on the pocket. With a steadying breath, I relaxed my shoulders, released my clenched jaw, and took the shot. My ball followed the intended trajectory, bouncing off the far wall before dropping neatly into the center pocket.

"Yes!" Henrik slapped me on the back. "Now do it again, woman."

A smile tugged at one corner of my mouth as I moved around the table to take my final shot.

"Please beat my brother," Mia begged. "He has the hugest head."

Tyr and Henrik practically fell into each other, their shoulders shaking with barely restrained hysteria.

"Oh, grow up," Elsa admonished.

"She kind of set herself up." Forse's chuckle lightened my heart. If he could find the strength to smile given everything he'd gone through, then any humiliation I felt would be worth it.

Though I was still going to kill Tyr and Henrik.

I called my final shot.

"Make it, make it, make it." Mia crossed her fingers.

"Miss, miss, miss," Brynn chanted.

I tuned them out, focused on the end game, and took aim. The ball rolled across the felt, bounced off the edge of center pocket, and rolled neatly toward the corner. With a definitive *clunk* it dropped into the hole, cementing our win and stripping Jason of his title.

"Yes!" Henrik swept me up in his arms, twirling me in a circle before setting me back on my feet. "Take that, Brynnie!"

"Ugh. Congratulations," Brynn muttered. "Thanks a lot, Freya. Now I have to do his laundry for a week."

"Gross." I wrinkled my nose.

"You're telling me." She grimaced.

"Congrats." Jason held out his hand. "That was impressive."

"It was, wasn't it?" I flicked my hair, sending a mass of strawberry-blond over my shoulder.

Jason's eyes twinkled. "You'll have to show me how you did it."

"Can't have you knowing all my secrets."

The second the words left my lips, I bit down on the inside of my cheek, pumping the brakes before I got both of us hurt. Jason was obviously flirting with me. But his *perfekt* match had to be somewhere nearby—it was the only explanation for the light show firing up *again* in my brain. And even if she wasn't, and even if I *did* have feelings for him, *which I absolutely did not*, then acting on those feelings would only end with...

Gods. It would be a disaster.

The Norns had waited until I was of age to confirm me as Goddess of Love and commander of the valkyries, because they'd wanted to make sure I fully understood the contract to which I bound myself. Unlike the rest of Asgard's titled gods, I performed twin roles that required not only understanding of souls' individuality and compatibility, but *perfekt* control over my own world. Forging matches and reducing fear through growing love, while *also* commanding my army required a focus and awareness one simply could not possess while worrying about a partner. For this reason, my titles came with a stipulation: I was allowed to live among Asgardians, form friendships, and even engage in casual relationships. But I couldn't align myself with my *perfekt* match— couldn't give my heart away—until the Norns decreed that my doing so wouldn't jeopardize the security of the cosmos. My job, my purpose for being—something at which I was currently *failing*—was to protect the realms from Chaos by infusing them with Love. It was my duty to safeguard my heart for the good of the realm, so that I would not endanger the security of Asgard.

And duty to Asgard came above all else.

"Tomorrow. You, me, a rematch. What do you say?" Jason pressed.

"I don't think so," I said gently.

"Got a better offer? Something more pressing to take care of?" Jason challenged.

I racked the balls while I racked my brain. *Duty to Asgard above all else.*

I cringed at the realization of what I had to do. Not to avoid alone time with the more irritating Ahlström sibling, which would just be a perk of exhausting my final healing option, but to take a proactive step toward *not failing* at my job.

"Actually, I have an appointment," I said calmly. "Or, I think I do."

"You *think* you have an appointment?" Jason raised one eyebrow.

"Yes." Though I'd felt better today than I had in months, I still wasn't whole. And with Ragnarok now imminent, it was more imperative than ever that I get a grip on my mind. There was one being I hadn't consulted who *might* be able to fix me. . . if she was still available. "Elsa, do you think Lornara's still willing to help us out?"

Elsa's mouth formed a pert *O*. I'd rebuffed her fairy friend's offer for months. But being out of options and out of time made a girl open to crystals, and *älva* dust, and all the crazy Alfheim's High Healer would surely bring with her. But if it meant helping my realm, I would do it.

For Asgard.

"Lornara?" Elsa tilted her head to the side. "I'm sure she'd love to help. I'll call her."

"Good." I nodded. "I'm ready."

"Who's Lornara?" Jason frowned.

"Work friend." I waved my hand. "Let's go. It's getting stuffy down here."

"Feeling tense again?" Henrik snorted.

I glared at Tyr's bodyguard before picking up the dessert plate. As I swept up the stairs, I bit into one chocolate chip cookie, then another, and chewed. "Did we vote on these yet? Mia's cookies are mouthwatering. Henrik's came out a little dry."

Henrik's mortified gasp made me relent. "Okay, that was a lie," I admitted. "They're amazing. But you're on notice, Andersson. Mess with me, I will go after your baking."

"Noted," Henrik grunted. As he jogged up the stairs after me, I heard him whisper to Brynn, "Told you she was mean when she played pool."

CHAPTER 5

GOOD GODS, JASON WAS brilliant. I'd always liked Mia's brother, but seeing the way he got under Freya's skin was fan-freaking-tastic. And infinitely entertaining. He was into her—*obviously*. Not only was Freya a fierce warrior and the living embodiment of love, but she was drop-dead gorgeous. And she was totally avoiding him, which, of course, made him want her even more. *Men.*

Jason was smart enough to play it cool. He spent the rest of the afternoon alternately ignoring Freya and giving her a hard time. According to Mia, it was his tried-and-tested Midgardian courting technique, and apparently, it had worked really well on the mortals at Jason's fancy East Coast college. But it just seemed to tick Freya off, which made her twitchy, and uptight and...frustrated.

The Goddess of Love was big time frustrated. Odin only knew how long it had been since she'd been on a date, and this sexy, smart guy was in her house driving her nuts. It was only a matter of time before she cracked.

I couldn't wait.

"Suit up, Brynnie." Henrik charged into the kitchen where I was eating another cookie and totally not watching Jason explain to Freya *again* how very uptight she was, and how she could really do with a spa day, *'or whatever you chicks do to unwind in California.'*

"Suit up?" I mumbled around a mouthful of crumbs. "Why?"

Henrik didn't say anything more, just raised an eyebrow at Jason before tilting his head to the hall-way. With a sigh, I shoved the rest of the cookie in my mouth and followed him out of the kitchen. Looked like my time enjoying the Frey-son show was over.

For now.

"Better be important," I said. Though with a mouthful of cookie, it sounded more like, "Mehhuhptttf."

"Say it, don't spray it, *sötnos.*"

I narrowed my eyes and swallowed. "Careful, or I'll say that cookie was dry. Might have been one of yours."

"Oh, please." Henrik rolled his eyes. "My cookies have never been dry. Freya's just in a mood because she hasn't gotten any in ages."

"Henrik!" I punched him in the arm. His bicep was so thick, he didn't even flinch.

"It's true. But it's also beside the point. Grab some

weapons and a travel pack, and meet me at the drop site in five. You, me, and Tyr are heading to Alfheim."

"What? We can't do that. Jason will see the Bifrost."

"Already on it." Henrik opened the hall closet and tossed me a jacket. "Mia's going to distract him in the basement—demand a pool rematch, since he called her soft. It'll keep him busy long enough for us to get out of here."

"Fair enough." I shrugged into my jacket. "Everything okay in Alfheim? Why are we putting on coats? Isn't it summer there?"

"Should be." Henrik zipped his own parka up. "But the weird winter pattern's hit more than just Midgard. Ragnarok is definitely coming."

I glanced toward the kitchen to make sure Jason wasn't listening. The last thing we needed was our mortal guest overhearing the end of the world was nigh.

"I'll apprise you of the situation on-site. Just suit up and prepare for the worst."

Awesome.

I charged upstairs, knowing full well details were inconsequential. It was always the same on these missions—drop in, dispel the threat, dispel the *secondary* threat lurking behind the primary, come home, celebrate with Henrik. All I really needed was my dagger, rapier, and possibly a piece or two of chemical tech. Just in case.

"Hey!" With my blades in place, I poked my head out of my room and shouted toward the man cave, where I assumed Henrik was weaponing up. "Grab the—"

"Already on it!" Henrik stepped into the hallway, shoving the closer into his backpack as he moved. "Who needs beta phase when you can test it on a dragon transfer?"

"Dragon?" I blinked. "I thought Nidhogg called off the dogs? Doesn't the dragon king owe us for not killing his team in Helheim?"

"He does. And he did." Henrik shrugged the pack over his shoulders before reaching into the man cave and grabbing his broadsword. We really had to stop leaving those things laying around when we had company.

"Then who's attacking Alfheim?"

"Rogue team. The scouts haven't seen this breed before, but odds are they're working with Hymir." Henrik holstered the sword and motioned for me to follow him down the stairs.

"I am seriously hating on Tyr's bio-dad. What's he done now?" I stomped after Henrik.

"We don't know. He's been hiding out since he lost the arm in Svartalfheim, but rumor has it he's teamed up with a subversive unit—one with access to off-the-grid dragons. No doubt he's been regrouping since we took Runa into custody."

I shuddered at the reminder of Runa, Tyr's biological sister, and the half-giant who'd both unleashed Fenrir on the Fredriksens, and held Elsa captive in her Svartalfheim nightmare-tower. At Tyr's insistence, Runa's execution sentence had been converted to a life imprisonment. It had surprised no one that Runa had refused all attempts at rehabilitation, and had spent the last year rocking in a corner of her cell, muttering to herself. Some of us worried she might be communicating with Hymir, but Forse assured us the prison was impenetrable, even by dark magic. And as Justice, he should know.

I *so* hoped he wasn't wrong.

"*Ja*, well. With everything going on, let's make sure Runa stays in our custody." I followed Henrik out the front door, leaping off the steps of our cabin's porch.

"My thoughts exactly." Henrik jogged alongside me, so we reached the drop site together.

"You ready?" Tyr's low voice barked. He stood at the edge of the drop zone, the vein over his jaw already bulging with tension. It was going to be one of *those* missions.

"Always am." I stepped into the clearing and bit down on the inside of my cheek. *Don't throw up. Don't throw up.* Someday, I'd be rid of my Bifrost sickness. Until then, I'd rely on sheer determination and dumb luck.

And Henrik's magic hands. He placed one on my lower back as he stepped in behind me. I leaned against him with a long-suffering sigh.

"You got this, *sötnos*," he said.

I wish.

"Heimdall!" Tyr leaned his head back and shouted at the sky. "Now!"

With a whoosh of air and a flash of multi-hued light, the rainbow bridge shot down from Asgard. My bones vibrated, nearly sucked right out of my skin, and in one nausea-inducing slurp we were swept out of Midgard, shot across the cosmos, and deposited in a painful heap at the edge of a waterfall in Alfheim.

The scene that greeted me when I managed to drag my eyelids open left me even more nauseous than the Bifrost.

"Hyro! Stop!" I stumbled backward, bumping into Henrik's back as I took in the sweet teenage fire giant we'd relocated from Muspelheim, breathing fire into the barely moving remains of a baby dragon. The little creature's chest shuddered with each fresh blaze, and its eyes flickered open to reveal a look of pure agony. I didn't care what the evil dragons had done to Hyro; *nothing* justified hurting their young.

"Hyro!" I screamed. "Disengage *right this minute!*"

"Stay back, Brynn! I don't want you getting hurt!" The adolescent fire giant held out one pale purple palm. She shot me a look of barely contained terror before turning back to the tiny dragon and sneezing on it. Her sneeze sent a fresh burst of flame across the dragon's chest.

"Stop it! If you kill that dragon, and it ends up being one of Nidhogg's, he'll—"

"It's not one of Nidhogg's." Henrik spoke up from behind me. "I've never seen barbs on a dragon's tail *and* head, or scales that glow—though that could be because she's incinerating it. Must be one of the invaders who came through that."

"Through what?" I asked.

"Turn around," Tyr grunted.

I spun on one heel to find the boys pointing to a dark, swirling shape that hovered a hundred meters away. Sparks shot from the edges of the wobbly rectangle, smoldering in the dirt of the once pristine meadow.

"Holy *skit*," Tyr swore. "Look at this place."

I glanced over my shoulder at Hyro and the now totally glowing dragon, then turned a quick circle to take in the blackened trees surrounding Alfheim's tallest waterfall. What had once been a sanctuary was now a war zone, with trees burned to stubs, soot where grass was once blanketed, and a thin layer of ash floating in the air like snow. A solitary green tree stood in the center of the former field, a testament to the beauty that had once thrived here.

"What the Helheim happened?" I raised my rapier to eye level and shifted so my back pressed against Henrik's.

"Questions later. Duck now." Henrik's hand on my arm tugged me downward. A whoosh of brisk air followed by a reptilian screech alerted me to the presence of a second, much larger dragon. This one swooped overhead in a wide arc. As I craned my head to get a better look it sent a stream of fire straight at the lone tree. The trunk went up in flames, incinerating in mere seconds.

Skit.

"*Ja,* definitely not one of Nidhogg's," I concurred. "Unless the treaty's null and void."

"Look out!" I shoved Henrik to the side and threw myself into the air, neatly somersaulting away from a fresh burst of dragon breath. "We have to get out of here. Hyro!"

"Don't worry about me!" She waved her hand again. "The cave behind the waterfall—they haven't breached the mountain yet. It should be safe!"

Ignoring the fire giant who apparently lacked a self-preservation gene, I leapt to my feet and unzipped Henrik's backpack. After removing a palm-sized item, I charged toward the gaping black hole in the sky.

"Where are you going?" Tyr shouted.

"I have the closer," I yelled over my shoulder. "You guys take care of that dragon—and try to keep Hyro from getting killed. Or killing that poor baby dragon. I'll seal the portal. I hope." I muttered the last words under my breath, but Henrik's warning let me know we were on the same page.

"Be careful," he called. "We don't know if it's stable."

"Don't I know it." I ran harder, my boots digging into the soft ash of the charred meadow. The portal was fifty meters away. Twenty-five. Not much longer and I'd be—

"Arugh!"

Searing pain wracked my ankle. I went down fast. My knee struck something hard, sending warm liquid pooling against the thin fabric of my cargos. I held tight to the closer with one hand, and gripped my rapier with the other. A glance at the ground revealed a tangled web of vines—I'd stumbled through what was left of a root system, and though whatever tree it had once belonged to now littered the air with ashy particles, its grounding structure was firmly intact...and firmly buried beneath a thick layer of soot.

Fabulous.

Ignoring the pain now shooting up my right leg, I extracted my boot from the root's stronghold and limped closer to the sparking rectangle in the sky. A second large dragon shot through the portal, and I threw myself onto the ground just in time to avoid being taken out.

"Henrik!" I shrieked. "Incoming!"

I had no way of knowing whether he heard me, and had no intention of taking more time than absolutely necessary to seal off this door to...to wherever the Helheim it led. I had to trust that Henrik and Tyr would have this. They always did.

Well, they usually did.

Except when they didn't.

Work fast, Aksel.

I hurriedly sized up the portal, sheathing my rapier while I worked out coordinates. It wasn't the standard circular model I'd seen before. This one was framed by four sides, and quartered with navy–grey beams. It more closely resembled an iron door to a hidden garden than an entryway to a dark realm. Only the reddish–purple sparks that shot from its edges, and the overwhelming feeling of despair that seeped through its surface, tipped me off to its dark origins. Well, that, plus all the chargrilled trees surrounding the waterfall. Nothing good could have come from this doorway.

It was time to shut it down.

Raising the closer to eye level, I tapped the button on its side and waited for the green diagram to emerge. Henrik and I had coded this feature to calibrate to the exact specifications of whatever portal it assessed. Once calibrated, it would emit a protoplasm that should envelop the full-scale portal, coat it in a light magic-laced film, and shrink it to the size of a pebble. The pebble could be retrieved and stored in the closer for delivery to Asgard, where it could be studied or destroyed, Odin's choice. It was one of the more brilliant pieces of technology the Brynnrik brain trust had developed.

Or it would have been, if it had worked.

I clicked the button again. A tiny green flicker appeared at the top of the closer. It flashed twice before extinguishing completely.

No.

My thumb pushed down harder as I willed more than just a spark to emerge. A thin line shot a full three inches from the closer's top, wavered pitifully, and snuffed out.

Skit.

I clicked again, then again, wondering what the Helheim we'd failed to anticipate when travel-proofing the box for inter-realm transportation. We'd used a

Nidavellir-procured metal that our dwarf friend, Berry, had assured us was genuine. That material should have been impervious to elemental adversity, so its functionality shouldn't have been affected by Alfheim's atmosphere or the surplus of carbon dioxide from the flambéed foliage. Henrik had placed a buffering charm around the device, so it shouldn't have been affected by the Bifrost forces, either. Unless I'd somehow screwed up the internal schematics, the tech should have been operational, just like it had been when—

"Brynn! Get down!" Tyr's roar pierced the air, and I threw myself onto the charred dirt. A flash of orange and a burst of heat let me know I'd been *this close* to getting singed by an angry dragon.

Again.

"Come on," I muttered, my thumb jamming the button in a frenetic repetition. On my twentieth attempt, a steady light burst from the top of the closer. It was so strong I snapped my eyes closed, grimacing as the bright beam seared through my lids.

"Hurry up, *sötnos*! Getting kind of—ouch!" Henrik's yelp set my teeth on edge. "Kind of burned over here!"

"I'm working on it!" I called. My teeth ground together, and I dug my elbow into the soot, careful to keep the closer as far from my body as possible. The light was meant to be a hologram—*not* a laser. Gods only knew what it would do to my skin if I angled it the wrong way.

I forced my eyelids open and thrust the closer in the

general direction of the portal. The green pulse that shot from the container was too intense for me to see around, and I seriously hoped it was shooting at its intended target.

"Look out, Brynn!" Tyr roared again.

Heat seared my back. I cried out in pain. It took everything I had to retain control of the device as I rolled on my back to extinguish the blaze.

"Get that dragon away from me!" I screamed.

"Just close the *förbaskat* portal already!" Tyr yelled back.

"I. Am. *Trying!*"

A coppery taste filled my mouth as my molars sank into my cheek. Gripping the closer with both hands, I wrenched it to the side and glimpsed the door in the sky. It was only partially open now, with flames lapping around its edges. A barbed tail whipped thorough the frame, extending the opening another foot. The doorway shook as the owner of the tail slammed into it, then raised its scaly head and shot a massive stream of fire toward me. I flung myself to the side, ignoring the rock that pierced the skin atop my bicep and rolling with my arms outstretched so as not to trade dragon burns for laser ones.

"Brynn!" Henrik hollered.

"On it!"

I raised my hands and angled the closer directly at the door. The dragon pushed its head through the frame, but before it could open its mouth again, the closer's green light morphed into a rectangle. It shimmered, adjusting to match the specs of the portal, then surged forward. *Thank gods.*

Light coated the door, the dragon, and the lingering sparks in a thick goo that hardened before emitting one final flash. The structure converged on itself, shrinking to the size of a golf ball—not the planned-for pebble, but hey, who didn't love a fix-it project? With a *plink*, the ball dropped to the blackened ground, all trace of the portal it had once been contained within its tiny sphere.

Mission accomplished. Now to retrieve the evidence.

I transferred the closer to my other hand, and took off. As I ran toward the pile of soot where the golf ball had fallen, I plucked the stone from my shoulder. A thick red ooze quickly coated my jacket, and I pressed my palm to the wound. My injury would heal itself quickly enough, but right then it hurt like a mother. *Stupid dragon.*

A high-pitched shriek and prolonged gurgle from behind made me turn my head. The knot in my gut released infinitesimally at the sight of Tyr atop a slain dragon.

"Mine's dead," he said unceremoniously. I kept running as Tyr withdrew his dripping sword and charged toward the spot where Henrik battled his reptilian attacker. "Don't worry, Andersson. I'll pick up your slack."

The roar of an angry beast muffled Henrik's retort. As much as I loved watching my man literally slay dragons, I needed to finish my job so I could help the guys with theirs—and if need be, evacuate the misguided teenager who was *still* breathing fire onto that poor baby dragon.

"Okay, little ball. Where are you?" My gaze roamed the ground until it came to rest on a green-tinted sphere slightly buried beneath black ash. "Gotcha."

I snatched up what was left of the portal, and popped the hatch on the closer. The ball fit snugly inside, and I sealed the door shut, pressing my thumb to the latch to activate the fingerprint seal we'd installed. Odin forbid this thing fell into the wrong hands, Henrik and I hadn't wanted anyone *not* on our team to gain access to it. Tyr, Henrik, Forse, and I were cleared for operation. If we all lost our left thumbs, the worlds were out of luck.

I shoved the closer into the pocket of my cargos and spun on one heel, intending to help Henrik and Tyr take down the remaining dragon. But the boys had the situation in hand—Henrik's broadsword made one decisive swipe through the creature's neck, slicing its scales and relieving the reptile of its head. Tyr's repeated stabs to its chest were suddenly rendered moot.

"Hey, War. I think it's dead," I called out.

Tyr served up his grunt with an award-winning glare.

"Seriously. It's hard to stay alive without your head," I pressed.

"But not impossible," Tyr countered.

Point, Fredriksen. We'd definitely seen stranger things.

"Heartbeat's gone, *kille.* That's both of them." Henrik wiped his blood-soaked sword on the dragon's cheek before stepping back to apprise our handiwork.

The dragons were dead and the portal was contained…but the meadow now boasted six additional bonfires, and the lone tree we'd spotted on arrival was no more. Whoever unleashed the beasts on Alfheim hadn't intended to leave any survivors.

Henrik lifted his head. "Do we know who we're dealing with?"

I closed the gap between me and the boys while Tyr jumped off the headless corpse. He raised his palms to the waterfall, and redirected the water so it extinguished the blazes lighting up the landscape.

I raised one eyebrow. "Showoff."

"Jealousy's not your best look." Tyr winked. "And no idea. I'm assuming Hymir's behind it, but Odin only knows where he's hiding out. And like we said, these dragons definitely weren't from Nidavellir. Still…"

Almost as one, our gazes swept toward Hyro. She still hovered over the small dragon, but at least she'd stopped breathing fire on it.

Finally.

"Hyro." Henrik's boots kicked up soot as he marched to the fire giant's side. "We need to get you out of here. We'll, uh, take care of that dragon."

"You can't kill it! I fixed it." Hyro blinked up at Henrik with wide eyes. "It's good now!"

"Excuse me?" Henrik and I shared a look. *Crazy teenager said what now?*

"I burned the evil out of it." Hyro drew her shoulders back, her chest lifting.

"That's not how evil works," Henrik offered gently.

"It is with feyndrals! When they're young, they don't have an affiliation—light or dark. They get to choose for themselves. Most of them go dark because, well, if you lived in Svartalfheim you'd go with the only thing you ever saw too, right? But—"

"Svartalfheim? There aren't dragons in Svartalfheim anymore." Tyr's authoritative tone carried a slight question. There hadn't been native dragons in Svartalfheim in recent history—Asgard had wiped them out during a war some centuries ago, though the occasional rogue reptile made it in via a portal...or was snuck in alongside a particularly vicious perp. But if any of the native species had survived...if they'd gone into hiding...

"Hyro, how do you know about feyndrals? They've been extinct since way before you were born." Probably. I still hadn't quite worked out the math on how fire giants aged.

"Two came through Muspelheim when I was really young." Hyro stroked the red neck of the little dragon beside her. "My parents took me to the forest to see their nest. They told me how rare they were, and that the dragons would be in danger if I told anyone they were there—dragon scales were worth a lot of money on my old realm. And they had three eggs..."

As touching as Hyro's story was, I needed to stop her from inciting some kind of a war with the feyndrals—if they even existed. We'd already killed two adults—granted, it had been in self-defense. But if Hyro was wrong about these creatures having the agency to choose a side, flambéing a baby definitely wouldn't help us keep the peace.

"Why do you think you can burn evil out of that dragon?" I asked gently.

"My parents told me I could." Hyro's eyes shone with such trust and innocence, for a moment I wanted to wrap her in a hug. Her parents had been killed a few years back in a volcanic explosion. She'd lived on her own in the forests of Muspelheim until our team found her and relocated her to Alfheim. She rarely spoke of her family—the pain of losing them was still too raw. And while I hated to disabuse her of one of her memories, I couldn't have her burning baby dragons in a misguided attempt to save them from themselves.

Henrik caught my eye, and I nodded.

"Listen, Hyro." He dropped to his knees so he could look her in the eye. "My parents told me a lot of things when I was young, too. But most of the stories they told me were just that—stories. Do you think maybe your parents were trying to make you feel better about those baby dragons you saw? I mean, since feyndrals are evil and all, your folks probably had to kill the monsters to protect you from—ow!"

Henrik rubbed the elbow I'd just kicked.

"Tact, Andersson," I hissed.

But Hyro shook her head emphatically. "My parents didn't kill the babies. When Surtr's guards visited the forest a few days later, we saw the feyndrals take to the sky to defend their nest. The guards killed them almost instantly, and my parents ordered me to stay in our house while they went to check on the babies. Sure enough, the guards weren't smart enough to see why the feyndrals attacked them—and they never realized they were protecting their young. My parents kept the babies in our house for as long as they could, and when they were old enough to pick an affiliation, two chose the light while the third chose the darkness. My dad was a healer, and he showed me how to isolate the dark threads trying to root in a soul, then burn them out. Like I just did with this guy."

We all stared at the small dragon lying peacefully on the ground. He'd nestled his head lovingly in Hyro's lap, and his round belly rose and fell with deep breaths of sleep.

"What happened to the babies after that?" I asked.

"They couldn't stay on Muspelheim—the guards would have found them and killed them for their scales. When they were big enough, my dad contacted a friend in Svartalfheim. That was the feyndrals' home world before they went—well, before we all thought they went—extinct. Dad got the babies off-realm, and apparently, there were others like them."

"Others who just tried to cook us for lunch," Henrik grumbled.

"It wasn't their fault! They grew up in the dark

realm—they'd never seen any other way of being. But this guy…I can show him how to be good. Honest." Hyro looked lovingly at the now-snoring dragon in her lap. Tiny puffs of smoke burst from his nose on each exhale. It was kind of cute.

"That's a big responsibility," Tyr cautioned. He stepped closer to Hyro, his broadsword still drawn.

"I can handle it." Hyro raised her chin. "It's not like I have anything else to do."

Henrik and I exchanged another look. We'd known the *älva* of Alfheim had been less than thrilled to have a fire giant planted in their midst, but I'd thought the meadow elves had been pretty welcoming. Even so, it was clear Hyro was lonely. And now she'd found a pet…

"Okay, here's the deal." I rubbed the stiffness in my neck. "Hyro, you can keep the dragon *if* you teach it to be on our team. We're going to need all hands on deck now that we've got random portals from Svartalfheim popping up in friendly realms."

Henrik reached for my neck, replacing my hand with his own and pressing lightly. My tension ebbed. "Seriously."

"Are you sure you can handle this?" Tyr pressed.

"I can handle it," Hyro asserted. "I promise."

I nodded. "Tyr, we're good here—you can go debrief Odin. Henrik and I will stick around and make sure everything's secure. We'll relocate Hyro some-where closer to the meadow elves' village, and make sure they administer extra doses of, uh, goodness to... are you going to name the dragon?"

"Marshmallow," Hyro said without hesitation.

"Marshmallow?" Tyr raised an eyebrow.

"Yes. His little breaths look like marshmallows."

I watched the white puffs coming from the dragon's nose. Hyro wasn't wrong. "Right. So you and Marshmallow will come with us. We'll get you settled in a new place, since this one's no longer secure—or habitable—and then we'll take off. Did any of your stuff survive this fire?"

"I moved it all behind the waterfall," Hyro said. "Forse warned me Ragnarok was triggered, so I figured better safe than sorry."

"He did?" That was news to me. I hadn't realized he'd continued running communications while grieving the loss of his father. That selflessness had probably saved Hyro's life.

It had definitely saved her stuff.

"Okay, grab your things, and we'll get you relocated. Tyr, that okay?"

"Yes." War nodded curtly. "I'll return from Asgard as soon as I can. But hurry. I don't like Mia being unattended for this long. Especially with everything going on."

"Agreed." Henrik eyed the snoring reptile on the ground. "Do we have to pick it up, or..."

"If you guys grab my stuff, I'll carry him. Everything's just behind the waterfall." Hyro pointed.

Henrik and I hurried to the water, returning

quickly with far less than we'd expected. "We only found the two bags," I apologized. "If you tell us where the rest of it is we can—"

"You got it all." Hyro lifted the dragon in her arms and cradled him while she walked.

I raised an eyebrow at Henrik. "You only have two bags?"

Hyro's shoulders rose and fell. Whether it had been a shrug or a sigh, I couldn't tell.

"Hurry," Tyr called after us.

"We will," I promised.

As Henrik and I followed Hyro over the charred field toward the wooded village where the meadow elves had lived for centuries, I made myself another promise. We'd failed Hyro when we relocated her. Once Ragnarok was behind us, I was going to find her the best home in all the realms—one where she could have a friend-family every bit as wonderful as ours. She'd just stripped the darkness from a dragon, for Odin's sake. She deserved that much…and more.

I would find a way to give it to her.

CHAPTER 6

FREYA

*D*ON'T PANIC. JUST DON'T *panic.*

"So, you're saying...what exactly?" I gripped the arms of my chair, as if digging my fingertips into the leather would down the tornado of fear in my gut. Lornara hadn't given an outright diagnosis yet. My anxiety was ungrounded.

For now.

Alfheim's High Healer pursed her lips. "What I'm saying...well..." Her wings fluttered as she turned to shoot Elsa a pleading look. "Maybe you can explain it."

Elsa knelt so her white-blond head was level with Lornara's raven curls. Both wore identical expressions of concern. Elsa opened her mouth, her clear blue eyes not quite meeting mine. "The thing is...uh..."

This was ridiculous. "Just tell me if I'm dying or not."

Elsa's sharp inhale ricocheted across my bedroom. "You're not dying," she said vehemently.

"But you're not thriving, either," Lornara cautioned. "Reach into your heart again—are there any reserves of love there?"

I checked my heart for the third time in as many minutes. The well had been mostly dry since the pool tournament, when I'd been so excited to be able to send something, *anything,* to Forse. Now…"Still just a few drops."

"Mmm." Lornara opened my palm and removed the gold-orange stone she'd instructed me to grasp. "And tell me truthfully, have you felt *any* different since we connected you with this?"

"No," I admitted. "Sorry, Lornara. I know you think rocks are magical, but—"

"Crystals," she corrected. "*Crystals* are *healing*—when the source of the injury is energetic, as I still believe yours to be."

Right. And I could be fixed by squeezing the magic rock. If Brynn were here, she'd have rolled her eyes with me.

"But she didn't respond to the peach aventurine at all," Elsa murmured. She pushed herself to her feet and paced at the foot of my bed. "I watched her centers—thought for sure the movement near the heart was a positive response. But whatever's clouding it still hasn't cleared, and if that stone didn't work…and my cleansings, essence applications, and affirmations failed too…"

"You're out of options," I said dully. So, I was dying, after all.

"No. Not out. Try these." Elsa shoved two more rocks into my hand. "I haven't paired clear quartz and black tourmaline yet. The former should channel energy into the tourmaline, and clear any negativity or toxicity to maximize the pair's healing capabilities."

I wanted to retort that I was neither negative nor toxic, but Elsa's eyes held such hope that I simply closed my lids and waited for the magic rocks to do...

Nothing. I loved Elsa, but this whole crystal thing was about as helpful as a scorned dwarf.

"How's it going, Freya? Any shift at all?"

I shook my head. "None."

"That's not good," Elsa whispered.

"So *now* we're out of options." I handed the not-so-magic rocks back to Elsa.

"We aren't giving up," Lornara said firmly. "We just need to regroup. Has there been a time—any time at all —in the last few months where you've felt *any* more like yourself? Or has it just been one huge fog?"

"I've felt better this week. Well, intermittently. I blacked out when I got back from Asgard—after Balder..." I shook myself. "But I felt a shift when I woke up yesterday—like the weight in my heart had lifted a few degrees. It's worse again today, but I guess you can see that."

"We can only see what you want us to," Elsa reminded me. And I wondered for the hundredth time if they *really* didn't peek. I would have.

"Did anything change in Arcata today?" Lornara's curls tumbled over her shoulder. "Protests at the university, artist festivals in town, maybe an influx of tourists?"

"Nothing's going on in town. We're lower on numbers here at the compound, but usually Freya responds well to a quieter environment so I don't think that's it," Elsa said.

"Lower in numbers?" Lornara asked.

"Brynn, Henrik, and Tyr are dealing with a situation in Alfheim," Elsa explained. "And I asked Mia to get her brother out of the house so we could work on Freya. She took Jason on a drive up the coast to show him that big fern gully from one of their favorite movies."

"Mia's brother is here?" Lornara blinked at Elsa. "Interesting."

"No, not interesting," I countered. "He didn't get Mia's awesome gene."

"How long has he been here?" Lornara asked.

I shrugged. "A few days?"

"He arrived yesterday," Elsa offered.

"Around the time Freya came out of her post-blackout fog?" Lornara raised one perfectly sculpted eyebrow.

Elsa's eyes widened. "Yes."

"Mmm." A silent communication passed between the two healers.

"Mmm, what?" *What are they driving at?*

"And has Jason been staying at the house while he's been here?" Lornara ignored my question.

"He has. But…he's not a…and she's…it's not an option." Elsa crossed to the window and stared outside.

"Maybe Ragnarok's changed the rules. Maybe the restriction will finally be lifted." Lornara ran her hands through her hair.

I growled in frustration. If they didn't loop me in, somebody was getting a pillow to the head. Or worse.

"Freya," Lornara said cautiously, "do you have…do you have feelings for Jason?"

"Jason?" My eyebrows shot to my hairline. "Are you insane? He's the most arrogant being I've ever met. And that's saying a lot, considering I know Thor."

"Are you sure?" Elsa turned from the window.

"One hundred percent," I declared. And I meant it. Jason Ahlström was arrogant and egotistical and didn't play by *any* of the rules that kept the mortals' society from imploding. He didn't seem to care one iota about the safety of others. And he had *zero* respect for boundaries. His "uptight" demonstration in the basement had proven as much. *Jerk.*

"Hmm." Lornara tilted her head.

"Hmm, what? Why are you both *looking* at me like that?"

Elsa's gaze shifted to Lornara, who gave a slight headshake. "No reason."

If they were suggesting that Jason had anything to do with my improved—and now regressive—health, then they were sorely mistaken. "Look, even if I *did* have feelings for Jason—which I most emphatically *do not*—it wouldn't matter. I'm under contract."

"The Norns prohibited you from uniting with your own *perfekt* match, *ja*. But doesn't that contract include a clause allowing for a removal of that restriction when the time is right?"

"Elsa, don't go there," I warned.

"I'm just saying with Ragnarok here, maybe this time—"

"Don't. Go. There," I growled.

Elsa's delicate hand flew to her chest. "I'm sorry. I only meant—"

"I know what you meant. And I can't go there again. Sorry."

"I understand." Elsa's voice was barely a whisper. "Lornara, I think Freya's had enough for the day. Let's set some crystals around her room and give her some space."

Lornara gave Elsa a curious look, but didn't ask so much as one question. She simply reached into her bag and withdrew a tied satchel. She loosened the ribbon, before crossing the room to dump the contents into Elsa's palms. "Set these at the corners, in pairs. I'll place complementary stones at the windows and beneath the bed."

The two of them set to work, quickly decorating my room with magic rocks. Elsa kept her head bowed as she worked, hastening around the room without making eye contact.

Remorse coursed through me. "I'm sorry, Elsa. I shouldn't have snapped at you."

"I shouldn't have pushed. I know how difficult that situation…" She looked up. "Well, I know it still hurts. I'm sorry."

I forced a thin smile, not wanting to hurt Elsa any further. "I'm fine."

Ignoring Lornara's worried glance and Elsa's pitying frown, I pushed myself to my feet. "Thanks for trying, but Elsa's right—I've had all the healing I can handle. I'm going to sleep this off, if you don't mind."

"Of course." Lornara picked up her bag and opened my bedroom door. "I'm going to stick around for the rest of the day, so just call downstairs if you need anything."

"Thanks." I folded my hands together, nodding politely at the fairy as she flitted into the hallway. Elsa moved to follow, but I called out before she slipped through the door. "Elsa, a word?"

Elsa paused. "Lornara, I'll meet you downstairs," she said. When the flutter of Lornara's wings were no more than a whisper, Elsa stepped back into the room and pulled the door closed.

"I was out of line," she apologized.

"No, you were right." I wrung my fingers together, hating the way my post-Helheim self continued to behave toward my friends. "It still hurts. And I don't know how to make it stop."

"I do." Elsa met my gaze. "Before you can release your pain, you have to embody it. It doesn't mean you're forgetting—it means you're evolving."

"I can't." I shook my head. "Not yet."

"I'm here if you change your mind," Elsa reminded me. She bit down on her bottom lip.

"Spill it, Elsa."

"If you are going to change your mind..." She exhaled. "Well, you might want to do it soon. Time's running out."

"I know." My too-thin smile returned along with the tornado in my gut. I didn't bother asking whether Elsa meant Ragnarok or my health; we both knew that time was running out on *all* fronts.

And unless I could make peace with my past, I was in for one Helheim of a fall.

Sleep was a welcome relief. I awoke to the sun sitting low outside my window and a savory aroma permeating my room—tomatoes and basil coming together in a *perfekt* dance of sweet and tangy. The Alfheim team must have sent Henrik straight to the kitchen on their return. My rumbling stomach served as a not-so-gentle reminder that I hadn't eaten since breakfast—ten hours ago, if not more. I climbed carefully out of bed, expecting either hunger or my condition to render me lightheaded. But to my surprise, the heaviness in my heart had lifted once again—a testament to the marvel that was Henrik's cooking. *Bless.* With a grin, I threw on skinny jeans and a flowy, sleeveless top, and hurried into the hallway.

"That smells incredible," I praised as I reached the bottom of the stairs and rounded the corner to head to the kitchen. "Henrik Andersson, every day I thank

Odin that your mother passed on all the family recipes to someone with such a brilliant gift—"

I stopped at the sight of the brown-haired, indigo-blue eyed *mortal* stirring sauce atop the stove.

"Don't let me stop you." Jason waved one hand. "Do go on about my gift."

"I thought you were Henrik."

"Nope. He and Brynn offered to cook when they got home—well, Henrik did. Brynn just laughed. But Elsa called and said she and her friend Lornara needed to talk to them, so they headed over to the cottage for dinner." Jason tapped the wooden spoon on the edge of the pot and set it on a plate. Then he poured the sauce over a pan filled with fried chicken and noodles, and put the whole thing into the oven.

"Uh-huh. So, it's just us, Tyr, and Mia for dinner?" I asked. Jason had clearly eaten with Tyr before. The pan could have fed ten.

"It's just us for dinner. Tyr took Mia out for pizza." Jason added a dash of garlic salt to a frying pan where green beans simmered in oil. Gods, chicken parmesan with green beans was my favorite of Mia's meals. It was her grandmother's recipe—apparently, Meemaw had shared it with both of her grandchildren.

Dim flashes pulsed in the back of my brain, and I wondered for the umpteenth time why the subsidiaries hadn't tapped into the resonance of Jason's *perfekt* match, already. I'd sent them the signal days ago, and followed up with a tersely worded call. They'd claimed they couldn't access the signal, the only reason for which would have been Jason's pairing with his match being somehow vital to the realms. Or…

No, Freya. No 'or.' You do not get matches. You just make them.

"Isn't Forse eating with us?" I threw out my final lifeline, knowing full well that where Elsa cooked, Forse ate.

"Brynn said something about Forse checking in on his mom. It's just you and me, love." Jason shot me a wink. "Lucky you."

"Maybe I already have dinner plans."

"You don't. Brynn told me." Jason carried two plates from the cupboard to the table.

I made a mental note to have *words* with Brynn.

"Well, then, maybe I don't feel like eating with you." I rested one hand on my hip.

"Please. My chicken parm is legendary. Most girls would die to have me cook it for them."

I appraised him coolly. "I think you'll find I'm not most girls."

Jason paused in front of the silverware drawer. His eyes moved slowly from my sleep-tousled hair to my bare feet and back up, lingering just a moment too long at the deep "V" of my neckline. I hurriedly folded my arms around my ribs. "No, Freya. You are *definitely* not most girls."

Harrumph.

"Put these on the table for me." Jason reached into the drawer and held out a fist full of flatware. "Gotta check on the bread."

"Fine." I took the silverware, ignoring the spark that shot up my arm when our fingers touched. And the way my heart pounded when he walked away. And the way my cheeks warmed when he bent over to check the oven.

"About five more minutes." Jason straightened up. "Were you staring at my butt?"

"What?" I said indignantly. "No."

Yes.

"Mmm-hmm." One corner of Jason's mouth pulled up in a smirk.

"I wasn't!" I insisted. I whirled around and stormed to the table, placing utensils haphazardly beside the plates.

"Hey, go easy on the flatware. Just sit down. If my butt didn't impress you, my dinner sure as hell will."

Oh, gods. I was never living this down.

Jason waited until I'd dropped into a chair before stepping closer. His thigh brushed against my arm as he reached across the table to light a candle. *When did we get a candle?*

Before I knew it, we were seated opposite each other, the space between us filled with steaming platters and an air of tension.

"Cheers." Jason raised his glass, a challenge in his eye. "To a night to remember."

"You wish," I muttered. But I begrudgingly raised my own glass and said, "To dinner."

Jason smirked. "So that's what you call it in Sweden."

Oh, *honestly.*

With a wink, Jason brought his glass to his lips. I did the same, then allowed him to place a generous portion of chicken parmesan onto my plate while I dished up green beans. The bread basket steamed between us as I raised my fork to my mouth, and tried not to moan as I took my first bite.

"It's good," I mumbled around a mouthful of sauce-drizzled chicken.

"Glad you think so." Jason grinned. "Better than Mia's?"

"I don't—"

Jason sat up straight, his face wiped clean of amusement. "Seriously, I need it to be better than Mia's. We've got a bet going, and I *cannot lose.*"

"Why are you two so competitive?" I forked another piece of chicken.

"Just are. Now tell me." Jason placed his forearms on the table and leaned closer. "Is there too much basil? Is the sauce too wine-heavy? Does it need more sugar?"

"You made the sauce from scratch?" I balked. No guy I knew had ever made sauce from scratch—except for Henrik, for whom cooking was therapy. I was impressed.

"Freya, focus for me. What does the sauce need?" Jason studied me intently.

"Hmm…" I chewed, giving myself time to think and totally ignoring the fluttering in my stupid stomach. "Maybe oregano? Another tangy thing to offset all the sweet."

Jason's gaze shifted from my face to the corner of the room. He stared at the ceiling, seemingly in thought. "Yes. Oregano. And...ah!"

"Ah, what?"

Jason didn't answer, just stalked across the kitchen, rummaged through the spice cabinet, and returned with two small jars. "Close your eyes."

"I was told to keep both eyes open around morally questionable boys."

"I'm not morally questionable." Jason rolled his eyes. "Between Mama, Meemaw, and Mia, I couldn't put a foot out of place. Bless their hearts."

Indignation ricocheted in my chest. "So, I suppose leaving an underage girl in the middle of a college bar to fend for herself was something they'd have approved of?"

"What?" Jason dropped into his chair, his quest for the perfect pasta sauce apparently forgotten.

"And I suppose ditching said girl because she wouldn't put out was in line with the enlightened view of women you picked up from your mother, grandmother, and sister?"

Jason's jaw went slack. "I have no idea what you're talking about."

"Does the name Rayn Vindahl ring a bell? Tall, blond transfer student you hit on about a year ago. About eighteen years old?" Actually, Rayn was circling eight hundred. But Jason didn't need to know that.

Jason frowned. "Rayn...oh. Oh."

"Oh's right, buddy. How many girls have you put in

compromising situations because they refused to sleep with you?"

"Is that what she told you?" Jason placed the spice jars on the table—oregano and red chili flakes. "Wait, how do you even know Rayn?"

"It's a small world."

"Yeah, well, she wasn't very honest with you." Jason ran one hand through his chocolate waves. "Rayn approached *me* in that bar. She wanted me to go back to her place, but she was completely blitzed. Wouldn't have remembered a thing in the morning. That's not how I work."

My eyes narrowed. "*Ja*, right."

Jason shrugged. "Believe me or don't, but it's the truth. I'd never sleep with a girl who didn't know what she was getting herself into. I told Rayn she needed to sleep off the alcohol—took her outside and called a car to get her home. But once she realized I wasn't going with her, she bolted back in the bar. Probably hooked up with some other guy, I don't know. I didn't see her after that."

My head buzzed. I scanned Jason's body language for telltale signs of dishonesty, but his eye contact was steady, his voice didn't tremble, and his hands rested easily atop the table, no tension in his veins. Either he was *really* good at lying, or Rayn was in *serious* violation of the valkyrie code. She hadn't made captain rank, and accordingly was prohibited from dating—and most definitely from propositioning the subject she'd been sent to investigate.

"Wait, is *that* why you don't like me?" Jason's eyes widened. "You think I hit on your friend?"

"I thought you *hurt* my friend," I corrected. Or put her in a compromising position. Or…My thoughts were all mixed up. I was going to have a *major* sit down with Rayn when I got back to Asgard.

"Well, I didn't hurt your friend." Jason leaned back and crossed his arms. "*Now* can you stop going all ice queen on me?"

I pursed my lips together. The truth was, what I'd thought happened between Jason and Rayn was only part of why I didn't like Jason. The other part was because I kind of did like him—he was the only member of the household who didn't treat me like I had one foot already in the grave. But the last time I let myself actually care for someone he'd…

He…

"Freya." Jason nudged my foot under the table. "Can you turn off the ice queen?"

I shot him a glare. "I'm not an ice queen."

"Prove it." The competitive spark flickered in Jason's eye. What was it with the Ahlströms?

"Excuse me?"

"Prove you're not an ice queen. Take a walk with me after we finish eating, and don't roll your eyes, or glare, or do anything other than *just be nice* the whole time. I dare you."

"Jason, that's ridiculous. I don't—"

"Man." Jason shook his head. "Couldn't even get through one sentence without an eye roll."

"That's not true! I—"

"And there's the glare." Jason crossed his arms over his chest. "You suck at this."

I opened my mouth to give him a piece of my mind, but the sparkle in his eyes caught me off guard. Despite my misgivings, I was enjoying Jason's company. And I was certainly enjoying his cooking.

"Fine. But if you're going to be so difficult, I'm going make it worth my while."

"I'm listening."

"If I win, you get your sister and her boyfriend to treat me *normally*. Like you do. I know they're worried, but the way everybody walks on eggshells around me is driving me insane." If Mia and Tyr backed off, the others would follow.

I hoped.

Jason leaned back in his chair. "Do I get to ask exactly why they worry about you so much?"

"No, you do not. Do you accept my terms?"

Jason shrugged. "Deal. And if I win, you have to sit down—*nicely*—and work out what this sauce is missing with me. This batch is already done; adding to it after the fact isn't going to be as effective as letting the flavors cook in."

"You really want to beat Mia, don't you?" I rubbed my fingers along the edge of my napkin.

"Desperately."

I shrugged. "Then it's on."

"It's on." Jason picked up his fork. "Now tell me, Freya, have you always tended toward the frosty side or do I just bring out the very best in you? Remember, all eye rolls result in an immediate forfeit."

"What? No. That starts after we finish eating. Those were your terms."

"Love, you're going to need *lots* of practice." Jason winked. "Best to pace yourself."

Dear gods. What had I gotten myself into?

A seeming eternity had passed since we'd left the warmth of the Arcata cabin. Despite Jason spending most of that time attempting to goad me, I'd maintained my non-judgmental face. Jason had finally relented, and we'd spent the last few minutes in somewhat companionable silence, walking through the thick ferns and towering redwoods. A light chill hung in the early summer air, making me appreciate my thin sweater. The coastal California region should have been a good fifteen degrees warmer than it had been all week—a sure sign Ragnarok loomed ever closer.

"So." I broke the silence, mostly to derail my morbid train of thought. "Cooking's your thing, huh?"

Jason's athletic figure moved effortlessly beside me. "Mama taught us when we were little. I wasn't that into it at first, but eventually I figured out it has its uses."

"Like when you realized girls like guys who cook for them?"

Jason turned his head with whip-like speed. "Come on. Seriously? No eye roll on that one?"

"I told you." I lifted my chin. "I'm not an ice queen."

"We'll see about that." Jason chuckled. "But yeah, girls do seem to appreciate my cooking. Got you to take a walk with me, didn't it?"

"Was that your plan all along? Dazzle me with your chicken, then lure me into the woods to…" To what? Jason was walking a solid four feet to my left—well out of touching range. He obviously wasn't planning to seduce me. Had I read him all wrong? Was I even his type? Tall redheads weren't for everybody. Gods, was Jason actually *not into me?*

"I have no plan." The object of my confusion raised both hands in mock surrender. "I'm just out for a walk, trying to win a bet so I can beat my sister at cooking. Nothing devious about that."

"Sure." Seriously, was he not into me?

You're not into him either. Remember?

Right.

"What about you? I don't know a thing about you except that you're my sister's friend, you grew up with her boyfriend and her roommate, and my chicken parmesan is the best thing you've ever eaten," Jason said.

"It was pretty good," I conceded. "But Henrik's hotcakes are better."

"Ouch." Jason clutched his hands to his heart as if he'd been stabbed. "Beaten by the beast."

"The beast?" I laughed. "Hardly. Henrik's a softie."

"Yeah, but he's massive. I've seen tree trunks smaller

than that guy's arms." Jason shook his head. "What's he bench? Two, three hundred?"

"I don't know." Admitting Henrik and Tyr lifted boulders back in Asgard would be oversharing. Secrecy was the name of the game when mingling with mortals.

Not that I was mingling. I was performing the necessary function of entertaining Tyr's girlfriend's brother, aiding the preservation of our safe house and identities. There was *definitely* no mingling to be had.

No matter what the stupid light show in my head had to say about it.

"Come on, give me something. What about your family? Are they good with you living in California? That's pretty far from Sweden."

"Ah, well." I studied the ground, careful not to step on the smattering of flowers breaking through the moss. Mia had done a good job feeding her brother our "exchange students from Sweden" cover story. She probably hadn't revealed any more about any of us than absolutely necessary, but I needed to test the water just in case. "Mia hasn't told you anything else about my family?"

"Nothing." Jason shook his head. "Why? Is there a good story there?"

Orphaned, raised by the Norn Verdandi, and guarded by the original valkyries probably constituted a good family story on Midgard. But since we were still flying under the radar, I gave a nonchalant shrug and just said, "Not really."

"Come on, love. Tell me about the young ice queen."

Jason didn't break his stride as he nudged me with his elbow.

"I'm not a—oh, forget it." A stream of air escaped my lips on a strong huff. "Fine. My parents died when I was young, so I was raised by…" I racked my brain for a plausible Midgardian substitute. "By my godmother."

"Whoa."

I'd taken several steps before I realized Jason had stopped walking.

"Whoa, what?" I turned around.

"I didn't know about your parents. Mia never told me. I'm sorry."

"Don't be." I shrugged again. "They died noble deaths. Both were warriors."

"No wonder you're so tough." Jason eyed me with something akin to respect. "I can't imagine growing up without my parents. Did you have any other family nearby?"

"My concept of family is pretty broad." I softened my tone. "To me, the family you choose is every bit as significant as the one you were born into. So, I didn't have biological aunts or uncles or cousins, but I didn't lack for family. My godmother had lots of… friends"—*valkyries*—"who lived with us"—*in the valkyrie compound the Norns created to protect me*—"and played with me."—*trained me to be a warrior so I wouldn't become my realm's greatest liability*. "And when I got to go to school, I met Tyr and Elsa and everyone, and my family got even bigger. So…it was good."

Jason let out a low whistle before raking his hand

through his hair. "I thought you said you didn't have a good story."

"It's a pretty tame story where I'm from." It was. My best friend was a half-giant who'd been adopted by Asgard's then-God of War, and a third of the valkyries under my charge had lost at least one parent in the defense of the realm. But Jason didn't need to know anyone else's story—or even the full version of mine.

Not yet.

My entire body stilled as I wondered what that meant.

"Freya? You all right?"

I shook my shoulders, forcing myself to focus. "Never better. What about you? What was it like growing up in…Connecticut, right?"

"Right." Jason shoved his hands into the pockets of his puffy vest. "It was pretty normal. Sunday dinners with the grandparents, summer camping trips, sports— lots of sports. Football and baseball were my favorites."

"Mia speaks very highly of your family. It's wonderful that you're so close."

"We're lucky that way." Jason eyed me. "Sorry—I didn't—"

"Please." I raised a hand. "Everybody has a story. I won't have anyone pitying mine."

"Fair enough." Jason took a few steps to his right and tilted his head to the sky. After a short silence, he shifted his gaze to me. "You like stars?"

"As much as the next girl."

"Come here." Jason motioned for me to join him. I stepped cautiously across the mossy forest floor.

"Yes?"

"Look right up there." Jason placed his hands on my shoulders. When he'd positioned me directly in front of him, he reached around with one arm to point to the sky.

I ignored the way my skin tingled where his shoulder pressed into mine. "What am I looking at?"

"Ursa Major—the Big Dipper." Jason's breath tickled my ear. I forcibly reminded myself that I'd yet to receive a contract update from the Norns, and therefore Jason was *not* for me. Though he was awfully good looking. Maybe I could just…

No, Freya. Bad idea.

Or is it?

"Everyone knows the constellation, but I like the story behind it," Jason said.

"Why's that?" It was purely a matter of balance that made me lean into him as he spoke. I was in complete control of myself. *Perfekt* control, actually.

Pursuant to the explicit terms of my contract.

"Because this particular constellation served as an eye test for ancient fighters. One of the stars is a double —if a man could identify which of the stars was the double, he was granted warrior status."

"Just the men?" I raised an eyebrow. "Patriarchal societies were so backwards."

"True, but they were also chivalrous," Jason countered. "Allowing someone to protect you doesn't make you weak. On the contrary, trusting someone enough to let them see your vulnerabilities is a sign of strength. And love."

The words loosened something in my heart, and released one of the infinite knots tethering me to my pain. But while Jason's sentiment rang true, he needed to understand something bigger.

"I don't need protecting," I said softly.

"Mia told me that you've been sick." Jason's breath was cool against my ear. "And it's obvious you're very independent, and that the way your friends coddle you drives you nuts. It'd drive me nuts, too. A constant reminder that I'm different from what they're used to? Not helpful. But from everything I've seen, your friends—your chosen family—really want to be there for you. Are you letting them?"

"I'm…" I closed my eyes. "I'm trying."

"Good." Jason lightly placed one hand on my hip. A bolt of energy resonated through my body, spiking my pulse and making me shiver at the same time. *Bad idea, Freya. Bad, bad, bad.* I quickly stepped forward, putting some distance between us. "Freya?"

"I—er—did you hear that?" I blurted.

"Hear what?"

"Nothing. Guess I imagined it. So, uh, the stars." *Lame.*

Jason's brow furrowed. "Hold on. Now I hear it."

What? "You do?"

"It sounds big." Jason pulled me behind him and

broadened his stance. "It's coming from the edge of the clearing. I'll look into it."

A low growl rang through the woods, sending blades of fear ripping into my gut. What if it was one of our enemies? They'd opened a portal in these woods before—and nobody knew better than me how terrifying capture would be. *I can't let Jason walk into that.*

"No, don't!" I blurted. "I'll go."

"Like hell you will," Jason objected. "Go back to the cabin. I'll distract it until you're gone, then follow you. But if it takes me down, run like he—where are you going?"

"Stay there!" I called over my shoulder as I charged into the trees. I was *not* letting Jason anywhere near whatever demon lurked in the woods. I ran faster, tapping the communication device on my wrist as I moved. "Tyr, possible hostile at the northeast corner of the clearing due west of the main cabin. I'm investigating, but Jason is unmanned. Extract him if I don't come back."

"What the Helheim are you doing?" Tyr's low voice came through my comm. "Freya, disengage. I can be there in—"

"No time. It could be a—" I blinked at the sight of the gigantic, furry creature rising on two legs. "Never mind. Don't send backup. It's just a bear."

An extremely angry, possibly offspring-defending bear, but a Midgardian mammal was infinitely more manageable than a raging fire giant. Or worse.

"You sure?" Tyr barked from my wrist. "Why are

you in the forest, anyway? Jason's supposed to be watching you at the house."

A surge of frustration shot through me. "I don't need watching. I am not a child!" The bear's ears flicked, and I forced myself to speak softly when I said, "I have to go. See you at home."

Exercising tremendous self-control, I tapped the communicator with one finger and lowered my head. Making sure to stay low to the ground, I slowly backed away from the enormous brown animal. At the same time, I scanned the region for cubs. Sure enough, two brown fur balls were tumbling in the ferns roughly twenty yards away from their mother. No wonder her hackles were raised—Jason and I had unknowingly posed a threat to the things she loved more than anything in the world. And biology mandated she protect that love with everything she had.

Using those massive teeth.

"Sorry, Mama," I murmured softly, still backing away. "They're safe."

I called up the last few drops in my reserve and pushed a wave of love at the bear. As a rule, animals were quick to pick up on energy, and this one was no different. Her lips curled back down over her teeth, and she dropped down to four paws and silently padded toward her cubs. Nudging them with her nose, she pushed them away from the meadow and deeper into the forest, glancing over her shoulder before disappearing into the woods. The whole exchange had taken less than a minute, and by the time I'd turned around Jason was running toward me.

"Freya! Jeez, I couldn't find you." Jason rushed to my side, an enormous stick in hand. "Where is it?"

Had he been planning to use that pitiful weapon to attack a bear? Or, if my gut had been right, a dark elf? *Bless*.

"It's gone. It was just a mama bear." I gently pressed the stick down until it hung at Jason's side. "And I told you to stay where you were."

"Well, I told *you* to go back to the house. A bear? Seriously, you could have been killed."

"I told you, I didn't need protecting," I reminded him.

"I guess you don't." Jason grinned. "You're something else. You know that?"

"Thanks." Even as I brushed off the compliment, a glow built deep inside my chest. "Come on. Let's go home before something else tries to eat us. You were telling me about the stars?"

"You sure you're okay?" Jason tossed the stick to the ground.

"I'm good. Honest. Come on." I walked back the way we'd come, confident Jason would follow. Sure enough, his footsteps fell softly behind mine. "So. Any other constellations I should know about?"

"Well, that's one of my favorites." Jason came up beside me and pointed to the patch of sky just above the tree line. "Corona Borealis. Those seven stars make up the Northern Crown."

"What's the story behind that one?" I pulled my sweater tighter around my chest, a pointless effort to ward off the summer's unseasonable chill.

"Once upon a time a terrible monster called the Minotaur wreaked havoc on Crete. The people were able to contain the Minotaur in a maze, but they were terrified it would break free. This hero, Theseus, set out to destroy the monster. But he didn't do it alone—he needed help from his true love." Jason shifted to face me. His twinkling eyes warmed my cheeks.

"Who was that?" I mumbled, ignoring the heat pooling just south of my navel.

"His brilliant, fierce, take-no-prisoners fiancée. Princess Ariadne knew that even if Theseus managed to kill the monster, he'd never find his way out of the maze. That was the whole point—the maze was created to make sure the Minotaur never, ever escaped. Ariadne gave Theseus a ball of string to unwind as he made his way through. After he slayed the beast, he followed the string through the labyrinth, where his love was waiting to marry him. The seven stars make up the points of the crown Ariadne wore on her wedding day. They appear in the sky every night as a reminder that respect, love, and teamwork are all we need to slay any monster—mythological or otherwise."

My heart thumped frantically against my ribcage.

Stand down. He's not your match.

I don't care.

Yes, you do. You can't do this to another guy. Remember what happened to—

I shut the thought down before the tsunami of pain drove me under.

"That's…beautiful," I whispered. I forced my gaze from Jason's smoldering eyes, and blinked up at the stars. "They taught you that in astronomy class, huh?"

"They taught me the names and designs of the constellations in astronomy class. But I like the stories behind the science. Things are rarely what they appear on the surface."

The rumble in Jason's voice pulled my attention from the sky. He'd tilted his head to the side, and now studied my face with unbridled curiosity.

"Wh-what do you mean?" I wrapped my arms around my chest.

"I thought you were an ice queen when I first got here. But it turns out you're a pretty cool chick. Smart. Intense. Strong as hell. And I think there's a softness deep, *deep* inside there that some lucky guy's going to get to uncover. If you ever decide to let anyone in."

"I…uh…" Jason Ahlström was fast breaking down my carefully crafted wall. And I wasn't sure I liked it.

I wasn't sure I didn't like it, either.

"Look at that." Jason stepped close enough that his woodsy scent filled my space. My heartrate spiked, the pounding in my chest now jackhammering against my ribcage.

I was so screwed.

"Look at what?" I whispered.

"The ice queen's blushing." Jason reached up, the backs of his fingers gently brushing my jawline.

Heat flooded my face anew. All sense flew out the window as I allowed myself to lean into the touch. Jason turned his hand around so his palm cupped my cheek. He ran the pad of his thumb along my jawline, and my lips parted.

"What are you doing?" I whispered. Whatever it was, it could only end in heartbreak.

Or worse.

"Freya," Jason murmured. He took the final step into my space, wrapping an arm around the small of my back. He pulled me into him in a swift movement, forcing the air from my lungs in a surprised gasp. He was so close I couldn't miss the pulse of his heart against my chest, or the electricity pinging from the too-intense eyes now lined up perfectly with mine.

"Jason, I don't think—"

"Exactly." Jason slid his hand from my cheek to the back of my neck. He laced his fingers through my hair, holding me in place. "Don't think."

I brought my hand up, pressing lightly against Jason's chest. "I—"

Jason stared at me, his hooded eyes communicating his desire in a way words never could. All I had to do was say the word, and he'd be mine for as long as I wanted him to be.

Or until the Norns took him away. By force.

In that instant, Jason's face morphed into my final vision of Rhylark's—the agonized pain in his eyes; the unspoken recognition on his lips; and the unflinching willingness to put Asgard first so the realm could survive. My hand trembled, and I quickly removed it from Jason's chest. I couldn't do this to him—there was only one way this could end, and he shouldn't have to pay that price. I couldn't do this to Mia—she'd been nothing but kind to me…and she brought unparalleled happiness to Tyr, who needed stability now more than ever. And I most certainly couldn't do this to myself. I was barely holding on to my sanity; I couldn't afford another loss of that magnitude.

Not when my healing was so fragile.

Not when my heart was already so torn.

And not when the future of the realms was on the line. The Norns had taught me that this kind of love was a vulnerability—one I could never afford again.

"Freya?" Jason's eyes widened. "Are you okay?"

"Yes. No. I—uh…" Jason's face blurred in and out of focus. I wouldn't be the reason our realm fell. I wouldn't be the reason the worlds went dark. And—I blinked back tears as the memory of the last time Rhylark held me flooded my vision. *No.* I would *not* be the reason Jason's future was taken from him. He deserved more.

He deserved to live.

"Freya! What's wrong? You're ice cold—"

But Jason's voice dropped into silence as my world narrowed to a single point. As I stared into twin orbs of unknowing, too-trusting indigo–blue, my head clouded and my thoughts swam. Strong arms enveloped me as the world turned black.

CHAPTER 7

BRYNN

"MIA! TYR! WHERE IS everybody? I need help!" Jason's panic blasted through the cabin. My fingers gripped the edges of the kitchen island. Henrik shot me a look that clearly said, *what now?* Gods, if I knew. We'd only just gotten home from dinner at Elsa's. We were about to help ourselves to second dessert from the never-ending mountain of Mia's baking, but apparently, duty called.

Again.

"We're in here." Henrik pushed himself off his stool. He gave the plate of white chocolate macadamia nut cookies a wistful look. "Any chance this is a low-level crisis and I can take a few of these to go?"

"There's always a chance," I offered.

"I don't know what happened to her!" Jason appeared in the kitchen doorway, a limp Freya in his arms. Her body was turned into him so we couldn't see her face, but her strawberry waves hung limply to Jason's knees, and she wasn't moving, save for the torso shifts that synched with his steps.

"*Skit*." I jumped to my feet while Henrik practically blurred to Jason's side.

"Take her to the couch and lay her down," Henrik commanded. "Brynn, get Elsa and Lornara over here. And if Tyr's not already on his way—"

"My ears are ringing." Tyr's voice carried more amusement than was customary. He and Mia must have had a *really* good date.

One we were about to flatline.

"Move, Jason. *Now*." Henrik nudged Jason back into the hallway.

Two sets of heavy footsteps stormed in tandem toward the living room. I hurried after them, tapping on my com to send a quick message to Elsa, and entering the hall just in time to see date night ruined. Mia and Tyr stood by the front door, twin statues of horror. Mia's delicate hands covered her mouth while Tyr's eyes narrowed in anger.

"Who did this to her?" he growled.

"Nobody did anything," Jason protested. He laid Freya gently on the couch, and pulled a throw off its back to wrap around her legs. "One minute we were looking at stars, and the next…"

Tyr's focus snapped. "The bear in the forest. Did you actually see it? Or was it…something else?"

"I, uh…" Jason took a step back as Tyr stormed into

the living room. I didn't blame him. Tyr was part giant —not that Jason knew that—and not only did he stand taller than six-and-a-half feet, but he did fury like no other.

"Tyr." I placed a warning hand on his bicep. He flexed the muscle hard enough to push me away.

Ugh.

"I want to know what kind of affliction we're dealing with," Tyr growled. "If one of the frost giants found a way through and—"

"Frost giants?" Disbelief danced across Jason's features. "Are you okay, man?"

"Rival gang!" Mia blurted. "There's this gang in, uh, Eureka." She named Arcata's neighboring town. "They're called the Frost Giants, and sometimes they do, uh, bad things around town."

I blinked at my friend. Mia was good. But a healthy dose of skepticism was vibing off Jason. He was her brother—he'd know when she was lying.

"Mia," Jason said in a low tone. "What's going on?"

"We're here! Where is everyone?" Elsa slammed the front door.

"This way," Henrik barked.

Elsa and Lornara rushed into the living room. Their faces were mirrors of concern as they dropped to their knees beside the couch. Elsa had to nudge Jason out of the way to claim her place beside Freya.

"I'm sorry, Jason, but we're going to need you to leave," Elsa said gently. "This is a family matter."

"A family matter?" Jason balked, whether at Elsa's words or Lornara's wings, I wasn't sure.

"Yes. Ours may be a bit unconventional, but families come in all shapes and sizes, each as unique as the multitude of beings that comprise them. Lornara, open up the healing bag and pull out the peach aventurine, a selenite wand, and a vial."

"You have wings." Jason stared at Lornara.

"Cosplay," Mia blurted. "Jason, meet Lornara. She works at, uh, a renaissance fair."

Right.

"Hi. And I'm not leaving Freya," Jason said firmly.

Elsa looked up in surprise. "You have to. Right, Tyr?"

Tyr shot his sister a look of frustration. "I don't give a *skit* anymore what Jason knows or doesn't know. The only thing I'm worried about is bringing Freya back. Again. *Forbäsket,* why can't you heal her already?"

"What do you think I've been trying to do?" Elsa threw up a hand. "That's been my primary focus for over a *year!*" She took the slightly cloudy crystal wand Lornara handed her, and ran it along Freya's body from head to toe. "Jason, I'm sorry, but you really can't be here right now."

"*Skit.*" Tyr glanced at his phone before turning on one heel to stomp out of the room. "Odin. I have to take this. Elsa, *fix her.*"

"I'm trying! Stop yelling at me!"

"I'm not yelling!" Tyr bellowed over his shoulder.

"Odin? Like Thor's dad, Odin? From the movies?" Jason turned to his sister. "What the hell is going on?"

"Odin's a, uh, very common name in Sweden." Mia's eyes darted to the side—her signature tell.

"Bull." Jason folded his arms. "You guys don't want to tell me what's happening here, fine. But I'm with Tyr. Do whatever it takes to get Freya better. I don't know what's wrong with her. I don't know what made her pass out. But I…I really like her. And I want to help."

Freya drew a shaky breath, but remained otherwise motionless.

Elsa and Lornara exchanged a glance. The two of them had always shared some secret healer code—one the rest of us never tried to understand. Without a word, Lornara passed over a peach-colored rock, and Elsa pressed it to Freya's heart. Elsa frowned as the rock pulsed with a brown haze, before resetting to its apparently-resting peach hue.

"Okay, Jason, come here." Elsa waved him down.

Jason knelt between her and Lornara. "Now what?"

"We want to try something," Lornara explained. "Take Freya's hands in yours, and tell her what you just told us."

"That I want to help?" Jason asked uncertainly.

"That." Lornara nodded. "And that you like her."

"Uh…" Jason eyed the comatose girl on the couch.

"Trust us," Elsa said easily.

"All right." Jason drew a breath and cupped Freya's hands between his own. "Freya." He shot a glance over his shoulder, where Henrik, Mia, and I watched with rapt fascination.

Oh. Right.

"Sorry," I blurted. "Guys, look away."

"Right." Henrik turned to face the window, pulling me along with him. Mia followed suit, and we all took a sudden interest in the twilight that filtered through the redwoods beyond our porch. Jason murmured behind us, too quietly for me to make out the words. *Dang it.* After a long pause, a sharp intake of air was followed by a swear word I'd never heard pass Elsa's lips.

"We were right," Lornara whispered.

"Right?" Freya's shaky voice made me whip right around. Forget privacy—what had Jason done to not only wake her, but get her upright? Freya was three-quarters of the way to being full-on sitting up when just seconds ago she'd been down for the count. What was in that magic rock?

"Careful." Lornara guided Freya so she could lean against the plushy cushions. "How are you feeling?"

"Dizzy," Freya admitted. "But good. The weight in my chest is gone, and so is the fear I've carried since Hel had me trapped in that cage and I thought I'd be stuck in Helheim forev—" She broke off as her focus zeroed in on the mortal kneeling at her feet. "Oh, gods," she whispered. "I didn't—I mean…"

"Thank God you're okay." Jason carefully wrapped his arms around Freya.

Her rigid shoulders softened in his embrace, and

she rested her head against his. Her strawberry waves brushed against Jason's brown ones, and her cheeks flushed a healthy pink as she closed her eyes in what was fast turning into a *very* personal moment.

I was about to order Henrik to turn around again, when Jason pulled his head back. "Did you just say someone named Hel trapped you in a cage?"

Freya's eyes flew open. "I…uh…"

"Metaphor," Mia blurted. "It's the metaphorical cage of Freya's, erm, depression?"

"I am not depressed." Freya frowned. "At least, I don't think I am. But *ja*, the cage was…a metaphor. For whatever's actually wrong with me."

"Uh-huh." Jason's expression was unreadable. I had the impression he wasn't fully buying into our cover story. To be fair, we weren't exactly being the best secret squirrels.

Henrik nudged my shoulder as footsteps thundered down the stairs. I followed my boyfriend's sightline to the entryway, where Tyr burst into the living room. His hair stood in wild tufts atop his head, the whites of his eyes were twice their normal size, and his nostrils flared with heavy breaths. He clutched his phone in one white-knuckled hand.

Something was majorly wrong.

"Tyr?" Mia flitted to his side. She placed a gentle hand on his bicep.

"It's begun."

The room was instantly filled with anxious antic-ipation.

"*Skit*," Henrik swore. He reached over to wrap one massive hand around mine. I let his warmth encase my palm, even as liquid ice coursed through the rest of my body.

It's begun.

The words settled heavily in my head. Ragnarok was here. And we most definitely were not ready. We'd need to hold a strategy meeting, find out where our team would be shipped to best serve Asgard, figure out who could orchestrate the valkyrie attack since Freya was in no condition to lead us, assemble all the tech we'd crafted and Bifrost it to the Elite Team captains stationed near the most immediate threats—

"What's begun?" Jason asked.

Right. And we'd need to figure out what to do about the worried human still kneeling at Freya's side. Anxiety pulsed fiercely off the four gods, one *älva*, and Mia. Jason knelt in the middle of a veritable storm of emotion, taking it all in.

Skit.

Elsa's phone beeped with an incoming message. She slowly drew it from her back pocket, her fingers trembling. "Forse must have heard. He's on his way back from his..." Her cheeks blanched as what little color she had drained away. "His mom," she whispered.

"What about his mom?" Tyr gritted.

Elsa's phone clattered to the floor. "No," she whispered. "Not Nanna."

"Elsa? Talk to us," Tyr ordered. Elsa's mouth opened and closed, but no sound emerged. With a nod, Tyr stared at his sister. No doubt he'd dived into her head, using the secret sibling communication system Odin had gifted them. Sometimes I envied their ability to read each other's minds.

Even when the message they shared was horrific enough to turn both Fredriksens' faces white.

"No." Tyr's hands trembled, whether with sorrow or rage, I couldn't yet ascertain.

Lornara reached for the fallen phone. She picked it up and read Forse's message.

"Mom passed minutes before I arrived. My brother says she died of grief. She and Dad will have a joint service."

"*Skit.*" Tyr pulled his shoulders back and barked orders like a drill sergeant. "He doesn't know it's begun. Elsa, go get Forse and bring him back here. Lornara, go with her—I don't want anyone traveling alone right now. Henrik, Brynn, go upstairs and take inventory of all the tech on hand. Pull what you'll need for our team, and prep the rest for distribution. Mia." Tyr's eyes softened as he looked down at his girlfriend. "Take your brother out onto the porch and tell him."

What?

Freya gasped. "Tyr!"

"Tell him?" Mia's lips formed a small O. "How much?"

"Everything." Tyr shrugged. "Somebody's going to have to stay behind and protect Freya until she's fit to resume her duties."

"And Jason did say he wanted to help," Elsa chimed in.

"Careful what you wish for around here," Henrik deadpanned. I elbowed him in the ribs.

"Right." Mia gave a firm nod, and crossed to the entryway. "Jason, come with me."

Jason raised one eyebrow, but followed Mia onto the porch without a word. Elsa and Lornara set a cluster of rocks in front of Freya before stepping back.

"He makes you better. You know that," Lornara said softly.

"I know," Freya whispered. "But I can't—I mean, the last time I…It's not an option."

"Things change," Elsa reminded her. "Maybe this time the Norns will—"

Freya shut her down with a firm, "I can't go there."

Elsa frowned. "I understand. But try to be open. We need you in the field as soon as you're ready."

"I'm ready now, so—"

"You're not fit to lead the valkyries into war. At least, not today." Tyr's tone left no room for question. "Look, I know what happened with Rhylark was Helheim for you. And I know you don't want to walk through that particular fire again. But I need you to do whatever is necessary to get yourself operational as soon as possible. The realms need Love. And the valkyries need their leader."

"You can't tell me to stay here!" Freya's wide eyes pleaded with Tyr. "I can't do that. Look what happened the last time I let somebody do my job! Nanna was so busy doing *my* work, she wasn't there for Balder when he needed her! And…and now she's—"

"You're benched until you've healed from whatever is happening with you. You need to appoint a successor. I'm sorry, but in this condition, you're a liability."

Freya's shoulders sagged. She dropped back into the cushions of the couch with a heavy sigh. "I understand."

Tyr's eyes filled with compassion. He crossed to the couch and sat beside his friend, taking her hand as she stared bleakly at the wall. After a beat, he looked up to where Henrik, Elsa, Lornara, and I still stood. "What are you waiting for? You have your orders, now go. Reconvene here in five."

Without a word, I turned on one heel and marched from the living room. I hung a left and jogged up the stairs, with Henrik close behind. The click of a door let me know Elsa and Lornara had left to retrieve Forse from Asgard, though how they were going to Bifrost in and out without Jason noticing, if that was even an issue anymore, I had no idea. They'd have to blur pretty far behind the compound to get an undetected pickup—though I supposed even harder tasks lay ahead of us.

Henrik and I entered the upstairs lab and immediately set about dividing the numerous devices we'd developed during our time in Arcata.

"I've got the aeros and the hydros over here. Three of each; we can keep one set, and send the others to whoever's captaining the Muspelheim team." I stuffed two sets of the fire-extinguishing devices into a bag I pulled from a drawer, and moved on to the next piece of tech. "And the vacuum—there's only one up here, but I think we have more in the garage lab, right?'

"Right," Henrik confirmed. He pulled a backpack from the closet and stuffed the extinguishers I'd earmarked for our team inside. "We'll go downstairs next. What about the meltexes? De-icers should go to the Jotunheim team, but it's cold season in Nidavellir. Maybe we'll send one to that captain, too?"

"It'd be easier to allocate if we knew where the hostilities were focused," I grumbled.

"We can change it up after our briefing." Henrik shoved one of the meltexes into the backpack, and nudged the rest to me. I placed them carefully into a new bag, and moved along to Henrik's right.

"Popples?" I asked. "Those transporters should go to whoever's closest to the open threat, for sure."

"Definitely." Henrik nodded. "We'll decide after we have more intel. Ugh, too bad we don't have more of the closers. Portals are going to be popping up all over the place by the time the heavy fighting's underway. I wish we could send these to every warrior."

"*Ja*, but we can only do what we can do." I shrugged. "Keep that one with us—you're protecting Tyr, and we can't afford to let War fall. Or get captured."

"He'll be okay," Henrik said softly.

I shot him a look, my eyes saying the words my lips didn't dare speak.

Would he?

I shivered. Tyr was more than just our friend—he

was the leader of our army; a key member of Odin's cabinet; and the last line of defense between the order of Asgard and absolute Chaos. As his bodyguard, Henrik had one of the most important jobs a warrior could have.

I placed my hand on Henrik's shoulder. "Be careful out there. I don't know what I'd do if anything ever happened to you."

"Oh, *sötnos.*" He wrapped thick arms around me. "You don't have anything to worry about. I'm the best at what I do. Remember?"

"*Ja.* But this is Ragnarok," I reminded him. "Rules don't apply anymore."

"I know," Henrik murmured. "But when it comes to you and me, Brynnie, there's one rule that's never going to change."

"What's that?"

Henrik pulled back to plant a light kiss on the tip of my nose. "I'm your *perfekt* match, remember? Whether it's in these realms or Valhalla, we're a team. And nothing, not even the mother of all battles, can separate us."

"I love you," I whispered fiercely before pulling Henrik in for a desperate kiss. Since I didn't know how many more moments we'd have together, I intended to take full advantage of this one.

But much too soon, Henrik withdrew his lips from mine and turned my shoulders toward the door. Duty called.

It always did.

"I love you too. Now get your cute butt downstairs

and start allocating the garage tech. I'll drop the bags we've finished at the front door, and be right behind you." Henrik slapped my behind. I turned around and took a mental picture of his playful grin, knowing I'd need something happy to hold on to in the days that followed.

Odin willing those days actually came to pass.

When we reconvened in the living room, the air was thick with anxiety. Freya, Elsa, and I were lined up on the couch, a trifecta of barely contained panic. Lornara hovered beside the arm of the sectional, her sparkly wings fluttering as she shifted from foot to foot. Tyr paced in front of the fireplace, hands clasped behind his back. And Henrik and Forse were positioned in front of the window, their arms crossed. We'd rushed to comfort Forse the minute he and Elsa stepped into the house, but he'd brushed our sympathy off in a rare display of sternness. I got it—he couldn't afford to break down with Ragnarok underway, and shutting us out was the only way he knew to keep it together. But I'd caught a fleeting glance between him and Elsa, and the complete brokenness in his eyes nearly tore me apart. Forse was one of the kindest souls I'd ever had the pleasure of knowing. He, of all gods, shouldn't have to experience loss on this level. He deserved joy. And light. And love.

He deserved everything.

Elsa would be there to pick him up when the dust settled and he was finally allowed to grieve—we all would. But for now, she sat beside me on the couch, careful not to look at her fiancé... though we all knew she was sending him whatever healer vibes were keeping him from completely breaking down.

I was so grateful they had each other.

Henrik winced at Mia's frustrated shout. He glanced over his shoulder, peering toward the porch where the Ahlströms were having it out. Through the window, I heard snatches of what sounded like an increasingly heated conversation. *Yikes.*

"How's it going out there?" I leaned over so I could whisper in Elsa's ear.

"Not great," she admitted. "Jason's worked through denial, and now he's angry Mia wasn't honest with him from the beginning."

"I think he's moved past anger and is just hurt she didn't trust him to protect her," Lornara said.

"Mmm. That may be," Elsa agreed.

"Is he angry with me, too?" Freya asked quietly from her corner of the couch. With her knees tucked to her chest and her arms wrapped around her shins, she looked more like a forlorn schoolgirl than the commander of a legion of elite warriors. Everything about Freya broke my heart.

"He's not angry with you." Elsa reached over me to place a loving hand atop Freya's. "And if he acts that way, remember—anger's not real. It's just a mask for a deeper, more vulnerable emotion."

"Ja," Freya muttered into her knees.

"Jason cares for you a great deal," Lornara chimed in. "But this is a lot for him to take in. Especially now."

Right. Now that the worlds were ending, we'd decided to throw Mia's brother into the ring. Not our kindest call, but what choice did we have? Freya needed protecting. And the rest of us had our own roles to play.

Roles that might buy us a one-way ticket to Valhalla.

Don't go there, Aksel.

"Listen up." Tyr stopped pacing. He folded his arms so his biceps popped against his T-shirt.

"We're listening," Henrik growled.

I glanced to the window, where he and Forse still stood. The pair mirrored Tyr's pose, down to the matching scowls. There was a very high likelihood I might drown in the whirlpool of testosterone.

"Odin's report was not good," Tyr summarized. "Fenrir's escaped. He's planning to kill Odin and Frigga. They've been relocated to a secure facility while Odin strategizes his next steps, but I'm going to send a few members of the Elite Team into the palace to take Fenrir down once and for all."

"Tyr." Elsa exhaled softly. "I'm sorry."

"Me too. Guess nothing I did was ever going to change who he was born to be."

Poor guy. Fenrir had been Tyr's pet once upon a time. The two of them had been inseparable, taking the kinds of adventures only a jotun-bred wolf and a giant-born god could conceive. Fenrir had had a bad start to life, but Tyr had truly believed he could teach the wolf a different way…until the day Fenrir killed Mr. and Mrs. Fredriksen. Since then, Tyr had worried that there was no overcoming destiny—that because his birth father, Hymir, was a monster, that one day Tyr, too, would give into some pre-programmed evil framework.

"You and Fenrir are *not* the same," Elsa reminded him. Again. "He chose his path; you chose yours."

"Here's hoping." Tyr moved on. "I'm sending a second team after the snake. Jörmungandr intends to put a hit on Thor, so he and Sif are also on the move. They can take care of themselves, but I'm sending backup anyway."

"Do you want us to take on the snake?" Forse offered.

"No. Elite Team can handle that, too. You and Henrik are going to take on Naglfar with me."

"Naglfar?" Elsa shot Forse a worried look. "What kind of monster is Naglfar?"

"A boat," Tyr answered.

"A boat?" Elsa wrinkled her nose. "What's so scary about a boat?"

Tyr eyed his sister. "This one's made entirely of toenails."

Oh, ew!

"Naglfar's a trigger. If it sails, it has the ability to open the sky, which initiates a sequence that will give it direct access to the Bifrost. According to Odin, once

Naglfar crosses the Bifrost, the bridge will break under its weight. That cuts Asgard off from the realms and leaves it isolated, so our enemies can attack. A certain giant volunteered to sail the ship. Any guesses as to who that might be?"

"Hymir?" I whispered.

"None other," Tyr confirmed.

Oh, gods.

"That's a *lot* of elements moving together," I said. "Who's orchestrating them all?"

"Loki."

"*Skit.*" Henrik, Forse, and I swore in unison. The God of Mischief *hadn't* been on his uppers like we'd hoped—he'd been plotting the demise of the entire cosmos while we'd been focused on Tyr's crazy birth father. *Double skit.*

"At least Hymir's daughter is still locked up." I clung to the one positive I could find. "Do you think Runa might finally want to help us? Give us intel on Hymir in exchange for...whatever passes for currency in prison these days?"

"Highly doubtful," Tyr said, "Seeing as how she escaped with Fenrir and is, in all likelihood, fighting for the other side."

Forse let loose with a string of curse words I'd never heard from his gentlemanly mouth.

"Once all the players are in place and they've executed their attacks..." The vein in Tyr's neck bulged. "They're going to burn the earth and swallow the sky."

"The prophesy," Freya whispered.

Gods, it was. The Ragnarok prophesy ended with fire consuming the earth and darkness swallowing the sky. Nobody, god or mortal, would survive.

Nobody.

But I didn't feel like dying today.

"Okay." I clapped my hands together. "Tyr, Henrik and Forse are taking Hymir down. Where does that leave the rest of us?"

Tyr rubbed his jaw. "Elsa, I want you and Mia as far from the action as possible. And preferably in a secure location. Can you set up scanners from the man cave and work your Unifier magic from here?"

"I suppose," Elsa hemmed. "But as High Healer, I'll need to be in the field."

"I'll take care of the field," Lornara offered. "I have a strong team of healers on Alfheim. I'll retrieve them and go wherever the casualties are. Tyr, can you put someone in communication with me?"

"Absolutely. Thanks, Lornara."

"Of course." Lornara offered a tense smile.

Tyr continued. "Freya's going to stay here and focus on getting well as quickly as possible so she can return to active duty. Or at least, resume commanding her warriors remotely." Tyr jutted his chin at the window, where raised voices let us know the Ahlström siblings were still *discussing* things. "Jason will stay here and look after Freya."

Freya winced. Before Helheim, she'd been the most

formidable warrior I'd ever met. She had to hate Tyr saying she needed *looking after.*

"What about me?" I glanced between Freya and Tyr. Freya was technically my commanding officer, but if she was out of commission I supposed I answered directly to Tyr.

"You…" Tyr lifted a hand to Freya. "You tell her."

"Tell me what?"

"You're going to lead the valkyries in my place." Freya raised her chin. It trembled.

"What?" I blurted. "Freya, I'm not a leader."

"Yes, you are," she countered. "You've guided Mia into the fold beautifully. You almost singlehandedly orchestrated my extraction from Helheim—with a little help from Henrik and Tyr, of course."

"Freya, I—"

"You can do this," Freya assured. "There's nobody else I'd trust to stand in my place. I believe in you. Now you need to believe in yourself."

My heart swelled, both with love for Freya and pride at her words. "I won't let you down," I promised. I shot a panicked look at Henrik, whose reassuring gaze all but screamed *You got this, sötnos.* Gods, I hoped he was right.

"Brynn, you'll catch the Bifrost to Asgard with me, Henrik, and Forse. You can head to the valkyrie compound and take command from there. We'll stay in contact through our coms—Henrik, do you still have any of the transparent ones we used on Svartalfheim?

I'd rather switch over to those in case any of us get captured."

"I tossed enough for all of us in my backpack. Even you, Lornara," Henrik confirmed.

"*Takk*," she said.

"Hand them out, and we'll move out in ten." Tyr drew an unsteady breath. "I just want you all to know that..." He exhaled forcefully. "It's been a pleasure serving Asgard with each and every one of you. And if, Odin forbid, this is the last time we're all together—"

"Don't talk like that!" Elsa admonished.

"I just want you all to know that I...that I love you," he said gruffly. "And it will be my honor to fight alongside you in Valhalla."

Oh, gods. Even Tyr thought we were all going to die. On the list of epic pep talks, this one landed firmly the bottom. Somebody had to step it up.

Somebody.

Anybody?

I guessed that somebody was me.

"Enough goodbyes." I jumped to my feet. "We've got to get moving. Let's eliminate these perps and prove the Norns wrong. Screw their stupid prophecy. I still have a *lot* I want to accomplish. And *not* from some stuffy seat in Valhalla."

"You and me both, Brynnie," Henrik chimed in. With a wink, he turned to face our friends. "You heard the lady. Let's go kick some bad guy butt."

I raised my palm and Henrik slapped it in a determined high-five. We gathered up our weapons, holstered our swords, pulled the less stable pieces of tech from the locked weapons closet in the hall, and handed our friends the bags filled with the best technology we'd developed in our time together. Once everyone was loaded up, we shouldered our own tech-laden packs.

And once again, we set off to save the worlds from imminent destruction.

FREYA

THE BRILLIANTLY HUED FLASH signaled my friends' departure. My right foot scuffed against the area rug at the front window—the spot from which I'd watched the first Bifrost shoot Lornara to Alfheim, and Tyr, Henrik, Forse, and Brynn to Asgard. Odin only knew what Jason had thought of our rainbow transport; he and Mia were still working things out on the porch. With everything they had to talk through, I wasn't about to interrupt them.

Elsa closed the front door with a firm click before hastening up the stairs. "Send Mia to the man cave when she's finished with Jason. I'm going to convert the space so we can start Unifying from there."

"Else—" I bit down on my bottom lip. "What do I do?"

Elsa turned on one ballet flat. Her sky blue eyes turned down at the corners as she apprised me sadly. "Can you open your heart to Jason?"

A vise squeezed my chest, constricting my breath. "It would be horribly unfair of me to do that. You know what it would cost him."

"We don't know for sure. It's Ragnarok—the Norns *have* to release you. They just have to. And if they do… things could go differently this time."

"Or they could go exactly the same." I wrung my fingers together. "And then where would we be?"

Elsa cast a pointed look out the window. "As it stands, we're on the brink of inter-realm annihilation. Things can't get a lot worse than they already are. And I'm sorry to bring this up, but we stand a much better chance of survival if we have our love goddess fully operational."

Ice shot through my chest. Elsa never would have spoken the words, but we were both aware there was nobody left to do my job for me. Nanna was gone—dead from a broken heart because she'd been fulfilling my title instead of protecting the husband she couldn't live without. And though I had absolute faith in Brynn's ability to command my warriors, I couldn't ask anyone else to pick up the mantel of Love in my place. Still, opening my heart to Jason—and releasing the hurt of my past—might be the fastest path to my own healing, but it would no doubt be the end of him. It would be my life for his, no matter how hard I tried to prevent it.

And love wasn't that selfish.

Elsa frowned. "I understand."

"I'll do my job," I vowed. "But I can't sentence Jason

to death. I...I care about him too much. And I care about Mia and Tyr too much. Losing Jason would destroy her—which would destroy him." *So much destruction...*

"You really are the embodiment of love, Freya," Elsa said softly. "We'll figure it out. Send Mia up when she comes in, have whatever talk you need to with Jason, and then join us upstairs. We'll find a way to maximize your love reserves, and you can direct them where we're Unifying."

"Thanks," I whispered. "For understanding."

Elsa shrugged. "I wouldn't be able to hurt someone I loved either."

With that she ran up the stairs, leaving me to wonder what exactly she meant. "You mean Mia and Tyr, right? Not Jason?"

"You tell me," she called over her shoulder. She disappeared around the corner, a blur of blond waves, pale blue chiffon, and ivory capris.

Wait. What?

Elsa clearly suffered from Ragnarok-induced delusions. I'd admitted I *cared for* Jason, but no way did I love him. I barely knew him. Love built slowly, over years of friendship and shared experiences and united dreams. It didn't just pop into your house for a visit, challenge you to a game of pool, and *boom*, worm its way into your heart. Love—*true* love—was more meticulous...more methodical.

And as Goddess of Love, I should know.

"None of this is okay!" Jason shouted from the porch.

Uh-oh. I stepped closer to the front door.

"Jason, I'm *really* sorry. But you have to understand why I kept this from you." Mia's harried voice carried through the wood. There was an edge to her tone that bordered on hysteria. Her family was everything to her—and if Jason was as angry as he sounded...I had to step in. None of this was Mia's fault.

"Mia?" I opened the door and poked my head outside. Poor Mia sat on the porch swing, her arms wrapped around her knees and her chestnut tresses covering her face. Jason paced angrily on the far end of the porch. An intervention was definitely in order. "Sorry to interrupt, but Elsa needs you upstairs. It's time."

Mia lifted her head to shoot me a panicked look. "We're not done talking."

I stepped onto the porch and offered a sympathetic smile. "I'll take it from here. You were keeping our secret—it's only fair that I bear some of the fallout."

"You're not my sister," Jason ground out. "You're not the one I've spent my entire life looking out for. You're not the one I'm upset with."

"No," I admitted. "But Mia was only doing what we asked her to. She was protecting us. If there's anyone you should be mad at, it's me. Or Tyr, but he's a lot bigger than you, so I'd go with me."

"If you think for one minute that—"

"Mia." I ignored Jason's outburst. "Go upstairs. The realms need what only you and Elsa can give them."

Mia glanced at her brother. "I really am sorry, Jason. I love you. And I hope one day you'll understand."

Jason's eyes bled hurt. "It's my job to look out for you, Mees. You're my baby sister."

"She's a lot tougher than you know," I said gently. "And your sister's got the job of her life ahead of her. She's going to fight with Elsa to bring the dark forces of the cosmos to our side. And she'll have a much better chance of succeeding if she has a clear head." I shot Jason a pointed look.

"Fine. I love you, Mia," Jason grunted.

"I love you too." Mia's lower lip trembled. She jumped up from the swing and crossed the porch in quick strides. Jason didn't say a word when she launched herself at him—he just wrapped his arms around his sister, and held her tight.

After a long moment, Mia pulled back to stare Jason in the eye. "We're good?"

"We're good," he confirmed. "But we're not done talking."

"I know." Mia held Jason at arm's length. "I really am sorry."

"Go." Jason jutted his head at the door. "Save the world. Wait. Did Freya say you're fighting the *dark forces of the cosmos*?"

"Remotely," I said smoothly. "She'll be realms away from the front lines. Mia, get to work. Jason and I need to talk."

Mia squeezed my hand as she scurried into the house. *"Good luck,"* she mouthed.

"Thanks," I mouthed back. Gods knew I'd need it.

I waited until Mia was upstairs before I closed the front door and walked to the porch railing. I rested my forearms on the wooden beam, and crossed one foot behind the other. "So, I'm not an exchange student from Sweden."

"I heard," Jason said drily. He gripped the railing at the far end of the porch. "Neither is Tyr. And Lornara doesn't work at a renaissance fair. And you guys dragged my sister into your end-of-days battle."

"I understand you're angry, but—"

"No, Freya. I'm not angry. I'm hurt. I get that Mia made a promise to keep your secret—which was an incredibly unfair thing to ask of her, considering the danger you've pulled her into."

"I know," I whispered. "But—"

"I'm not finished." Jason held up one hand. He stalked closer. My heart stilled at the coldness in his voice. "What I don't get is why you'd let her carry on that lie for you. You and I just met, but I've known Tyr and Henrik and Brynn for the better part of a year and a half, now. In all that time, they didn't think I was a decent enough guy to let in on the secret? So my sister didn't have to deal with all of this all by herself?"

"I know it seems like a lot—it *is* a lot." I fingered the ends of my hair. "But Mia's handled everything brilliantly. Believe it or not, Elsa talked with her last year about bringing you in on all of this. When Mia started training in her role as Unifier, Elsa worried the strain might be getting to her. Do you know what Mia said?"

"What?" Jason's hands balled so tightly, his knuckles cracked.

"She said she loved you too much to ask you to keep this secret for her. She chose us—chose this life. But she wouldn't force it on her brother."

"I'm her family. I should have been there for her."

"We're her family too," I said gently. "We love Mia. We've never met a human quite like her...well, not until you."

Jason's eyes darted to mine. "What's that mean?"

"You're different—both of you. You somehow fit with us. Be honest: you knew we weren't exchange students before Mia told you, didn't you?"

Jason shrugged. "I knew you guys were more than you let on. But I wouldn't have guessed you were... gods." He spoke the last word with almost a reverence. "Jeez, all these years going to church and...well, it's not what I expected."

We'd been through this with Mia. Tyr and Brynn had borne the brunt of helping her orderly mind try to place us in an unimaginable box. "What you learned in church wasn't wrong—not exactly. The human viewpoint is limited, which makes it hard to comprehend that a singular divine entity has the power to reveal Himself to different civilizations in the ways they can best comprehend Him. For you and Mia, that was God. For other mortals, it's Allah. Or Buddah. Or—"

"Or the Norse Goddess of Love?" Jason raised one brow.

"I'm not the Supreme." I shook my head. "I'm just one of Odin's titleds, with a singular function to serve. Well, two, once I get my act back together."

"What do you mean?"

I frowned into the twilight forest. "I don't know what Mia told you about my job, but in addition to serving as Goddess of Love, I'm supposed to be high commander of the valkyries—Asgard's elite all-female fighting squad. But last year I was captured by Hel. She kept me in a cage in Helheim, and whatever she did to me left me unfit to perform either of my jobs. Brynn's in Asgard right now overseeing my warriors. And the goddess who tried to take over as Goddess of Love...it didn't end well for her. So, I have to figure out what I need to do to get well, so I can get back to work like, yesterday."

Jason studied me from beneath long lashes. "You were captured by Hel? Like, the ruler of the under-world, Hel?"

"To us, she's just Hel."

"Jeez, no wonder you're sick. And you guys don't have any idea what she did to you? Or how to get better?"

"Well..." I bit down on my bottom lip. "Elsa has an idea. But it's not worth the price."

"Not worth the..." Jason's eyes widened. "From what Mia just told me, the world—uh, worlds, are on the brink of war. Whatever the price is, you need to pay it."

My heart tugged. "It's not me who'd be paying," I said softly.

Jason's eyes narrowed. "What aren't you saying?"

No. Absolutely not. I was *not* doing this to him.

"Freya," Jason growled. "Worlds are ending. Spit it out."

"Fine. Elsa thinks if I let myself…fall for you, then I'll get my love mojo back and everything will be back on track. There. Happy?"

One corner of Jason's mouth tugged up. "Is this for real?"

"In Elsa's head, yes." I rolled my eyes. "Stop smiling."

"It's not every day a guy hears he's the key to the Goddess of Love's happiness." Jason's gaze traveled the length of my body, lingering longer than necessary at my chest. *Men.* "If you need to use me to get your juices flowing, then by all means. Do what must be done."

With a laugh, I reached out to swat him. Before I could touch him, Jason wrapped his fingers around my wrist and pulled me to his side.

"I mean it. In times of war, every man must do his part to serve his country…uh, world. Worlds? Whatever. I'm here to serve you…Goddess of Love."

"Jason!" My laughter died in my throat. I tried not to notice the way my pulse quickened at his touch, or the way my thighs tingled pressed this close to his. But even as my blood heated up, my heart sent a chill through my veins. *Remember the last time…*

"Mmm?" Jason didn't release me. Instead he moved even closer, wrapping one arm around my lower back and pulling my hips to his.

Oh, gods. "You don't know what you'd be signing up for," I whispered.

"I don't care," he whispered back. He ran his nose along my jaw, sending a wave of heat to places that had been long dormant. My pulse quickened, and I placed my palms to Jason's chest before things got out of hand.

"You should care." With a groan, I extricated my thighs from his and took a step back. "My title doesn't come without conditions. One of the terms of my… employment is that I'm not allowed to give my heart away."

"Never?"

"Not until the Norns—our prophets—decide to allow it. I've been around a long time, and so far…"

"They haven't allowed it." Jason cocked head. "Have you ever asked them?"

"Once," I whispered. The memory flashed in my head. I pushed it back down. *Not today.*

"And how did that go?" Jason pressed.

Not. Today.

"Not well."

Seconds ticked by, and finally Jason said, "I see."

"I can't give you what you deserve, Jason. I don't know what you're looking for from me, but if it's a partner, I can't be that for you. At least, not now. And possibly not ever."

Jason stepped closer, cradling my head in one hand. "What do you want us to be to each other, Freya?"

I leaned into his touch. "What I want doesn't matter. My duty must always be to my realm, and until the Norns release me from their terms, I have to be extremely careful about how much I allow myself to care for you. We can date, but things between us can never get too deep. All I can offer you is a casual, no-strings relationship. Not that you've said you want anything else. Gods, I'm probably way ahead of myself, and—"

"There's nothing casual about my feelings." Jason rested his forehead against mine. "I like you—I mean, I *really* like you. Girls never get under my skin, but you're something else. You're stubborn, and independent, and fierce as hell. Which I get now, since you have your own army and all."

"All-female army," I couldn't help correcting him. I was proud of my girls.

"Right. Point is, those prophets have to release you eventually, right?" Jason shrugged. "When they do, I'll be waiting."

"They might not," I pointed out. "It's been centuries."

"You're that old?"

I punched Jason in the chest. Hard.

"Ouch! Okay, I deserved that." He chuckled. "Look, we'll figure it out."

"I can't let myself fall for you, Jason," I warned. "Not

the way I want to. Not until they release me. And you shouldn't fall for me. Not completely."

Jason cocked his head. "You're serious about this casual thing?"

"Dead serious," I confirmed.

"Huh. I'll be honest, this is not the way this conversation usually goes. Normally I'm the one asking to keep it casual, and the girl, well…" Jason shrugged.

A bubble of laughter ripped from my throat. "You're impossible."

"I've heard worse." Jason pulled me close again, and lowered his head to mine. My heart thundered in my chest as I closed my eyes, tilted my head back, and—

"Freya!" Elsa's voice carried from the house. "We need an assist!"

A frustrated huff escaped my lips. I opened my eyes to Jason's bemused grin. "Duty calls?"

"It usually does. And at the least opportune time. Welcome to Asgard."

Jason's dimple popped. "Then by all means, I'd better let you go. I'll just hang out here for a few. Cool down."

My cheeks heated as Jason stepped back, and his words took on a new meaning.

"Good idea." I forced myself to look away from what promised to be a *really* good time. "But come inside soon. Our compound's secure enough, but things have breached the perimeter before. Better safe than sorry."

"Sounds good." Jason nodded. "If you need

anything…anything at all…for the good of the worlds, I mean."

"I know where to find you." I winked before heading back into the house. I stopped in the kitchen for a glass of ice water before heading up the stairs. Jason wasn't the only one who needed cooling off.

Elsa had been right—after months on months of darkness, opening up to the possibility of Jason, even knowing I couldn't completely give myself over to any feelings we developed for each other, had filled me with hope…with the dream of a future. For myself; for my friends; for my realm. Whatever became of things with Jason, at that moment I felt every bit the love goddess the Norns had decreed I would be.

And it was time for me to get to work.

"Fenrir's a dead end. He's not receptive to the energy I'm sending him *at all*. Who's next?" Mia leaned back on the thick meditation pillow beside the leather loungers in the man cave. Brynn and Henrik's lab equipment had been pushed to the left side of the room, leaving much of the floor space open. The girls had scattered three large, white pillows, along with a sea of crystals, through the space. The room thrummed with a serene vibe, and if the end of the worlds wasn't upon us, I would have appreciated the peaceful flow they'd created.

As it was, I crept silently into the room to take my

place on the lone unoccupied pillow. I blinked at the basketball-sized pink rocks set in a horseshoe directly behind me. They were some of Mia's favorites—rose something-or-other. I knew they were meant to resonate love.

My friends were amazing. I wouldn't let them down.

Love. Love. I am Love. I activated the center in the back of my head, connecting it to my heart and intending both spaces be filled with love and light. *I am Love. I am Love.* I repeated the mantra until it overtook me and vibrated through every cell of my being in an absolute truth.

I am Love.

For the first time in a long time, I *knew* it to be true.

I was Love.

"Elsa?" Mia pressed. "Did you hear me? Fenrir's a dead end. Who do we work on next?"

"Sorry." Elsa's twinkling voice pulled me from my trance. "Something's just shifted. It was beautiful."

"Elsa?" I was ready to work. "What's the assist you need me to focus on?"

"I...oh, Freya. Your heart's shining. Finally." Moisture brightened her blue eyes. "I've missed you."

"I've missed me too," I said honestly.

"Did you work things out with Jason?" Elsa asked.

"As much as I can."

"So that's the shift." Elsa beamed.

"Ja, ja." I waved my hand at my friend. "Save your *told you so* for *after* we save the worlds."

"Very well." Elsa closed her eyes. "We failed to connect with Fenrir, so Runa's next. Focus your energy on her."

"Runa?" Mia balked, as if Elsa's suggestion bordered the insane.

In a way, it did. As a child, Runa had performed tremendous acts of bravery to protect Tyr from their tyrannical father. But as she grew older, she took on more of her father's traits. Elsa's pure heart always trusted that Runa could be brought into the light—even *after* Runa had escaped Asgardian prison and, apparently, run straight to Daddy Dearest. To end us all.

Skit.

"Yes. Runa." Elsa re-crossed her legs and rested her hands palms-up on her lap. "Send unifying energy to her soul while I try to connect with it. Freya, if you're ready, send love to Runa's heart center."

"On it." I crisscrossed my legs, mirroring Elsa's pose atop my pillow. "Where are we directing this?"

"I think she's on...Jotunheim?" Mia hedged.

"I get ice, too," Elsa confirmed. "Do you sense her, Freya?"

"Got her." I nodded. "Okay, here goes."

With a breath, I soaked in more energy from the pink stones, filtered it through my heart, and beamed it out into the cosmos. It shot through the darkness, pierced the icy atmosphere of Jotunheim, and funneled into a soul I recognized from my brief visit to Asgard's prison chamber. Runa's body was thinner than I remembered it, her once vibrant skin now a sallow white. She was filled with darkness, an angry fog clouding what I understood had once been a beatific heart. Her circumstances had been far from ideal, but I'd hoped—as we all had—that we'd be able to bring her around. She'd been Tyr's first *protektor*; the first being who fought for him. She deserved so much more than the fates had given her.

"She's not open to receiving," Mia murmured.

"I'm getting the same," Elsa confirmed.

"Let me try a different angle and—ouch!" I cried out as my warm, pink energy shot back at me. Runa had rebuffed the love I'd sent her. She'd returned it with a white-hot edge.

"Are you okay?" Mia asked.

"*Ja*, let me just…wait. Do you feel that?" My muscles locked up as the thick cloud of dark energy encroached on my space. My eyes flew open, and I scanned the room for the threat. Nothing.

"Feel what?" Elsa opened her own eyes.

"That darkness. I don't think it's Runa. I think it's coming from outside the cabin…" My eyes met Elsa's and Mia's in a moment of pure terror.

"Jason," Elsa whispered.

Mia jumped to her feet a split second after me. "Go," she urged.

But I'd already blurred halfway down the stairs.

"Stay where you are!" I screamed over my shoulder. "Elsa, initiate the lockdown procedure *immediately*."

I didn't bother to wait for Elsa's confirmation. The

whirring of the bulletproof—and dark magic-proof—encasing let me know the man cave was transforming into the safe room. My feet thundered toward the entry, leaping across the floorboards as I flung the front door open and charged from the porch to the clearing.

"Freya! Go back in the house!" Jason's cry stopped me in my tracks.

"Where are you?" I whirled around, scanning the darkened forest. "I can't see...you." The last word came on a whisper.

Because while I could barely make out Jason's nearly limp form, painfully crumbled on the ground, I could easily see the whirling black portal that emitted silver and purple sparks directly behind him.

And beside the hovering portal stood the half-blue figure of the monster who'd held me captive in her Helheim prison. Her palms pressed joyfully together as she threw her head back in jubilant laughter.

"Freya." Hel cackled, one stiletto-booted foot atop the mortal who held my heart in his hands. "I believe I have something that belongs to you."

BRYNN

THE VALKYRIE COMPOUND WAS a lot bigger than I remembered.

Granted, I'd spent the last few years stationed on Midgard—and things on Midgard were *significantly* smaller than their Asgardian counterparts. But I'd forgotten the grandiosity, the elegance, the ethereal design on an absolutely massive scale that was the architecture of the V.C. From the marble pegasuses guarding either side of the carved front door, to the gold etching in the winged eaves of the roof—which was enchanted to appear invisible, maximizing natural light and providing an overall airiness to the complex —the compound was the epitome of refinement.

I tried not to gape at the massive ivory courtyard that stretched the length of the football-field-sized entry. Or at the clusters of anxious valkyries who scurried along the balcony, where the training center fed into the dormitories. Or at the way the bronze fountain in the courtyard's center sparkled beneath the gentle Asgardian sunlight. The fountain was the likeness of a valkyrie mounted atop a winged steed, her sword raised and her lips parted in a battle cry. It awed me every bit as much as it had on my first day as a junior valkyrie, in no small part because of the message it imparted: *For honor. For love. For Asgard.* The words were etched into both the sword, and around the lip of the fountain—a double reminder of what we valued—of what we fought for.

Of what we were.

"General Aksel?" The low voice from behind made me jump.

"Oh, I'm just a captain." I turned to find one of the senior valkyries standing at attention. Behind her, a surge of uniformed girls hurried across the entry, swords holstered at their hips. No doubt they were heading to the first-floor briefing auditorium to await their orders.

It was go time. I just had to issue the command. *No pressure.*

"My apologies, General Aksel." The valkyrie at my side raised her hand in salute. The flexible armor of her suit gleamed in the light, its silver a nice contrast to the pale blue fabric resting beneath. "But the high commander's orders state you are to be addressed as General. They further state I am to escort you to the war room."

General? Last year I'd considered myself lucky to leapfrog up to captain. Was Freya for real?

"Right." I wiped the awe from my face and did my best to look imposing. "Escort away…uh…Svaira?"

"Svetana," she corrected. "I oversaw your technical team when you joined up."

"Svetana!" I shifted my tech-bearing backpack to my other shoulder before palming the hilt of my sheathed rapier. "Oh, my gods, you smuggled us the *älva* dust we needed to complete work on that exploding portal! We never could have shut down the dark forest leak without it. Man, those were good times."

Svetana nodded tightly. "We'll stop by the laboratory on our way to the war room. I'd imagine you'll want to suit up before meeting with your lieutenant generals, and the tech team's just finishing their updates to your battle uniform."

"Right. Thanks. Uh, at ease," I added, because Svetana hadn't lowered her hand from her forehead. "And you can call me Brynn."

"Please follow me, General Aksel." Svetana turned on one knee-high booted foot.

We were salmon moving upstream as we made our way through tight groups of suited-up valkyries, all heading to the briefing room. Those who broke focus enough to register who we were parted to let us through, the respect and awe on their faces enough to make me avert my eyes. I might have been acting in my friend's place today, but I was no Freya. I was just a soldier who loved my realm, and felt lucky to have been chosen to be a valkyrie at all. Leading our forces was an honor I hadn't asked for. None of this seemed real.

But it was. And a lot of lives depended on me not screwing it up.

After a slow eternity, Svetana and I reached the twin staircases that twined around a statue of Freya herself. My friend hated having her likeness cast in marble—hated being the focal point of the V.C.'s entryway. But the rest of us loved the visual reminder of our strong, fearless, leader—the literal embodiment of love, who championed spreading Asgard's light throughout the realms. Gods, I hoped I didn't let her down.

My feet were heavy as I trudged up the marble stairs. Girls scurried out of my path as I climbed, and I wondered how much they knew about my role—about this temporary transition of power. *Temporary*. That was all this would be. Freya would return to lead her army in no time. She'd been the driving force of our team for as long as I could remember, and soon she'd be back to standing in the briefing room in her battle-tested high commander uniform, issuing her cry, and inspiring our warriors to diffuse tensions cosmos-wide.

Speaking of uniforms…

"Welcome back to the lab." Svetana made a sharp left outside a set of frosted glass doors. She raised her palm to the discreet scanner nestled on the wall. The door blurred, then disappeared with a chime, and the two of us stepped into the open space.

It was every bit as impressive as it had been when

I'd served here on the Junior Valkyrie Tech Team. Some of the battle valkyries had called us nerds, but we'd known how vital our work was to the order. Freya had been our biggest champion, constantly reminding us that strength of mind was every bit as important to our cause as strength of muscle. She'd given us a generous budget, and a generous workspace in which to create technological masterpieces. And her faith had allowed us to develop pieces that had contributed to inter-realm peace.

Now I scanned the enormous laboratory, over-flowing with the latest Asgardian developments. A tiny part of my mind wondered how Henrik and I had managed to create so many brilliant pieces of tech in our cramped, tiny Midgardian workspace. The things we could do here…

"General Aksel, we need to keep moving."

Right.

I nodded at a young recruit manipulating a holo-gram—a schematic of an imploding device, from the looks of it. "You've enhanced the impact radius with a mini rocket? That's brilliant," I encouraged. She glanced up at my words, her amber eyes widening behind thick goggles.

"Thank you, Bry—uh, General," she whispered, her mouth gaping slightly.

These girls were pinning all their hopes on me not getting us killed. Gods, I really needed to pull this off.

"Is the uniform complete?" Svetana called to the room.

"It's hanging from the general's old locker," one of the valkyries piped up.

"Very well. This way." Svetana pointed toward the changing room in the back of the lab.

"Thanks." I slipped past the multi-dimensional printer, raised my own palm at the scanner outside the changing room, and stepped through the entry as soon as the door wavered and disappeared. My locker was just as I'd left it, with one exception: hanging from its door was a uniform so exquisite, I looked around to double check it was mine. Since no other uniforms hung in the room, and since it was attached to my locker, I deduced this was, in fact, for me…and I couldn't believe my luck.

A suit, made of the traditional valkyrie silver and blue, hung elegantly from a padded hanger. But instead of the customary Kevlar-weave I'd worn as a junior valkyrie, this fabric looked thicker—richer. My fingertips grazed its surface, and I realized it was crafted from fibers I'd never worn.

"Is this…"

"It's a breathable, organic fabric interwoven with Nidavellir iron," Svetana said.

"You don't mean…" I exhaled heavily.

"*Ja*, General. It is threaded with the same fibers that formed Thor's hammer."

Holy skit.

"How'd you get the dwarves to give you *that*?" I gaped.

"As you may recall, they have a soft spot for Freya."

Svetana grinned—the first smile I'd seen from her that day. "I visited Nidavellir to inform them of her troubles, and to let them know that her substitute would need the strongest suit we could fashion. They gifted me a chunk of the iron for our tech team to manipulate, and reminded me that if Ragnarok were truly upon us, Freya would do well to call on Skidbladnir and Gullinbursti."

"Excuse me?" Did Freya have secret boyfriends she'd never told us about?

"Skidbladnir—a ship the dwarves crafted for Freya. I knew nothing of it; they gifted it to her in secret. The ship always has a favorable wind, and it can be folded up to hide in a pocket."

Seriously?

"Who's the other guy? Or, thing?" I asked. "Gillen…Gullen…"

"Gullinbursti—a golden-haired boar who beams light into darkness, and runs seamlessly through any substance, including air and water."

Hold the com. We had access to a glowing, space-traveling pig, and a magic, wind-shifting boat at the exact moment we were trying to stop a killer toenail-ship from sailing on Asgard?

Sometimes the Norns were just too good.

"Excellent. I'll get changed and we can relay that to the lieutenant generals." I sat on the bench to unlace my combat boots.

"Your shoes are in your locker. I'll give you a moment."

Svetana slipped discreetly from the room, leaving me to drop my bag and sword, and strip the rest of my clothes. My legs slid easily inside the upgraded fighting suit, its armor nearly weightless against my muscles. I reached behind me to tug up the zipper, but the suit closed itself, seemingly intuiting my desire. *Whoa.* What else could it do? I shoved my clothes inside my locker and removed the coolest pair of shoes I'd ever seen. They were crafted of a silver-hued leather, with some kind of blasters fixed to the heel.

Blasters. There were *blasters* on my *shoes.*

Why hadn't Henrik and I made these yet?

When my shoes laced themselves—because that was a thing now—I slid my rapier into the suit's iron-lined hilt, slipped my dagger into the hidden compartment in my blaster boots, fluffed my Nidavellir iron-lined cape behind me, and marched determinedly into the lab, my backpack over one shoulder. "Who designed this outfit?" I called out.

Svetana's lips tugged up at the corners as she scanned me from head to toe. "You look exquisite, General."

"I was going for deadly, but I'll take it." I shot her a grin. "Seriously," I called again. "Suit designer—and shoe designer—step out!"

Two goggle-clad girls shifted tentatively around a work table. One rubbed her cocoa-colored fingertips together. "I—I, um, designed the suit. Is there a problem with it? We didn't have time to send it through beta testing, so if the iron's not sitting right we can—"

"You made this?" I gripped the cape between my fingertips, holding it up. "This exquisite piece of art?"

"Um…yes," the girl squeaked.

"It's freaking brilliant," I praised. "Its intuitive features…I've never worked with those before. What can you tell me about them?"

Behind her goggles—and the glasses beneath those —the girl's warm brown eyes lit up. "The metal was only supposed to be weapon and dark-magic resistant. But it turned out that it was a conductor for a secondary system we'd been developing—one that read brainwaves and translated them to movement. Sort of like what you and Commander Andersson worked on for the God of War's prosthesis."

"Fred. Of course!" After Henrik and I finished work on Tyr's prosthetic arm, I'd sent a full report back to the V.C. for the tech team to analyze. We'd also dropped off a modified version of the specs with one of the human research facilities—there was no reason to keep our scientific advancements to ourselves. "So, the same neuro-conductors resonate with this suit?"

"Exactly." The girl's curly ponytail bobbed excitedly. "I'm Kyrea, by the way. I'm a huge fan of the work you've done with Major Andersson."

"Don't let Henrik hear you say that. His head will—" I spread my fingers apart, miming an explosion. Kyrea and her lab partner giggled.

"What's your name?" I asked the likely shoe

designer. She was Kyrea's slightly shorter doppelganger.

"I'm Kinsea," she offered shyly. "The boots are fitted with the same intuitive tech—rigged to fire explosives at close range, so mind your temper if anyone close to you makes you mad."

"Seriously," Kyrea muttered drily.

"Lab mishap?" I raised one eyebrow.

"You could say that." Kinsea flushed. "I kind of almost blew my sister's hair off."

"I shouldn't have been examining the boots with their safety off," Kyrea said.

"Just know this button here"—Kinsea knelt down and tapped a nearly imperceptible nodule at my ankle—"locks the safety. Once its unleashed, anyone within fifty feet is fair game."

"Good to know. Seriously, you guys did great work." I made a mental note to have Svetana send letters of commendation to their parents, as well as to Freya. Incorporating my own tech into my suit on a day when I felt totally out of my element…the sisters deserved a bump in rank, for sure.

"General," Svetana murmured. "It's time."

"Keep up the good work, everyone," I offered as I strode toward the lab door. "Tech's been the key to saving my team over and over—this department means more to the realm than you can possibly imagine. Know that what you're doing has the power to save countless lives—no matter what the battle valkyries have to say about it."

"Preach," muttered one of the girls. Their entire department burst into giggles.

With one last grin at the tech team I strode down the hall, Svetana on my heels. I paused outside the war room, drew a breath, and raised my hand to the scanner beside the double doors. They glimmered, then disappeared. I stepped into the room to take my place before the four lieutenant generals who made up Freya's War Cabinet.

Odin willing, I wouldn't let them—or the warriors under their command—down.

"The Elite Team has warriors stationed in Helheim, Muspelheim, and Jotunheim. But Loki dispatched additional forces to Nidavellir and Svartalfheim, where our allies are underrepresented. His monsters are currently funneling dark energy from Nidavellir to Vanaheim through a portal Asgard's warriors have been unable to seal. We expect a full-scale attack on our sister realm soon." Mariana, the tallest of Freya's lieutenant generals, stood at the opposite end of the war room to me, gesturing to the holographic screen atop the wooden conference table. The screen showed the nine realms, with red lights illuminating the areas under threat, and blue lights highlighting our allied forces. She glanced at the three other lieutenant generals, all of whom stood in full battle uniform, hands clasped tightly in front of them.

Nobody looked happy to be here.

"We'd planned to allow Svartalfheim to fall at Ragnarok—unleash a cataclysmic device that would reduce the realm to stardust. But before the fighting broke out, the elves opened a portal in the dark forest and gained access to our primary school. There are almost two dozen Asgardian younglings in their custody." Mariana reached up to tuck a chestnut strand behind her twice-pierced ear, then folded her hands in front of her. "The darkness spread quicker than we'd anticipated, and our forces will be scattered across the existing skirmishes. Saving the children may cost us the chance to level Svartalfheim. How do you want us to proceed, General?"

Well, *skit.*

My short fingernails dug into the polished wood of the conference table. We were a formidable army with numbers that rivaled any dark realm's, but the way Loki had structured his attack meant our resources would be stretched completely thin—even if we didn't send anyone into Svartalfheim. But how could we abandon our young—the very innocents we'd taken a vow to protect?

Think, Aksel. What would Freya do? What would Love do?

When I put it that way, it was exquisitely simple.

"Okay. Here's the plan." I raised my arm and swiped the screen to my right, revealing a close-up of Svartalfheim. "Extracting the younglings is priority one. We'll send an assassin squadron into Svartalfheim, eliminate the threat, and remove the children through a cloaked portal—one with a dark-magic trigger, so it annihilates any malicious beings that may try to break through. I assume that tech's still functional?"

"It is," Svetana confirmed.

"Mariana, can your team handle the extraction?" I asked.

"It would be my honor, General," she replied.

"Good." I swiped the screen again, bringing up the image of Nidavellir. With my right hand, I plucked the hologram of Vanaheim and brought it into focus beside the dwarves' realm. "Now, the dark energy siphon from Nidavellir to Vanaheim is concerning, not only because it puts Vanaheim at risk, but because it's also likely setting our sister realm as a staging area to attack Asgard. We'll send a squadron to Nidavellir to put down any skirmishes and seal off the leak. That should take care of the secondary threat, provided we get forces on the ground in Vanaheim to take out any hostiles we *haven't* prepared for. But the primary threat to the Bifrost is still the ship Naglfar. Let me touch base with the team tasked with taking it down."

I pressed my fingertips to the camouflaged com on my wrist. "Call Tyr." Seconds later, my friend's face appeared on my forearm. I swiped up so his hologram was visible to the entire council.

"What? I'm kind of busy," Tyr snapped.

"We all are," I retorted. "Do you have Naglfar under control or will you need backup?"

"I've got Henrik, Forse, Odin, and an Elite Team squadron on boat duty with me."

That meant *skit.* Everybody knew my girls could kick Odin's warriors' butts—including the bad guys.

"Do you need any valkyries?" I rephrased.

"I don't plan to." Tyr looked over his shoulder. "I have to go."

"Be safe." I swiped down, and Tyr's holo disappeared. I pulled my shoulders back and rolled my neck to the side, eliciting a loud crack. *Much better.* "We'll reserve five senior warriors to assist Tyr when he changes his mind."

"But the God of War said—"

"I know what War said." I turned my attention back to the screen. "And when he realizes he was wrong, he'll be glad we didn't listen to him. Five of our best—Sigrunn, can your team spare anyone?"

"Of course." Sigrunn nodded.

"Good. Have them remain on standby in the V.C. And send two of your warriors to evacuate the danger spots in Vanaheim. Now, returning to the Nidavellir uprising, if we send in a squadron here"—I pointed to the base of the mountain that was the heart of the dragons' nesting region—"and extract any allies we uncover through a portal here"—I tapped the east edge of the alder forest—"we can seal off the leak and stop the flow of dark energy into Vanaheim. Sigrunn, I'm entrusting the rest of your team with this mission."

"We will not let you down."

"Excellent. Now, between War's team and Sigrunn's

girls, the ship should be disabled before its launch. If it never invades the Bifrost, we don't need to worry about Asgard's isolation from that front. The dark forest remains a threat, so let's send in four valkyries to assist the Elite Team there." I glanced around the room, waiting for a volunteer.

"I have a small task force in my squadron who can handle it," Tessyra said. "I'll issue the dispatch order now."

"Good." I stared at the holographic screen while Tessyra spoke into her com. "Heimdall's well guarded, as is Frigga. And we're sure Thor has a handle on Fenrir and the snake?"

"He tells us it will be a clean kill on both fronts," Mariana confirmed.

"Right. That just leaves..."

"Muspelheim."

All eyes shifted to Xatnari, who placed a fist over her heart. "On my honor as a valkyrie, I will crush any fire giant who seeks to harm Asgard."

"It's not going to be easy," I warned her. "They're filtering in feyndrals from Svartalfheim."

The four lieutenant generals swore in one collective breath.

"I thought those were extinct," Xatnari hissed.

"So did I. Until I found one of our evacuees burning the evil out of a baby one on...hold on. That's it!" I pressed my fingertips to my wrist again, barking a command into the shimmering flesh. "Call Lornara."

The face of my fairy friend appeared in the waves,

and I swiped the image up so Lornara's hologram hovered inches above my arm. "Brynn? Are you hurt?"

"No. I need you to find Hyro," I ordered. "Can you track her down?"

"She's with me in the southern elderberry grove." Lornara's wings fluttered behind her. "I'm healing her burned arm."

"What?"

"It wasn't Marshmallow's fault," Hyro wailed in the background. "He's still a baby!"

"Hyro," I gritted. "Can you control him?"

"Usually!"

"Lornara, let me see the dragon. Please."

The hologram pulled back, revealing the winged reptile who'd more than tripled in size since our last encounter. He was big enough for Hyro to ride…if he didn't accidentally char one of her limbs, first.

"Hyro," I hedged. This mission would either be Xatnari's glory…or her undoing. "I need you to help a friend of mine. She's leading a group into Muspelheim, and she could use someone to help her diffuse the feyndrals. They can only be turned when they're babies, right?"

"Ouch! Be gentle!" Lornara cried out as Hyro's face filled the hologram. Hyro must have grabbed the fairy's arm and pulled it to her.

"No! They can be turned as adults, too! I didn't know until a few days ago, when I made contact with a rebel cell on Muspelheim. Turns out they've been turning the feyndrals they come into contact with—it takes five fire giants to turn one dragon, but it can be done."

I gripped the table with my free hand. "How many members are in that cell?"

"About thirty?" Hyro guessed.

"*Perfekt.* Lornara, keep Hyro safe until I send someone in for her. And good luck healing the wounded."

"Absolutely. Thank you, Brynn." Lornara logged off.

I looked at Xatnari. "Quick detour to Alfheim's southern elderberry grove to pick up my friend Hyro and her flame-breathing pet?"

"Of course."

"Svetana, have the tech team isolate the location of the rebel camp on Muspelheim and instruct Heimdall to direct the second Bifrost drop there. Send a representative ahead to let them know the incoming squadron will be a friendly one."

"Yes, General." Svetana turned on one heel and marched from the war room. The door wavered, then re-solidified as she passed through.

"I almost forgot. Do any of you know anything about a space-traveling pig and a magic ship? Apparently, the dwarves gifted them to Freya, and they could really help us out." Odin knew we'd need every conceivable advantage.

"Gullinbursti and Skidbladnir?" Xatnari asked. "We know of them, but we've never seen them. Freya keeps both hidden."

Of course she does. "All right. I'll figure something

out. We need to move. Ladies…" I pressed my fist to my heart. "Make Freya proud."

"For Freya," Mariana chimed in. The rest of the lieutenant generals gently raised their fists to their chests, and we echoed the sentiment as one.

"For Freya."

CHAPTER 10

"**DON'T LOOK AT ME** like that, love goddess." Hel's lips formed a delicate pout. They were the palest of pinks beneath the thick moonlight. "You didn't really think I'd let you have your happy ending, did you?"

"What do you want with him?" I stalked carefully toward the ruler of the underworld. A perfectly sculpted black brow rose atop the cerulean half of her face. The other side was chalky, powder blue—the Midgardian sky on a summery day. But there was nothing peaceful about the rage that seeped from Hel's silver eyes, or the darkness rolling off her thick, black mane. Hel was lethal—I'd seen it firsthand during my capture.

And she had her sights set on Jason.

"He's only a human. Let him go." I raised my palms, trying not to sob at the sight of Jason on his knees before Hel. From the way his hands fisted the earth, I had zero doubt that the monster had inflicted unimaginable levels of pain to lock him in place. But Jason didn't cry out—he barely even flinched. He just turned his eyes to me and mouthed one word.

"Run."

Absolutely not.

"Only a human?" Hel's sharp inhale left hollows between her high cheekbones and sharp jaw. "If that's the case, then why are you fighting for him?"

"Because he's innocent." I stepped closer to Hel, to Jason. "He's done nothing to you, and he has no role of consequence to play in Ragnarok. Let him go."

"But you're wrong, Freya." My name came out on a hiss. "Your human pet has quite the substantial role to play."

Hel closed her eyes and loosed a breath. Jason's back arched, his face contorted in pain, and he unleashed an agonized cry that set my teeth on edge.

"Stop it!" I yelled. "You'll kill him!"

"Precisely. I am not partial to obstacles." Hel exhaled again, and this time Jason's scream brought me to my knees.

"He's not an obstacle. He's only a human!"

"That's what I thought, darling, but your kind seems to have quite the fondness for these weak, insipid creatures. I'd have thought War would have jumped at the chance to rule in darkness by my side, but that mousy little mortal seems to have quite the hold on him. Pity. I'll have to force War's hand. With you gone, he'll descend back into that black space he so nearly inhabited before. And when he does, Ragnarok will be won. Everyone he loves will be dead, and he'll have no choice but to rule with me. But first..." Hel unleashed a new wave of agony onto Jason. His screams reverberated through the trees.

How do I make her stop?

"Jason!" Mia's voice pierced the night. She and Elsa appeared on the porch, the horror of Jason's torture mirrored on their porcelain faces.

"Stay there," I ordered my friends before returning my attention to Hel. "Is that why you're doing this? To get back at Tyr?"

"Partly." Hel sneered. "But most of all, to destroy you. I can't have this...*toy* healing your heart and stopping my rule before it begins."

"What do you mean?" I inched forward on my knees. If I kept her talking long enough, maybe I could get to Jason, and release him from whatever dark magic she held him in.

"Haven't you wondered why your healers have failed you? Why you haven't been 'yourself' since you came back from your little trip with me?" Hel's silver eyes flashed in the twilight. "Your heart is poisoned with ketane—a substance I placed within its chambers during our time together. The mist feeds on fear, its strength multiplying every time you allow yourself to feel the darkness. The stronger it gets, the better it's able to block love, and prevent you from *ever* healing."

"Ketane..." I'd never heard of it. And if the gasp from the porch was any indication, Elsa hadn't either.

"It is a…newer substance." Hel examined her silver fingernails as if she'd grown bored. "And one that cannot be overpowered with herbs, or crystals, or diets." She snorted. "But it can, sadly, be overpowered by love. And the fact that this human draws love from every fiber of your pathetic Asgardian being, and that that same love threatens to eject my mist…obviously, I can't stand for it."

Hel turned her palm to the sky, and Jason flew up. He hovered just in front of Hel's face, his feet inches off the ground and his hands grasping at his throat.

"Any last words, human? No? In that case…" Hel broke into a wicked grin as she slammed Jason to the ground. I leapt to my feet, poised to charge when a voice from the porch pierced my focus.

"Freya! Catch!"

I spun around, my hands opening instinctively to retrieve the small orb Mia threw. Odds were high it was some kind of explosive, or implosive, or whatever deadly thing Brynnrik had developed recently. And odds were even higher it would hurt Jason if I launched it directly at his captor.

Sending a silent prayer to Odin, I flung the ball at the ground ten feet behind Hel. And I waited.

It only took a second for the thick, black mist to ooze from the orb, and another second for it to transform into a translucent oval. Silver sparks shot from what seemed to be a portal. The light forced Hel's attention away from Jason in one beautiful, brief moment of distraction.

I seized it.

My muscles exploded in a burst of energy as my legs moved of their own accord. Three steps and I leapt into the air, covering the distance between me and Hel almost instantly. My arms framed her shoulders as I knocked her to the dirt, pinning her with a fierce knee to the groin. She let out a groan, her legs curling into her chest, and for the briefest of moments she was debilitated.

Then her magic kicked in.

"No." She hissed. A thick gas seeped from her lips, taking the form of a snake. The pseudo-reptile lurched at Jason, wrapping around his legs and flattening him before he managed to scramble to his feet. Jason clawed at his ankles, trying to remove the binding, but Hel's dark magic held him tight. Jason stilled, seemingly realizing his effort was futile.

"Freya, get out of here!" Wild indigo–blue eyes found mine. "Protect yourself!"

I grunted as I wrestled with Hel. "That's not how things work around here."

Hel turned her magic on me, and it took everything I had to dodge the snake mist that wove and darted from her mouth. As I swung my leg up to deliver a fierce kick to her jaw the mist faltered, blood taking its place. Hel swiped at her chin, and I took the opportunity to jump to my feet. "Elsa! Shield Jason!"

A burst of energy shot from the porch, its white light and electric jolt knocking me back. I scrambled to resume my assault on Hel. A series of roundhouses kept her grounded for a moment, but before long she was on her feet, pacing the forest in a tight horseshoe. Unfortunately for all of us, she remained too far from the whirling black vortex for its presence to be of any use. How were we going to get her into it?

"Oh, Freya." Hel clucked her tongue. "When will you learn? I cannot be defeated."

"Is that so?" I catalogued our surroundings: mammoth trees, a handful of boulders, and two absolutely terrified squirrels. Nothing immediately useful, but I'd done more with less. All I had to do was keep Hel talking long enough to come up with a plan.

"Accept that your place is with me, either as my pet, or as one of the many souls ignoble enough to serve me in eternity." Hel raised her palm and hurtled a fireball at my feet. It ignited a patch of drying leaves, and I leapt back so far that I jabbed myself on a low-resting tree branch.

Bingo.

Without hesitating, I reached behind to wrench the branch off the tree. I shoved it into the blaze at my feet, and charged. Hel didn't look up from the ball of fire forming in her hands. I lunged. She finally met my gaze. Her lips parted in surprise as the burning stick pierced her thigh. Hel cried out in shock.

"How dare you?" Her silvery eyes narrowed and she drove her hand at my chest. The fireball at her fingertips quickly burned through the thin fabric of my T-shirt, and I dropped to the ground to extinguish the flames. Ignoring the blistering pain in my torso, I arched my back and again leapt to my feet.

"How dare *you?*" I ripped two branches off the nearest tree and drove them into the smoldering blaze on the ground. Fire sparked from the ends of the sharp sticks as I raised my arms in a cross. I spun them violently as I circled the clearing, my fiery trajectory forcing Hel's back to the portal. "Tyr will never agree to be with you." I took calculated steps forward. "You're going to die miserable and alone, without even your guard dragon to keep you company. I heard Nidhogg defected to Nidavellir just to get away from you."

Hel hissed, the angry sound escaping pinched lips. "You know nothing of my life." She threw a fireball, and I sidestepped it easily.

"Thank the gods for that," I replied. Hel shot again, and I spun the flaming sticks in front of me, two circles of fire forming a blazing shield against her onslaught. She stumbled as I drew closer. It was working.

I pulled my arms to my sides, shifting the shields to unleash a series of front kicks that knocked Hel off-balance. She stumbled again, and I drove my hands together, the fire of both sticks uniting in a fierce surge of heat. Hel faltered, and with a final kick, I knocked her backward through the portal. It sparked, spun, and closed inward with an explosion that knocked me across the clearing and extinguished the energetic shield surrounding Jason.

What the Helheim?

"Jason, get down!" I screamed as the portal erupted

in a second burst, sending a storm of dirt and rocks raining on my back. Shards dug into my forearms as I army-crawled to where I'd last seen Jason wrestling Hel's translucent cords. My fingertips grasped his leg as I raised my head, careful to cover my eyes against the continued onslaught of rubble. "Where are the cords binding you?"

"I think they're gone." Jason wrenched himself around to throw his body over mine, shielding me from the last of the downpour. It was a sweet gesture, but he was the mortal. And I wasn't entirely sure Hel was gone.

"Up," I ordered, pushing Jason off me. Once I was clear I jumped to my feet, scanning the area for any sign of the dark goddess. "Elsa, where is she?"

"Gone, but I don't know to where." Elsa's voice carried from the porch. "The portal sealed with her inside it."

Footsteps crunched on the rabble as a disheveled Mia made her way to my side. She had bark in her hair and a deep cut on her right cheek. Elsa moved into place beside her, having fared slightly less poorly.

"What was that thing?" I asked.

"Brynn once mentioned a piece of tech from her early valkyrie days—a portal that destroys itself after one transport. I'm guessing it was that?" Mia offered.

"I guess." My attention shifted to the mortal pushing himself off the ground. "You okay, hotshot?"

"I've been better," Jason admitted. "Anybody want to explain to me who the blue chick was?"

"That was Hel—goddess of the underworld, and daughter of the monster who's organizing Ragnarok. I hope Loki doesn't have access to wherever that portal led. The last thing we need is a family reunion." I picked a branch out of Jason's hair, and studied his steady eyes. "I'm sorry Hel hurt you."

"I can take it." He shrugged. "Sounds like she did way worse to you."

"Ketane." Elsa shook her head. "I've never heard of it. Mia, do you know anything about it?"

Mia tapped her finger to the translucent com atop her forearm. When it lit up, she studied the image, then swiped up to transform the screen to a hologram. "There's nothing on the human internet about it, but Brynn and Henrik's database has an entry. Looks like ketane is a dark-matter substance of minimal density. It thickens in the presence of certain hormones— norepinephrine and cortisol, the basic fear/stress cocktail. Oxytocin and vasopressin counteract it—the love mix."

"So, if I wanted to isolate the ketane, I'd need Freya doped up on love," Elsa mused. "Then I could extract and contain the toxin, in...do we have anything that can contain fear?"

"No." Mia frowned. "But we do have something in the upstairs lab that can contain dark matter. Think that'll work?"

"It's worth a shot." Elsa turned to me. "Freya, you know what I'm going to say."

"I know." I stared at my feet. "Fine. Give me five

minutes to talk with Jason, and I'll meet you in the lab. But let's shield the compound first in case Hel comes back."

"She won't come back," Mia confirmed. She swiped her hologram down so the screen returned to her arm, then shut down. "The electromagnetic current of the portal should debilitate her magic for at least two hours. Brynn said she built that into the specs. And by then, if we're smart, we'll have relocated somewhere far away. Is the northwest compound still secure?"

"The only compound I'm trusting with our lives is the valkyrie compound." I shook my head. "Five minutes with Jason, five more to extract the ketane, and then the four of us are heading to Asgard."

Mia's eyes widened, but she gave a tight nod.

Beside me, Jason let out a sound that closely resembled a bleat. "Asgard? Like, from the movies, Asgard?"

"Asgard, like home. Get inside, Ahlström. You and I need to talk." I gestured toward the house.

Jason fell into step beside his sister and muttered, "You ever been there?"

"They said I wasn't allowed," Mia hissed back.

She wasn't. Neither of them were. But with the worlds at war, I couldn't think of anywhere else they'd be safe.

And I wasn't risking *either* of the Ahlströms' lives again. Not when so much depended on both of them.

"Jesus Christ, Freya. You saved my life out there." Jason stood in front of the window, shaking his head.

"It was nothing." I crossed to the fireplace. "I'm just glad you're okay."

"It was not nothing. Hell, is that what you guys do? Fight monsters like the blue chick, and nearly get yourselves killed?" He ran one hand through his hair.

"Some days," I admitted. "Other days we do…less exciting things."

Jason's awed expression hadn't changed since we'd walked into the cabin. Mia was upstairs packing an evacuation bag, while Elsa had blurred to her cabin and retrieved one of her own. Now she was upstairs, prepping the man cave for our next task. I had only minutes before we'd need to extract the ketane, call for Heimdall, and Bifrost to the security of the valkyrie compound. But before I could relinquish the darkness Hel had forced into me, I had to release at least a portion of the darkness I'd forced upon myself. It had taken me a while to figure it out, a fact that caused no small amount of mortification, but I'd finally realized there was no mortal match waiting for Jason in Arcata. The reason my brain lit up like a marquee whenever he was around was because he was *my* match—nobody else's. The subsidiary Norns couldn't trace the signal because it wasn't theirs to service. And keeping so much of myself from the soul who, it turned out, was meant to complement me, was creating a whole new layer of haze around my heart. I'd have to stay on my guard—keep perma-walls erected to avoid putting Jason in a situation that could cost him his life. I would *always* have to be mindful of the contract that prohibited me from giving my heart away. But I would offer Jason as much of myself as my deal with the Norns allowed...and pray that things worked themselves out from there. It was the only way to keep Jason alive *and* allow enough love into my heart for Elsa to extract the ketane. I just needed to god up—to lay my cards on the table, and let Jason decide what he wanted to do with them. Then I could go upstairs, let Elsa evict Hel's poison, and return to Asgard with as much of myself intact as I could physically and spiritually manage. Whatever happened after that would be up to the Norns. And to the warriors and valkyries in whose able hands our future now rested.

Odin help us all.

I walked over to the window, took Jason's hands in mine, and finally opened up—about how allowing myself to fall in love had nearly cost the worlds everything. About the guilt that I still carried with me, and the fear it might never go away. About the loneliness inherent in identifying *perfekt* matches, while knowing I might never be granted the privilege of uniting with mine. About my worries of failing the elite team of warriors who depended on my decisions to keep them alive. I told Jason about my unconventional upbringing inside the valkyrie compound—a structure built by Verdandi, Urd, and Skuld with the purpose of not only protecting me, but fortifying me so that one day I'd be strong enough to protect my realm…both as a bringer of light, and a harbinger of death.

And I told Jason about the depth of my love for my family of choice—Tyr, Elsa, Forse, Brynn, Henrik, and now Mia. About how I'd do anything to protect them… including walking away from a shot at my own happily ever after if, Odin forbid, it came down to that.

When I was finished, Jason pulled me into his arms, pressed his palms to my back, and held me in his steady gaze. "Don't walk away," he said fiercely. "There has to be a way for us to be together."

"We can be together," I reminded him. "I just can't…"

"You can't give me your heart. I remember." Jason lowered his forehead so it rested against my brow. "We'll just have to share mine."

As he spoke, Jason slid one hand up my back. He cradled my head and drew it to his, sweeping his nose lightly against mine. A surge of heat shot due south, and my eyelids fluttered closed. Jason's lips brushed against my cheek, trailing a line to my earlobe. I couldn't quiet my moan when he nipped at the tender flesh. His lips were absolutely divine. They moved lower, peppering a trail of feather-light kisses along my neck until my nails began to claw at his back. His mouth moved slowly upward, sucking gently at the skin below my jaw. When I started to believe I might actually combust, he pressed his hips against mine and withdrew his lips.

No! Why?

I opened my lids to find him studying me, staring into my eyes as if asking my permission to proceed.

He didn't have to ask me twice.

My tongue traced my bottom lip, and I pushed my hips harder against his.

With a groan, Jason crushed his lips against mine in a kiss unlike any I'd ever known. It was forceful yet sweet, passionate yet pure, completely in the moment and absolutely...*perfekt*. It was Jason, expressing his feelings in a way words never could—claiming as much of me as he knew I'd allow, while letting me know there was *so very much more* he withheld. All I had to do was say the word...

Good gods, I wanted to say the word. This kiss was saturated in such overwhelming intensity, it took everything I had to remember to hold the barrier around my heart; to not completely give myself over to this human and escape into a fog of blissful surrender. But reality nudged at the back of my consciousness, its weight heavy against the lightness of my joy.

Stupid Ragnarok.

I let the kiss go on...and on...and on. Even as my blood heated up, my heart sent continual waves of iced water dancing through my veins, keeping both my hormones and my emotions in check. The organ simply wouldn't allow me to fully submit to the present moment, an anomaly I could finally attribute to Hel's unwanted gift. Jason's arms tightened around me, sending a fresh wave of tingles flooding below my navel. *Good gods.* His tongue danced along my bottom lip. My blood surged again, and I shifted against him, reveling in the contact.

Ragnarok is coming.

Skit.

I moved to pull away, but Jason groaned and tugged me closer. My knees weakened as his hands moved down, palming my butt and pressing to him.

Get upstairs and get that ketane removed. Now.

With tremendous effort I finally pulled away, my breath coming in ragged gasps.

"That was"—*pant*—"I mean"—*pant, pant*—"just wow."

Jason ran his nose lightly along my jaw, the low rumble of his "mmm-hmm" evoking a wave of delicious shivers.

"I know you have to go," he murmured. "But I'll be waiting when you're done."

If the end of the worlds hadn't literally been upon us, I would have demanded Jason take me to his room right then. But things being what they were, I just reached up and pulled his head back to mine for another toe-curling kiss. There would be plenty of time for demanding *after* we'd saved the worlds. If we managed to come out of Ragnarok alive, things might even be different enough that we could have a real future—one in which rights to my heart reverted fully to me, and I could give all of myself to whomever I chose.

I could barely allow myself the hope.

With a sigh, I turned my attention to Jason, running

my fingertips along the planes of his chest. "Stay inside the house, no matter what happens. This won't take long."

"Take all the time you need, love." Jason kissed the tip of my nose. "I'm not going anywhere."

With tremendous difficulty, I extracted myself from his arms. I made my way toward the stairs, shooting one last look over my shoulder at the mortal I'd only just met, yet could easily imagine building a future alongside. Jason stood in front of the window, his broad shoulders straining against his grey T-shirt, and an easy smile tugging at the lips that had, moments ago, nearly driven me to madness.

I'm not going anywhere.

He had no idea how desperately I hoped his words were true.

Tyr would have been horrified had he known his man cave was aglow with pink. I had no clue where Mia and Elsa had procured that many rocks on such short notice, but when I entered the room, thin sheets of pink crystal lined the windows, dangled from the lights, and even covered an entire wall. Massive, cracked rocks with pink, shark tooth-like innards stood in each corner of the room. A creation that looked to be half chandelier, half wind chime, hung from the ceiling.

"Jeez, Else. You don't mess around." I lowered

myself into the leather chair Mia pointed to, and tried not to gape at the sheer volume of pinkness. "Was this just lying around somewhere?"

"Valkyrie delivery. Came in while you were downstairs. Mia learned ketane's averse to rose quartz, so…" Elsa didn't look up from grinding some glowing concoction—pink, of course—in a thick mortar atop the lab table. "Are you and Jason all squared away?"

"All squared away?" I raised an eyebrow. "It's not a business transaction."

"You know what I mean." Elsa sprinkled a sparkling powder into the bowl before walking it over to me.

"*Ja.* Things are good, considering…" My shoulders rose to my ears. "Well, considering he's a mortal and I'm, well, me." *A goddess under contract. Possibly forever.*

Elsa knelt before me. Her eyes scanned mine, her stare so intense I squirmed. "You look clearer. Good— you're resolved to release the past. We'll make this a quickie, not only because you're you and, frankly, you won't make it through the prolonged version—"

"Hey!" I protested.

"It's true. But also, because we are *super* short on time. Close your eyes."

I did as I was told, allowing Elsa's calming presence to fill my space.

"I want you to picture a massive river—one that's a thousand miles deep, and a thousand miles wide. Position Rhylark on one side, and yourself on the other."

"But I don't want to forget—"

"Do it," Elsa pressed. "We're not forgetting *him.*

We're forgetting the negative associations you've attached to him. Can you trust me?"

My nod was so slight, I wasn't sure she'd register it. But Elsa continued painting her mental picture until Rhylark and I stood on opposite shores of an endless, surging river.

"Excellent. Now create a sphere that contains all of the memories surrounding you and Rhylark that cause you pain—don't look into them, don't analyze them, just place them into the sphere and float that sphere over the center of the river."

It took everything I had not to recall the pain, the hurt, the absolute heartache such a sphere would contain. But I did as Elsa asked, shoving my memories into a crystalline ball and sending it over the surging tide.

"Now drop it," Elsa said.

She couldn't be serious. "What?"

"Drop the ball. Let the river carry it away, to be recycled into the earth like the fertilizer it is. Those memories don't serve you in present time, Freya. They tether you to the past, and prevent you from moving into your future. That is not what the Norns want for you. It's not what Rhylark wants for you. And it's not what you want for yourself. If it was, you wouldn't have agreed to do this."

My fingernails dug into my palms as I took a deep breath, permitted myself one moment of hesitation, then dropped the ball. The river surged, pulling it under and sweeping it downstream so quickly that I didn't have the chance to mourn its loss. It was just… gone. In its place was an empty space, waiting to be filled.

But with what?

"Now, I want you to take another ball. Fill this one with all of the memories surrounding you and Rhylark that brought you joy. Don't look at these either, or analyze them—just place them into the ball, and float that sphere over the river."

Oh gods. Was she going to make me release this one too? I loaded up the ball, sent it into the space above the river…and I waited.

"Now, I want you to picture a beam of light shooting from one side of this ball directly to Rhylark, a thousand miles away, on the other side of the river. And I want you to picture a second beam shooting from the ball back to you, on your side of the river. Allow these memories, this happiness, to fill you both —to be the *only* thing you carry forward with you on your journey. That which nourishes your soul and serves your highest good—*that* is what you may take forward with you. Nothing more. Nothing less."

My cheeks dampened as tears ebbed from my eyes. With a sigh of gratitude, I allowed the light to fill my heart, to fill my entire body, and then, to expand to touch *all* of the space encompassing my side of the riverbank. A thousand miles away, a brilliant light showed me that Rhylark, wherever he was, was doing the same. The knowledge that somewhere, somehow, we were both harvesting all that was good from our time together with the intention of evolving into our fullest, lightest selves filled me with a peace I hadn't known for a long time—if ever.

"And now, my beautiful love goddess…" Elsa's voice cracked. "Gift all of Rhylark's energy back to him. Call all of your energy back to you. Release the ball into the river, for you have taken from it all that can serve you in the present time. And know that from this moment on, you are in *perfekt* command of your energy, as it relates to this portion of your past."

"Thank you," I whispered. I released Rhylark's energy, called back my own, and let the sphere drop into the raging tide. I felt no sadness as it was swept away, only gratitude for all it had given me. Every part of me was full, and light, and whole.

Every part but one.

"What about my heart?" I asked. "The ketane…"

"We can release it now," Elsa said gently. "Mia, do you have the containment vessel?"

My eyes fluttered open. *Mia.* I'd forgotten she was there.

"The vessel is here." Mia held out her hand. A small, round box rested atop her palm.

"Good. Extend it in your right hand, and use your left to hold our space at a golden–pink resonance. Intend that clarity and love fill Freya's aura. Freya, drink this. *All* of this." Elsa handed me the bowl, which was now full of glowing, pink liquid. "When it's gone, I'll begin the extraction."

I raised the fizzing drink to my lips and swallowed,

trying not to giggle as the bubbles danced across my tongue. "It tickles."

"Faster, please," Elsa urged.

I downed the rest of the drink, licking the last of its sweetness from my bottom lip. When I'd finished, Elsa took the bowl from my hands and placed it on the ground. She stepped back, held her hands in front of her, closed her eyes…and hummed.

The humming was new. Elsa's ministrations were usually silent.

Elsa flicked her fingers at me and continued her humming. I closed my eyes and nestled my head into the leather back of my chair. A second, slightly higher pitch chimed in from my right, and I was hit with a wave of calm as Mia and Elsa worked in tandem. When they'd learned to do this, I did not know. But I found myself encased in a cocoon of complete and utter peace.

Finally.

"Keep your eyes closed, Freya," Elsa advised. A few seconds later, her slender fingers rapped lightly on my chest. A force surged inside my ribcage—the dark weight that had held my heart seemed to recoil.

"I don't think it likes you," I offered.

Elsa hummed again, and a jolt of effervescent energy shot from her palm into my heart. Heat filled me from the inside, and the ketane whipped back and forth with such force, the backs of my ribs grew tender.

"Ouch!"

"Sorry. It should take only a moment longer. Mia? Open the box and bring it closer."

Mia's shoulder brushed against my forearm as a small click rang through the room. The containment vessel was in place. If the tornado in my torso was any indication, the ketane knew.

And it wasn't happy.

"Hold the armrests, Freya. This might be uncomfortable. I'll extract on three. Two. One."

A vicious curse ripped from my throat. Leather wedged into my nails as I dug my fingertips into the chair. Blazing agony tore through my chest, blistering my insides and filling me with the desperate desire to crawl out of my own skin. "My gods, it hurts!"

"Don't move!" Elsa's normally sanguine tone had a decisive edge. The part of my brain not consumed with my imminent demise prayed the ketane wasn't hurting Elsa, too. "Mia, close the box when the tail extracts. You'll see its barbed surface and—"

"Holy *skit!*" I screamed as tiny blades pummeled my heart, then ripped through my ribcage. I opened my eyes just in time to see the mace-like end of what appeared to be a snake fly into the little box in Mia's hand.

"Now!" Elsa cried.

"Got it!" Mia shut the box with a loud snap. It rattled violently, nearly toppling to the floor before my friend slammed her other hand on top of it. "There's a containment mode. I just have to find the switch..."

She slid her thumb over the lid of the box, and it stopped shaking.

My hands, however, trembled with the force of an angry frost giant. I shot Elsa a *look*. "That was more than *uncomfortable*."

"I know. I felt it with you. That thing was *horrid*." Elsa shuddered. "Its energy was so dark...as dark as Hel's own."

"She said it was a new substance. Do you think it was a piece of her?" Mia locked the box in the wall safe, and turned to us with wide eyes. "Good Lord, Freya. Did you have Hel's soul imbued in your heart all these months?"

"Gods, I hope not." I shuddered at the image of a piece of Hel's soul somehow contained within mine. But instead of amplifying, curling into itself, and thickening to weigh down my chest and cloud my head like my fears had done for months on end, this piece of anxiety flickered and died. My head remained mercifully clear, and my heart...

The black hole of darkness was gone. And in its place was the warm, pink pulse of complete and total, unconditional, brilliantly glowing...*love*.

I drew a deep breath, reveling in the way light surged into spaces I'd believed were lost to me forever. The love expanded, its warmth filling me with peace and gratitude and grace. Lightness danced across my torso, the sheer joy within it enough to make me sob with relief.

"Scan me, Elsa. I think we got it all."

Elsa raised her palm a few inches from my head. She ran it down my body and back up, hovering for an extra moment at my heart. "No residual energy. You're clear."

"Good." I pushed myself off the smooth surface of the chair to stand on shaky legs. "Let's call Heimdall and get to Asgard immediately. Brynn may have the valkyries under control, but I have a feeling our girls will need the backup of their love goddess."

"You're ready to go?" Mia asked. "Don't you need recovery time? You had *Hel's* energy inside of you, for God's sake. That must have been horrific."

"It was. But time's a luxury we don't have." I rolled my shoulders back and drew myself up to my full six feet. "The realms need us. And I'm finished letting them down."

I asked for a moment alone with Jason before we departed for Asgard. I took his hands in mine and assured him that though things were about to get substantially crazier, I'd be there for him in every way I could. Then I kissed him. In the sixty seconds we had to lose ourselves in that moment, my toes curled and my blood absolutely singed with heat. The ketane was *definitely* gone, thank Odin. And if Elsa hadn't charged down the stairs *right then* announcing the arrival of our rainbow transport, things would have gotten deliciously heated.

Stupid rainbow transport.

Jason, Mia, Elsa, and I left the Arcata cabin together, stepping as a unit into the multi-hued light of the bridge. The Ahlström siblings masked their uneasiness with shaky grins, though Jason definitely yelped as Heimdall raised the Bifrost. I held tight to his hand, offering what little reassurance I could to the human who, for all purposes, had left the only realm he'd ever known for the first—and possibly last—time. Odin only knew what Midgard would look like post-Ragnarok…if it survived, at all.

We accelerated on approaching Asgard, and as the force of descent increased the pressure on my body to near-unbearable levels, I reminded myself that we would face this battle as we had every other—with the fierce determination that had defined our society since the beginning of time. We'd survived countless attacks, each with the same end—Asgard victorious, rising again to lead the realms to peace. This battle would be no different. Love—and our warriors—*would* conquer all.

I believed this with every fiber of my being until we touched down outside the valkyrie compound. In that moment, I realized how very greatly the odds were stacked against us…and how truly heinous the horrors of Ragnarok had become.

CHAPTER 11

A S REALM-ENDING BATTLES went, this one was a major *skit* show.

The V.C. was absolute chaos—girls racing from the arsenal to the tech distribution center to the staging areas, where they were dispatched to dispel the seemingly infinite threats to the light realms. But inside the war room, the vibe was one of calculated calm. On departure, Mariana, Sigrunn, Tessyra, and Xatnari had each taken a set of birdies—the drone cameras Henrik and I had developed. Now, their missions played out on the four holo-screens atop the center of the enormous conference table. My gaze shifted from Mariana's team, who'd wasted no time eliminating the horde of dark elves standing between them and the younglings they'd been sent to extract, over to Tessyra's team, crouched low as they set deactivators around a portal in the dark forest.

In the Muspelheim screen, Xatnari stood in a blackened clearing with Hyro and her dragon, Marshmallow. The still-smoking tree trunks suggested that either fire giants or feyndrals had recently blazed the forest, which accounted for the additional valkyrie sentries who joined the regulation two in scanning the horizon from atop their pegasuses. The equines' wings fanned the dark smoke, creating a screen that blocked Xatnari's team from outside view. And just inside the screen, a cluster of two-dozen fire giants stood huddled with a handful of our valkyries. One of the giants knelt in the soot to sketch some kind of diagram. She must have been part of the rebel cell our girls had come to enlist. *Nice.*

Secure in the knowledge that our Muspelheim plan was in effect, I checked in on Nidavellir. Sigrunn and her team crept silently around a nest of sleeping dragons. A handful of dwarves cowered in the upper-right corner of the screen, where two of our higher-ranking valkyries waved them forward. No doubt they had an extraction plan in place, and provided they didn't wake the sleeping...*skit.*

"Sigrunn, live wire at your two o'clock." I tapped the Nidavellir screen to zoom in on the yawning reptile. Its eyes flickered open, the third lid sliding sideways as it registered the dwarf's movement. "Get everybody out of there, *now.*"

"Copy that." Sigrunn held up a fist. She lifted one finger, and a second later, three valkyrie-bearing pegasuses swooped across my screen. The girls on the ground lifted the dwarves one by one, depositing them on the backs of the horses before drawing their swords and turning on the dragons. Flames shot from the now *very much awake* reptiles' mouths. Though we generally honored a no-kill policy with Nidavellir's dragons, Sigrunn's team quickly dispatched the more aggressive creatures. Wren, one of our animal whisperers, set about calming the others—*thank gods*—and the skirmish was over before I'd unclenched my white knuckles from the edge of the table.

"Good work," I praised. "Keep an eye on the second nest—the one to your ten o'clock. The purple-backed dragon over there may be waking up."

"Got it. Thanks, General."

"Birdie, scan to the south," I ordered. My screen panned to the left, where the valkyries ushered a dozen dwarves toward a silver portal. "Exit looks good. Once evac's complete, you're moving on to debilitate the dark energy siphon, *ja*?"

"Half of my team is setting up detonation," Sigrunn confirmed. "This was the last of the captives. Once they're clear, the rest of us will head west and assist."

"I'm here if you need anything." I logged off and shifted my attention to the Muspelheim hologram, where Marshmallow snorted bursts of fire from his scaly nose. I was so focused on the flame-breather, I jumped when the door clicked open behind me.

"Ouch!" I rubbed my kneecap. Table edges were *hard*.

"Sorry," Freya apologized. I raised a curious eyebrow at the sight of my commanding officer—who was *supposed* to be in Arcata—scooting into the room with a rueful smile. "I know how crazy it gets."

"Svetana's running intermediary, and I told her I only wanted updates every five minutes. So, it's fairly calm in here. But out there?" I jutted my chin toward the now closed door. "Yikes."

"Total chaos," Freya confirmed.

"Seriously. The tech team's pulling all available devices and shipping them with each Bifrost departure. The arsenal team's ramping up transfer of weapons, and the contemplatives are reallocating adverse energy from the meditation center. From all appearances, Jotunheim's about to unleash total mayhem on…somewhere."

I pointed to the fifth screen—the one I'd set away from the others. It showed waves of frost giants charging across an icy field. They assembled in front of an actively sparking portal. Our strategists hadn't yet traced its exit point, but anywhere that many jotuns were heading was in for one Helheim of a shock.

"Any chance you brought our Unifiers with you?" I asked.

"Mia and Elsa went straight to the meditation center. The contemplatives said they had a separate room they could use for Unifying."

"Good. And Jason?" My eyes flicked from screen to screen, monitoring for imminent catastrophes.

"The contemplatives will keep an eye on him while Mia and Elsa work. He wasn't thrilled about being babysat while his sister and her friends saved the worlds, but once the contemplatives showed him a holo from the second Battle of Jotunheim, he understood he might need more training before going into the field." Freya chuckled. "Bless."

"No, I mean how'd he take all of this?" I waved my hands in front of me. "Kind of a lot, finding out Asgard exists and visiting it on the same day."

"He did okay. Well, he did throw up after the Bifrost." *Preach.* "But he recovered quickly—or at least, he pretended to. I appreciate the effort."

"I'll bet you do." Gods, I loved that Freya had fallen for Mia's brother. *So perfekt.* "And Mia? How'd she react to seeing this place for the first time?"

"Mia's Mia." Freya's eyes crinkled in a smile. "You could practically see her brain split in half when we touched down—one side memorizing everything to analyze later, the other trying to figure out how any of it could be real."

"Gotta love our human." Sharp movement from one of the screens drew my eye, and I quickly advised Sigrunn to have Wren take care of the purple-backed dragon who was now snorting fire. Once Wren was on her way, I blinked at Freya. She shouldn't have been in Asgard—none of them should. Something awful must have gone down. "So, I'm taking it you're in Asgard because something happened in Arcata?"

"You might want to pull up a Midgard screen," Freya offered. "Hel showed up at the compound."

I swore. Loudly.

"We sent her through a portal, but we don't know

where it took her. In case she makes it back to Midgard, it would help to have a debilitation team on standby." Freya crossed to my side. She pulled an additional screen from the air and set it in the center of the tabletop ones. "Set Midgardian scan to wide. Access all known dark portal sites. Revolve." The screen did as she asked, flickering through feeds in five-second intervals. "I can watch this one if you want," Freya offered. "Frees up more of your attention to focus on the Jotunheim situation."

"That'd be great." I raked my fingers through my hair. My curls had gotten a *lot* messier since I'd arrived in the war room. "I don't know how you've done this for so long. It's a ton of pressure."

"You get used to it." Freya shrugged. "But it's been hard to balance both jobs—I'm glad you're in command today, so can I focus on being Love."

I tilted my head from shoulder to shoulder, breathing deeply into the taut muscles in my neck. "You're ready to take that job back on?"

"Absolutely." Freya's voice carried a resolve I hadn't heard in a long time.

Thank gods. "I'm really happy to hear that," I said softly. And I meant it. The worlds were dimmer without Freya's light, and we needed that light today, more than ever.

"General!" Xatnari's sharp voice barked in my ear. "Permission to engage."

I transferred my focus to the Muspelheim screen, where four dragons crept through the forest toward the smoke. They appeared to be larger versions of Hyro's Marshmallow—they must have been the feyndrals. The lethal, dark-magic-wielding, god-killing feyndrals.

It was go time.

"Permission granted. Four dragons, your one o'clock. Having the rebels turn the feyndrals would be a win, but remember, if it's your lives or theirs, protect the rebels and our girls."

"I won't let you down, General. Wave one—move out!" Xatnari charged, her sword drawn. Her team spread into an attack formation before following her through the smoke screen. They bore down on the feyndrals, who reared back on their hind legs and shot fire from their gaping maws.

"Wave two!" Xatnari cried, and the rebel fire giants burst through the smoke. They broke into teams of six, circling around the feyndrals and drawing their heads back. The giants' bellies expanded just before streams of flame shot from their noses. The feyndrals fired back, and in no time the forest was a sea of red and orange and black. Flames lapped at the ground, up the charred trunks of the trees, and along the smattering of fauna that somehow managed to bloom amidst the unforgiving Muspelheim atmosphere. The equine team circled the dragons from the air, directing smoke at the reptiles and obscuring visibility so the rebels could approach.

"Feyndrals are swiveling their heads from side to side," I said. "In other dragon species, that signals disorientation. Give it another few seconds, and have the rebels go in for the turn."

"Copy that, General." Xatnari waited several beats before shouting, "Turn them!"

"Airborne, shift the smoke pattern to increase visibility for the rebels," I commanded. "If the feyndrals come close enough to attack, take out the threat."

Xatnari relayed my order to her pegasus team, and the valkyries shifted position. By the time the smoke cleared, three of the feyndrals had begun to buckle under the blaze of the rebel giants. The fourth angrily bobbed his head back and forth, firing at our allies. Two fire giants fell to the ground, shrieking as their skin was coated in thick, orange flames. A third moved in closer to the beast, shooting a stream directly at the feyndral's heart. The dragon staggered backward before regaining its composure and incinerating its attacker.

"Xatnari, the southern-most dragon is unwilling to comply. Three casualties. Eliminate by air strike, but protect the remaining rebels," I ordered.

"Air team, take out Feyndral Four." Xatnari charged into the flames, broadsword at the ready, while the pegasus team swooped in from the sky. They dove at the dragon in waves, slicing its neck on alternate sides. The monster whipped its head from side to side, registering each attack a split second too late.

"Rebels, clear out!" Xatnari demanded. The flames surrounding Feyndral Four dissipated, and the dragon drew its head back just as Xatnari leapt in the air and drove her sword into its chest. Thick, black blood gushed from the puncture, coating the valkyrie's weapon and her uniform in a tar-like goo.

"Air team," Xatnari panted. "Terminate!"

In a fierce flash of wings and swords, the airborne valkyries swarmed the dragon's neck. With synchronized precision, they drove their swords into the beast and wrenched them sideways, decapitating the feyndral. The beast's head tumbled down, narrowly missing Xatnari before landing with a thud. Thick, black soot puffed upward, obscuring my lieutenant general from view.

"You okay?" I barked.

"Never better." Xatnari coughed. She stepped through the cloud to study the other three dragons. Each knelt in submission, as if pledging fealty to the rebel giants.

"Send in Hyro," I ordered. We'd kept the young giant back, not wanting to risk her safety. But now that the turn had been successful—on three fronts, anyway —it was time for her to instruct the rebels on feyndral command. Having four formerly dark dragons on our team would be a huge boost to our fleet. Odin knew, we were going to need it.

Xatnari briefly communicated with our friend before Hyro and Marshmallow approached the three kneeling dragons. Since things seemed to be under control in Muspelheim, I turned command back over to Xatnari, and signed off.

"You handled that well," Freya praised. While I'd

been focused on the fiery realm, she'd relocated the Jotunheim and Midgard screens to the far side of the table, and settled herself into one of the captain's chairs.

My spine crackled as I rolled my shoulders. "Like I said, I don't know how you do it. Do you have a trace on the jotuns' portal exit?"

"Possibly." Freya's brows knitted together. "While I've been working, I've also been sending love to our allied realms. The additional light is being absorbed everywhere but here."

Freya plucked the Midgard screen from the air and zoomed in on an expansive beach house atop a stretch of white sand. She drew back to show lush foliage of the private island, an oasis awash in every conceivable shade of green. Surrounding the island was a sky blue sea, its surface barely marred by a gentle wind. "This location's reflecting all of the light I'm sending it. It seems to be encased in some kind of a blocker. Possibly one strong enough to cloak a staging area for jotuns."

What?

"That makes no sense. Why would they go to the middle of the Caribbean? Unless…" My heart thudded as I remembered the location of one of our lesser used Midgardian safe houses. "Do we have anyone on Asgard Cay right now?"

Freya blanched. "We did."

"Who?"

"I'll fill you in later. The short answer is that the Cay's last visitors evacuated when the fighting began.

But the jotuns must know we still have Asgardians on Midgard. And they're either going to use the Caribbean as a staging area for a realm-wide attack, or…" Freya's head snapped up. Our eyes met in a moment of prolonged anxiety.

"It's a diversion. They'd know we'd protect the Cay—though Odin knows how they found *another* one of our safe houses." I pulled the Jotunheim screen away from Freya and gave it a place of prominence in the center of the table. "Is there anything in Jotunheim that's particularly vulnerable? Something they'd send *an entire legion of warriors* to protect?"

I scanned the screen, swiping up with my fingertips to shift regions, and periodically drawing a city out for a closer view. It wasn't until I reached the southern sea that my blood ran cold.

"Naglfar," I whispered. I jabbed my pointer finger into my wrist. "Call Tyr! Now!"

Freya went white at the end of the table. "The jotuns know we'll be watching our safe houses—the dark magic screen around Asgard Cay is just a distraction. They're going for the ship."

I grimaced.

"Tyr doesn't have enough manpower to overcome an entire army," Freya whispered. "Does he?"

"He said he didn't need any help," I gritted. "Good thing I never listen to him."

The skin atop my forearm wavered as Tyr's face came into focus.

He didn't look pleased. "I'm busy, Brynn."

"You're about to be a lot busier. Give me your coordinates. I'm sending in a team."

"I don't think that's a good idea. I—hold on." Tyr leaned out of the frame. "Repeat that, Henrik. I can't hear when you're both talking at once."

Henrik's low tenor murmured incoherently from somewhere offscreen.

"I see," Tyr growled.

Henrik's face popped up on my wrist. "Give 'em Helheim, *sötnos.*"

"Right back at you!" I caught Henrik's grin before Tyr wrenched his arm away.

"Brynn." Tyr frowned. "I'll take that team you offered after all. Henrik just got a tip that the boat's more heavily guarded than we believed. Apparently, we're going to need the best crew you can give us."

"That's why I called you! Freya and I think a battalion of jotuns are heading your way."

"Jotuns I can handle. But those airborne aviary assassins?" Tyr shook his head. "Krugers are a different ballgame. Wait. Freya's with you?"

"We're in the V.C. war room."

"Bring her in," Tyr barked. I pinched my fingertips together and pulled his image up to hologram mode.

"I'm here." Freya moved to my side.

"Freya." Tyr stared into the screen. The brief flicker of emotion behind his game face caused his eyes to shift from grey–blue to almost navy. "Are you back?"

Three words. So much pressure. Without moving my head, I diverted my attention to my friend. Freya stood calmly, hands clasped, carrying herself with every ounce of the poise I'd admired from the first day I met her. Now she pulled her shoulders back, lifted her chin, and met Tyr's gaze. "I am."

"On both counts or just one?" Tyr pressed.

Freya's determined gaze said it all. *Thank gods.*

"Good. Take back command of the valkyries, and send Brynn to me. I'm going to need her."

Freya glanced at me. "Is that okay with you?"

"Yes," I squeaked.

Freya nodded. "Then consider it done."

Air escaped my lips in a rush, and without thinking, I threw my arms around my friend. "Good. Because this job is *hard.*"

"You were doing great," Freya assured. "I wouldn't have trusted anyone else to lead our fighters. And with everything that's going down, well…it may be time for the valkyries to have *two* high commanders."

My heart pounded in my chest. Was Freya asking me to be her equal? To *co-lead* Asgard's elite female squadron? Did I even want to do that?

"Discuss it later," Tyr barked. "Brynn, get here with that team. Freya, do your Love thing on Jotunheim. You have my coordinates?"

"I do. And I will. Stay safe," Freya urged. "And take care of our family."

"You know I will," Tyr said gruffly. His hologram flickered and disappeared.

"Well, then." Freya turned to me. "You know what to do."

"My reserve team is on standby in the stables." I clasped Freya's hands. "You sure you're up to this? That…darkness—sorry, I don't know what else to call it. It's really gone?"

"It's really gone," Freya confirmed. "Go. Help our boys. Don't let Tyr do anything stupid."

I squeezed Freya's fingertips before turning on one heel, my cape billowing in my wake. "Like I've ever been able to stop him. Oh!" I paused with one hand on the door handle. "Svetana said something about a golden boar and a magic ship—any chance you can send those with me?"

Freya's pale skin lightened a shade. "Gullinbursti and Skidbladnir? I'll retrieve them and have them sent to you. Go, quickly."

"Aye, aye." I saluted my friend before storming through the door. My movements earned a gasp from a furrow-browed Svetana.

"General Aksel!" She jumped up from the temporary post she'd erected outside the war room. "Where are you going?"

"I'm taking a team to Jotunheim. Freya's in command, now." I rested one hand on the hilt of my rapier as I hurried toward the staircase. Svetana jogged to catch up. "Run the same interference for Freya that you did for me. Don't let *anyone* in that war room."

"Yes, General." Svetana stopped at the top of the stairs and called after me, "Please be careful."

"Always am."

With one last nod, I charged the rest of the way

down the stairs and across the main floor of the V.C. I took the southeastern exit, running the short distance toward the stables. I was halfway there when a glittering white oval appeared directly in my path. I ripped my rapier from its sheath, preparing to attack whatever stepped out of the portal. But a blue-and-silver-clad leg broke through the shimmering white plane, followed by the torso, arms, and head of a sword-wielding valkyrie. She carried a young girl on her back.

"Mariana." I exhaled sharply. "Gods, you scared me to death. The children...are they..."

"We got every single one of them." Mariana reached up to pat the girl's head, then moved out of the way of the portal. "Keep moving, everyone. We're nearly there."

Towheaded twins climbed out of the oval, their little hands clasped tightly together. They were followed by three crimson-haired boys who looked similar enough that they must have been brothers, and two olive-skinned girls who clung tightly to a valkyrie's leg. One after another, the children and the warriors came through the portal. There were so many of them. And they were so young—so innocent. Soot smudged their faces, and their clothes were dirty and torn, but thankfully, they showed no sign of physical harm. Their time in the dark realm had to have been an absolute nightmare—Svartalfheim had long ago extinguished all sources of love, joy, and light. Odin only knew what they'd seen...and how long it would take their little psyches to recover.

"Where are you taking them?" I murmured to Mariana.

"We'll find an empty conference room in the V.C. and try to keep them calm while we contact their parents. Hopefully, a few of the contemplatives can come down and ease their anxiety." Mariana waited until the very last valkyrie had passed through before tapping the top of the white oval. It closed in on itself, dropping to the ground as a thin, silver ball.

I bent down to pick it up, then handed it to my lieutenant general. "Ask the contemplatives to send Mia Ahlström downstairs to help the children. She's one of our Unifiers, and she'll be able to help them in ways the others can't. She has a huge heart, and a very unique approach to…difficult situations."

Mariana saluted. "Thank you, General."

"Thank *you*." I rested my fingertips on her shoulder. "For looking out for those who are weaker than us. For helping those who need our protection most of all."

"It is truly my honor."

I blinked back a tear as I looked into the eyes of the tiny Asgardian on Mariana's back. Thank gods she was safe and sound…for now.

Back to work, Aksel. A lot of lives are depending on you.

Right.

"Freya's upstairs in the war room." I sheathed my sword. "She's handling ops while I assist War in Jotunheim. If you need me, she'll know how to reach me."

"Be safe," Mariana urged. "It sounds like things are heating up quickly in the icy realm."

"You have no idea," I muttered. "If things go south, I'll call on your team for backup. But until then, I want your girls looking after the children. Odin forbid anything comes for them here..." I shuddered. "They've been through enough."

"Agreed. We'll remain on standby." Mariana tapped the communication device on her wrist. "And we will ensure no further harm comes to our young."

I nodded to the rest of Mariana's team, and smiled softly at the children. I was tremendously grateful that they were home, safe and sound.

With one more tight nod, I resumed my trek. Inside the stables, five white pegasuses stood ready to mount, each with an armed valkyrie at its side. The warriors' eyes widened as they registered my presence, but they quickly regained their composure.

"General Aksel." The senior member of the team raised her hand to her forehead in salute.

"We're going into battle. War needs backup on Jotunheim." I scanned the stable for my familiar silver-maned pegasus, but Fang was nowhere to be found. With a frown, I drew a deep breath and bellowed, "I need my horse!"

"I'm so sorry." A breathless girl emerged from one of the stalls. She was young—definitely one of our newer recruits—and even shorter than me. "Freya's never left the valkyrie compound during a skirmish, and since you're in charge we thought it would be okay to let Fang graze. I'll retrieve her for you."

"No need." I brought my fingers to my lips and let out a piercing whistle. The stable hand winced. "Fang!"

Seconds later, my enormous pegasus swooped into the stable in a blur of white wings and glittery silver hooves. Her long mane had been woven into her favorite intricate braids, and her tail swished happily as she landed at my side.

"There you are! Ready to get to work?"

Fang whinnied, rubbing her head against my arm until I reached up to scratch the happy spot at the top of her head.

"I missed you too," I whispered into her ear. Fang nudged me joyfully before dropping to one knee so I could climb atop her back. Careful not to trip over the sheathed blade of my rapier, I swung one leg over Fang's haunches and settled into riding position. She rose to her full ten-foot height, and stepped into place before the line of valkyries.

"Mount up," I ordered. "The God of War is attempting to destroy the ship Naglfar before it sails for the Bifrost. He's expecting increased hostilities, and needs our finest warriors to keep him from getting killed. You ladies with me?"

"Always." The senior member nodded. She clicked her tongue, and her horse stepped forward. Once the other riders were in place, their pegasuses did the same.

"Ride toward the forest in tight formation. I'll call for the Bifrost to pick us up once we're on the move." I nudged Fang with my heels, and she trotted forward.

The click of hooves let me know the rest of my team was close behind. Fang took to the sky the minute we'd cleared the stable, her enormous wings flapping fiercely through the crisp Asgardian air. When five pegasuses flanked me, I tilted my head back and shouted, "Heimdall! Bifrost to War!"

The brilliant, multi-hued bridge shot down from the sky, encompassing us in a deafening wind tunnel.

"For Asgard!" I shouted. The rest of my team echoed my cry, and the next thing I knew, I was soaring across the cosmos, trying to ignore the churn in my stomach as I barreled toward Tyr, Henrik, and Forse—the male members of the family I'd chosen. The guys I'd gladly give my life to protect. And the...*oh, gods.*

My heart dropped as the Bifrost shot me onto an icy field with a perfect view of the dock, the ship, and the horde of monsters moving through the water toward Tyr, Henrik, Forse, and...Odin.

Double gods. Odin's way *too close to the front line.*

My friends were in seriously deep *skit.*

"Tyr!" I screamed as the Bifrost spat me into the Jotunheim atmosphere. "Watery incoming! Your two o'clock!"

Fang's strong wings flapped viciously, closing the distance between us and the enormous ship, Naglfar. My gut churned, whether from fear or Bifrost travel or the stench coming off the watercraft made entirely of the toenails of the dead—*ew!*—I wasn't sure. Tightening my grip on Fang's mane, I lowered my head and nudged her forward with my heels. She dove faster, halving the distance between us and the boat.

Tyr, Henrik, and Forse looked up in surprise as my pegasus and I touched down behind them. Seconds later, five more sets of hooves pounded the wooden boards of the dock as my team landed behind me. We'd made it in time.

Now, to slay all the monsters.

"*Dritt, sötnos.*" Henrik's eyes moved slowly along my skintight suit. "You are *hot* in that outfit."

"Thanks!"

Henrik's eyes lingered on my chest for an extra beat before he shook his head. "But weren't you supposed to come in from the east?"

"I was, but things changed." I pointed my rapier at the water. "You can't see them yet, but you've got hostiles."

"No *skit*," Tyr growled. He twirled his broadsword as he spoke.

"That's why they're here." Forse jutted his chin at the squadron surrounding Odin.

"Your Grace." I bowed my head to Asgard's white-haired, one-eyed ruler, before turning back to Tyr. "Yeah, Odin's guards can take care of the krugers and sink Naglfar once you get control of it. But can they handle a jurgmat?"

"There's a jurgmat?" Henrik whipped his head

toward the water. "I've always wanted to see one. Well, not like this, but—"

"What's your plan?" Tyr zeroed in on me.

"Me and the girls will take care of the bottom-feeder. The three of you knock out the water-bound attackers who *aren't* acid-spewing sea monsters. I saw them change trajectory when I was flying in. Now they're a hundred meters due west, about a fathom below the surface. Same number so far—three jotuns, three dwarves, two trolls. One air-containment vessel. They'll be here any minute."

"Odin!" Tyr called over his shoulder. "Is your team ready for that onslaught of krugers?"

"My guards have debilitated more avian assassins than any team in Asgard." Odin's regal nod earned a salute from his warriors.

"Good. Because the first flock is incoming…and I doubt it's the last." Tyr jutted his chin at the sky over the ocean, where a group of winged beasts approached. As the krugers drew closer, their sharp talons, blade-lined backs, and leathery, black appendages came into view. The claws atop their wings sparked with electric charges, and I knew that if they made it any closer to the dock, they'd either electrocute or stab us to death. We had to act. Fast.

"Attack!" Odin bellowed. A dozen guards drew bows from their backs and fired at the winged assassins. Two dropped from the sky, their enormous corpses eliciting equally sizeable splashes in the ocean below. Bolts of discharged electricity shot from their claws as their lifeless bodies bobbed to the surface, and I briefly wondered if the force of their charge had managed to kill the jurgmat. *Live to dream, Aksel.*

"Again!" Odin ordered. With a flash of light, a crimson haired figure emerged in the sky a hundred yards from Odin's forces. A burst of lightning shot from his hand, and I breathed a bit easier knowing Thor had arrived to assist his father. As the guards fired in tandem with the God of Thunder, I shifted my attention back to Tyr.

"I spotted the jurgmat in the water on my way in. It's not far off, so I'm taking my girls to the sky for a better vantage point." I nudged Fang with one heel. "We'll do what we can to disable it before it reaches you. Will you be okay with the rest of the hostiles?"

"*Ja.* Thanks, Brynn. You dropped everything to back me up."

Emotion swelled in my chest, but I tamped it down. *Not the time.* Instead, I returned Tyr's nod with a shrug. "What are friends for?"

"Take this." Henrik stepped forward, a small black cylinder in his palm.

"A basifier? *Takk,* babe."

Since the jurgmat's primary offense was spitting hundred-foot streams of acid, the neutralizing device would come in major handy. Assuming the jurgmat surfaced long enough for us to drop this bomb.

"Be careful." Henrik closed his hand around mine as he handed off the tech.

"Back at you." I bent low to brush my lips against

my boyfriend's. A tantalizing shiver danced along my spine as he slipped his tongue into my mouth. But much too quickly, he pulled away, and I was left slightly dizzy, rapier in one hand, and acid-neutralizing device in the other. "I'd better go."

"We'll finish that later." Henrik's wink sent a pulse of heat straight through me. *Oh yes, we will.*

"Valkyries, charge!" I slipped the basifier into my collar, and pointed my sword to the north. Fang took off, circling away from the krugers and leading our team over the spot we'd last seen the jurgmat. The water was dark below me, but hopefully my Asgardian sight would be strong enough to see through the—

"Arugh!" A shout from behind made me spin around. One of my soldiers tumbled off her pegasus. The animal's neck wrenched from side to side as it spiraled toward the shore, while the girl's hands clawed at her face. In the sea below, an enormous, blubbery creature splashed angrily in the water. *The jurgmat.* I could either kill the beast or save my soldier. There wouldn't be time for both.

Unless I was fast.

With a cry, I wrenched Fang's head to the left and altered my course. "Catch her!"

Fang lowered her head and dove. She reached my soldier at the same time I wrenched Henrik's gift from my collar. When the valkyrie landed atop Fang's haunches I reached back to steady her with my sword hand, careful not to nick her with the blade. Once her arms were wrapped securely around my waist, I calculated my trajectory and flung the basifier into the gaping jaws of the jurgmat. The black cylinder hit its target, exploding in a wave of sparkling mist the moment it made contact with the acid. *Excellent.* One less offensive tactic to worry about. Now we just had to dodge the jurgmat's lightning shots.

Lightning shots…oh, gods. I was well within firing range.

"Fang, get us out of here!" I bellowed.

"We'll cover you, General." My team circled above me. Those with bows drew arrows from their backs. They fired on the jurgmat with choreographed preci-sion. The beast let out a fierce groan as it shot a bolt of electricity at me. *Skit!* The lightning passed just inches from Fang's right wing. She swung to the left, narrowly dodging a second bolt. And then a third.

By the time I reached my team, the monster had fired off half a dozen bolts. The seventh grazed my thigh, and I yelped as the energy exploded against my leg, anticipating imminent anguish. Whatever the tech team had done to my suit must have been working, because instead of singed flesh, I only felt the begin-nings of a raging bruise. The part of my brain not consumed with survival made a note to promote my designers—a two-rank bump, minimum.

My hair whipped at my cheeks as I looked over my shoulder. I shouted at the injured valkyrie atop Fang's haunches. "Your pegasus looks stable, and she's circling back for you. If I get you close enough, can you jump to her?"

"I think so," she shouted back.

"Good." I steered Fang closer to the all-white mount, and turned my head again. "Whenever you're ready."

The girl pushed herself up and leapt for her pegasus. Despite the nasty acid burn on her face that had to be causing all kinds of pain, she gripped her horse's mane and rode hard toward our attacker. Pulling an arrow in her taut bow, she took aim and fired at the jurgmat. The arrow pierced the sea monster's eye. With a fierce shriek, the creature slapped the water with all four of the tentacles surrounding its head. It disappeared beneath the surface, and for one joyful moment I thought it might be dead.

Then it shot out of the sea, its powerful tail fluke lifting it a full twenty feet above the surface. As it soared, it shot lightning from each of its tentacles, caging my team within a deadly energy field.

Oh, Helheim no. It did *not* go there.

"Take it down!" I shouted.

My girls drew their weapons. The sky became a blur of flying arrows and glinting swords. Two valkyries swooped down on the jurgmat, their swords held high. As the creature dropped back into the ocean, my soldiers sliced through two tentacles, removing half of its lightning canons, and coating the sea in a surge of black blood. The jurgmat resurfaced, now moving considerably slower.

A staticky bolt shot from the water, and I knew it was now or never. I dug my heel into Fang's ribcage to drive her lower. Her massive wings quickly closed the distance between us and the sea monster. When we were directly above it, I reached down to unlock the safety at my ankle. I angled my heel so it was clear of Fang's wing, prayed my boot designer had crafted a kickback-free model, and cleared my mind of all thoughts but one.

Fire.

A blast immediately burst from my boot. The jurgmat let out a gurgled squeal, and I looked down to find a fresh stream of black liquid oozing from between its eyes.

"End this! Now!" I ordered.

A sea of arrows pierced the jurgmat's blubbery back, and the two sword-wielders swooped in, removing the last flailing tentacles that slapped haphazardly against the water. With a final *glurg*, the life flickered from the jurgmat's arrow-pierced eye. It sank slowly into the tar-colored liquid now surrounding its massive form.

We'd done our job. We'd decommissioned our threat.

Thank gods.

"Regroup," I commanded. I hurriedly reactivated the safety on my boot.

My team flew higher, out of range of any unseen aquatic hostiles, and formed a loose, airborne circle.

"That was excellent work," I praised. "We're clear to assist with the other two situations."

I glanced at the shore, where Odin's team was

under siege by a fresh flock of krugers. Holy Helheim, how many were there? Things hadn't fared much better on the dock, where Tyr, Forse, and Henrik were moving *away* from Naglfar. They were being driven back by three jotuns, three dwarves, and two shockingly frightening trolls. *Förbaskat.* We'd disabled our threat, but our brothers in arms hadn't been as lucky. And they were *badly* outnumbered. It would take a miracle to turn this battle around.

But we had to try.

"Bring it in, ladies." My girls drew a tighter circle in the air. "Okay. Odin's guards have higher numbers, so they stand a better chance of defending themselves. Getting War's team on that ship—and making sure they sink it—is our new priority. We'll attack from behind, taking out the dwarves first and—"

My throat closed up as a sparking, black portal opened at the end of the dock. It expanded while Tyr, Forse, and Henrik retreated unaware. The battalion of jotuns that Freya and I had seen from the war room emerged, one member at a time, their weapons drawn and poised to strike.

My boys were about to be slaughtered. And I was too far away to do a thing about it.

CHAPTER 12

"**S**VETANA, GET ME MY** horse and a battle suit!" I ripped my shirt over my head and shouted into the empty war room, knowing full well my assistant was listening.

Sure enough, Svetana burst through the door a half minute later, blue and silver uniform in one hand and a data pad in the other. She tossed the neatly folded fabric at me, and pulled up an image of each of the nine worlds from her device. "Shall I reroute any of the teams?"

"Send the half of Mariana's team and the full Muspelheim team to the Jotunheim dock, and make sure they bring the feyndrals," I ordered. "I want the rest of Mariana's team to stay here protecting the compound…and making sure nothing comes for those children." I removed my shoes and pants, and slipped easily into the updated suit. It was thicker, yet more pliable than our previous model. "Do you have War's coordinates?"

"Yes, and I'll remain on standby so you can let me know if I should request that additional support be sent your way. Any other instructions?"

"*Ja,*" I said. "Get Heimdall to drop the Bifrost outside the entry *now*. And make sure Starla's waiting for me by the time I get outside."

"Your pegasus will be in transit momentarily."

"Good. My friends need me." I reached instinctively for the handle of my sword, but of course it wasn't in its sheath. "*Skit,* I need weapons. Call for—"

"They are at my desk," Svetana offered gently. "I had them sent up when you arrived as well."

"Thanks, Svetana." I leaned forward to speak to the holo-screens. "Muspelheim team, reroute—coordinates will arrive shortly. Mariana, keep half of your team where they are and send the other half to the location Svetana forwards you. The rest of you, continue with your missions as planned. Svetana will hold down the V.C. while I assist with the situation in Jotunheim."

"High Commander!" Svetana squeaked. "I'm not qualified to—"

"You'll do great. I have to go." I charged across the room, pausing at the threshold to set up a drip for my *other* job. After rooting my energy to the core of Asgard, I sent a heavy pulse of love at each of the nine realms. Then I bolted through the door.

My battle belt was waiting on Svetana's desk, and I

wasted no time strapping it to my waist and barreling down the wide, winding staircase of the V.C. My fingertips grazed the pockets of the belt, confirming my broadsword, dagger, slicing disc, and secret weapons—the encapsulated and miniaturized Gullinbursti and Skidbladnir I kept in a hidden pocket —were all in place. Secure in the knowledge I was as armed as I could be, I swung a sharp right at the foot of the stairs, and quietly entered the room where Mia was addressing the once-captive children.

"You all did beautifully. Now, remember." Mia smiled. "If you need me, I'll be just upstairs, finishing some work with my friend, Elsa Fredriksen."

"I love Elsa," a knee-high girl squealed. "She helped my dad when he got hurt."

"Elsa's the best." Mia rubbed the pad of her thumb along the girl's cherubic cheek. My subtle wave caught her eye, and she nudged the girl back toward her friends before coming to my side. "Everything all right?"

"You're needed in Jotunheim. Tyr's in trouble, and your gift is much more effective in person."

Darkness cloaked Mia's eyes. "How do I get there?"

"Come with me." I opened the door and slipped through it. Mia paused to address the children.

"Slight change of plan—I'll be back shortly. Elsa will help you if you need her. I'm so proud of *all* of you." With that, Mia emerged through the doorway, her long denim-clad legs making quick strides across the marble floor. "Let's go." This tone was considerably more abrupt than the one she'd used with the children.

Skit. If our mortal was going into war, she'd need sturdier battle wear than jeans and a sweater. "Svetana!" I barked into my communicator. "I need a suit for my Unifier. Can you have one sent down?"

"Absolutely," Svetana replied. Seconds later, a curly haired girl charged down the stairs and thrust a valkyrie uniform at me.

"High Commander! Here," the girl said breathlessly. "The tech team's been working on this model since Balder fell. Its fibers are reconfigured for maximum protective capabilities. It's not equipped with the same attack features as our regulation model, but it is a fully operational defensive suit. Ideal for safeguarding a valuable asset."

Her eyes slid over to Mia. A Unifier was definitely a valuable asset. But a *mortal* unifier…I shivered at the thought of my friend going into battle without protection.

I took the suit from the girl and passed it to Mia, then pointed to the door to my right. "That room should be empty. Go put this on and meet me back here." Mia hurried off to change while I turned back to clasp the young valkyrie's hand. "Thank you. That suit may well save my friend's life."

The girl's curls slid in front of her eyes as she ducked her head with a shy smile. "It is my honor to help." Then she withdrew her hand from mine and scurried back up the stairs, in the direction of the lab.

Mia emerged quickly, now wearing valkyrie-issued silver and blue. "Where do we catch our transport?"

"We'll Bifrost in on my pegasus, Starla," I briefed her as we moved. "Brynn's teams debilitated the sea monster, but there are assassin birds targeting Odin, and a new team of jotuns bearing down on Tyr, Forse, and Henrik. Odin's guards are working on the birds, but I need you to send energy at the jotuns—try to slow them down enough to give our boys a fighting chance. They're massively outnumbered."

"I understood about half of that, but I know what I have to do." Mia broke into a run, darting in front of me through the now open door of the V.C. The rainbow bridge shone brightly in the compound's expansive drive, and my all-black pegasus knelt beside the Bifrost, ready for boarding.

"Follow me." I eased myself onto Starla before offering my hand to help Mia up. She'd mounted the horse herself before I'd fully turned around.

"Let's go, Freya," she barked.

With a cry, I urged Starla forward. The pegasus flapped her massive wings and rose from the ground, her head barely entering the Bifrost before we were shot across the cosmos and into the icy realm.

Gods, I hoped we weren't too late.

"Tyr! Break left!" Brynn shrieked.

I quickly scanned the ground, where Tyr dove just in time to avoid a sparking arrow. A full three dozen jotuns stampeded across the dock where he, Forse, and Henrik were positioned, their backs together in a tight triangle. A second jotun attack team moved in on their other side, its members opening fire with weapons that ranged from arrows to electrocution cannons.

"Mia," I said through clenched teeth.

"On it." She wrapped one hand tight around my waist. Her other arm shot out toward the fray, palm open. A surge of warmth nudged at my back, and I had no doubt she was already doing her thing. *Good.* We needed all the help we could get.

In the distance, Odin shot me a wary, one-eyed glance. I knew Tyr had apprised Asgard's ruler of Mia's involvement as Unifier, but it had to be a shock for him to see a mortal riding into the heart of battle. I'd likely have some explaining to do back in Asgard if things ended in our favor...and in Valhalla, if it didn't.

Here's hoping for the former.

I angled Starla downward, and she dove for the dock. With my chest pressed flat against her spine, I drew my broadsword and held it perpendicular to my body. Starla flew near enough to the jotuns that I was able to slice one in half on our first pass. I'd just circled round for another when Brynn's frantic wave caught my attention.

"What?" My second pass took out another two jotuns. Brynn tapped frantically on her collarbone before extending her thumb and pinky to her ear. Did she want me to…*call her?* On my collar?

Recognition dawned as I realized our new uniform contained a neck communication device. *Thank gods.* Turning on my wrist com would have been impossible with my sword in one hand and Starla's mane in the other.

"Got it." I managed to activate my suit com by rolling so my collarbone pressed against Starla's spine. "Talk to me, Brynn."

"Did you bring the boar and the boat? The guys need an escape route, stat!"

I looped around and eliminated a fourth jotun just as its comrades turned electrocution cannons on me. Starla flapped viciously, darting in a serpentine pattern until we were out of firing range.

Skit, that had been close.

"Unleashing the boat and the boar now." I wrapped my sword arm around Starla, and used my other hand to pull the tiny capsules from the hidden pocket of my belt. With great care, I raised them to my lips and blew lightly. A tiny thrill shot through me as each capsule transformed in a wash of glittering, gold powder—one became a golden-haired boar, and the other a wooden, dragon-headed ship. The ship dropped into the ocean, its subsequent wave crashing over the dock and extinguishing the charge of the electric canons. One of the jotuns flailed, thrown off balance by the surge of the sea. As he fell in the water the boar took off, running easily through the air before snatching the jotun in her snout and wrenching his head clean off. The remaining jotuns took trepid steps back.

Good.

"That. Was. Awesome." Brynn squeaked into the com. She raised her rapier. "Valkyries, attack!"

Brynn's team swooped down, circling the dock in a whirlwind of blades and arrows. The jotuns' numbers quickly dropped. Those remaining were so sufficiently weakened that Tyr, Henrik, and Forse shifted focus to the second attack team.

Gullinbursti charged to their aid. The boar quickly dispatched the trolls before being struck by one of the dwarves. She stumbled, rolling onto her back with a squeal. As she struggled to right herself, I caught a spark of colors pouring through the clouds. The Bifrost broke through, shooting a team-and-a-half of valkyrie-backed pegasuses, and four fire giant-wielding feyndrals into the sky. My chest caught at the sight of the teenage fire giant and her juvenile pet at the front of the dragon team. Hyro and Marshmallow soared fearlessly into a battle that, in all likelihood, was going to get them both killed. *No!*

Activating my suit com, I issued my orders. "Sigrunn, protect Odin. Take the krugers down. And *please* look out for Hyro—it's her first battle."

"Yes, High Commander." My lieutenant general's voice was steady as her pegasus looped around, drawing near enough to the feyndrals to relay my command to their riders. Seconds later the dragons dove, swooping down on the closest flock of aviary assassins and lighting them up with streams of fire. The scent coming off the birds reminded me of the afternoons we'd spent around Henrik's barbeque in Arcata. I had no doubt those particular assassins had been eliminated.

With a shout, I dove back into the fray. By the time I neared the dock, the boys had taken out all three of the jotuns in the initial attack party. Only the dwarves separated them from Naglfar. My chest loosened as something akin to relief seeped through me. We were literally a few feet away from sinking the ship—from stopping the trigger that would have isolated Asgard from the realms, and led to our demise. In mere moments, we would turn the tide of Ragnarok to our favor—despite the prophesies. Despite the odds stacked against us. Despite *everything.*

"Mia, hold tight." She squeezed my waist as I urged Starla closer to the dock, intent on impaling at least one of the dwarves standing between my friends and survival. We were close—*so very close.* Victory was nearly ours.

And then Hymir arrived.

Tyr's biological father dropped through a portal just above Naglfar. He landed on the bow of the ship, the weight of his eight-foot-plus frame crashing a wave over the dock. Tyr, Forse, and Henrik raised their dripping swords to Hymir's cruel face. Despite the chill, the giant wore a sleeveless tunic that revealed the scarred stump of his severed right arm—the one Tyr had relieved him of in Svartalfheim. He raised his remaining arm as if in welcome, its pale grey skin covered in bulbous knots.

"My son," Hymir boomed. "Come quickly, and I won't kill *all* of your friends."

"I'm not your son," Tyr corrected. "And you're not killing *any* of my friends."

"No?" Hymir ran thick fingers through his unruly white hair. "Very well. Perhaps I'll leave that to your sister."

No!

A flash of black leather and crimson curls burst from the portal. Runa landed silently on the ship, her knee-high boots touching down at her father's side. "Tyr," she sneered.

A growl was Tyr's only response. Though I was fifty feet away, I easily made out the whitening knuckles around the hilt of his sword, and the twitching vein atop his jaw. Tyr was furious.

And he was about to let everyone know it.

"That's Tyr's dad?" Mia's squeak gave me a start. I'd forgotten she was behind me.

"Don't let him intimidate you. Your Unifying is working—we were about to take the ship. Keep going." I nudged Starla with one heel, directing her slightly away from Naglfar so Mia was obscured from Hymir's view. If he realized what Mia meant to Tyr, capturing her would become his top priority. And I wasn't letting anybody hurt our human.

Especially not the monster who made my best friend doubt himself at every turn.

Brynn and her team circled me and Mia. But the herd of pegasuses drew Runa's attention—she pointed one crimson-tipped fingernail at Mia.

"That's her," she drawled.

"Excellent," Hymir hissed.

Mia screamed as Hymir twisted his palm. Before I could reach around to grab her, my friend was thrown onto a terrifying trajectory directly into the arms of the killer who'd imprisoned Elsa; who'd delivered Tyr to Hymir on Svartalfheim; who'd escaped Asgardian prison; and who'd plotted to kill us all. Mia writhed in Runa's grasp, her body frighteningly frail in the half-giantess's muscular arms.

No!

"Let her go," Tyr seethed. "She means nothing to you."

"True." Runa shifted Mia, locking my friend's neck in the crook of one arm. She used the other to twirl a finger through Mia's hair. My friend jerked against Runa's touch, but kept her chin high. "But she means everything to you. And since you still refuse to join our side…we thought you could use a little motivation. What do you think, brother? How would your girl-friend like to die?"

"Get your hands off of her," I ordered. Brynn's team followed me closer to the dock, until we hovered just behind Tyr, Henrik, and Forse. The boys' swords remained pointed at the two dwarves while Gullinbursti snarled behind them, her injury keeping her grounded. "We outnumber you. And we won't hesitate to kill you."

Despite my words, Tyr motioned for us to stand down. *What?* I squeezed my eyes shut, then opened them. It was ten on four, not including the boar and the boat—was I hallucinating?

"I'll do whatever you want. Just don't hurt her," Tyr pleaded.

Was he serious? Negotiating with terrorists had *never* been on the table.

"Tyr! We can easily take them both out. What are you doing?"

"You can't know that for sure." Tyr's face was ashen.

"Don't worry about me. Just protect the realms!"

My heart shattered at Mia's words. She had embraced our life so fully that she now lived by the basic tenant of Asgardian existence—duty to realm trumped duty to self. But in her generosity, she'd forgotten the *other* tenants of Asgardian life.

We didn't leave family behind. And we *never* let the bad guys win.

I set my attention on Tyr, hoping he wasn't so far gone he'd shut off that extra sense inside his head. *Gullinbursti can right this,* I pressed.

Relief coursed through me as War used another of his Odin-given abilities to speak directly into my mind. *How?*

She beams light into darkness. Hymir's long gone, but Elsa said Runa still had a flicker of goodness inside her. If the boar can reach that tiny bit of light, maybe she can expand it enough to get Runa on our side.

Tyr's skin paled another shade so he matched the Jotunheim snowfall. *I'll give the boar thirty seconds. But if they put so much as a scratch on my girl, I'm taking her place. I won't let him hurt her.*

Neither will I. My eyes narrowed in determination as I pressed a finger to my collarbone. "Gullinbursti, share your light."

At my command, the boar burst into a shimmering, golden beam. She shone from her spot near the dock all the way to the mountains, illuminating the blue-black waters of the ocean and bathing the sky in a blinding light. I threw my forearm to my eyes as the beam intensified, the white-hot light burning my lids. When I finally opened my eyes, Tyr had positioned himself atop the bow of Naglfar, within striking range of Hymir and Runa. His rage bubbled in sparks of absolute fury as he roared at Runa. "Let her go!"

Runa didn't release her grip. "Make me."

With a cry, Tyr pulled back his sword. As he swung it in a fierce arc, Hymir let out a roar. The monster withdrew a dagger and thrust it toward Mia's heart. *Gods, no!* Tyr's weapon was moving with too much force; even with his Asgardian strength he wouldn't be able to change course. Hymir's blade moved too quickly, and Tyr's strike was simply too set.

Mia was going to die.

My world view shifted into slow-motion. Tyr's knuckles whitened, his anguished cry filling the sky.

Mia squeezed her eyes shut, as if bracing herself for what was to come. Brynn and I leaned forward, urging our pegasuses to close the insurmountable gap between us and the girl we'd come to love as a sister. And Runa…

Runa's jaw slackened as she looked between the girl in her arm and the god she'd once protected from a ruthless father. Her resolved glare flickered as Tyr's face contorted in pain, his agony palpable beneath the fierce warrior's façade. His love for Mia poured so ferociously from his heart, it coated everything—and everyone—in its wake. Etched within every agonized crease of Tyr's face was his desire to protect the being he loved more than any other.

And that love, that desire to protect, coupled with the light of the boar, and the unifying energy lingering in the air, must have triggered some long dormant instinct in Runa. As a single tear streamed down her brother's cheek, Runa's face transformed. She ripped a dagger from her own belt, extended her arm, and spun so her back was to Hymir. In the split second it took for her to position her body between her father's dagger and Mia's heart, her eyes locked on Tyr's. Compassion flickered in their chocolate-brown depths, and with a surge of awe it hit me.

Runa was protecting her brother one last time.

Hymir's dagger pierced his daughter's spine, lodging at the hilt. A crimson trail seeped through the leather of Runa's vest as her back arched. The spasm was just enough for her to unleash her grip on Mia. Tyr lunged forward to catch his girlfriend as she tumbled toward the ground, at the same time Runa flung her hand out. She jammed her blade upward, striking Hymir's groin and wrenching the dagger down as she fell. A thick stream of blood shot from Hymir's thigh— Runa must have pierced an artery. The giant dropped to his knees.

"Valkyries!" I shrieked. "Seize him!"

Brynn led the charge for Hymir. By the time we'd dragged him from the ship to the dock, where Henrik restrained him with an immobilizer, the light had already left his eyes. They blinked once, twice, and with a weak exhale, whatever had passed for Hymir's spirt left his body. Tyr's biological father was gone. And if the amount of blood covering the bow of Naglfar was any indication, Runa wouldn't be far behind.

Bless you, Runa. May your soul finally know peace.

"Mia." Tyr buried his face in his girlfriend's hair. "Thank gods you're all right."

Starla's wings flapped silently as we hovered at the edge of the bow. Beside me, Brynn gave a delicate sniff.

"I am," Mia said softly. "Thank you, Runa."

Tyr lifted his head. At the sight of Runa folded over on the dock, his face crumbled into a mask of sorrow.

Mia raised her palm to his jaw. "Go to her."

Tyr carefully released his hold on Mia. He crawled on his knees, quickly covering the few feet separating him from the girl he'd once known as his sister. With painstaking care, he lifted Runa's head onto his lap, and grasped one of her hands in his. "You saved Mia," he whispered. "Why?"

"Because once upon a time, your happiness was everything to me. I got lost along the way, but..." Runa's words gave way to a gurgling cough. The blade must have pierced her lungs.

"Shh." Tyr used the hand not holding Runa's to brush the hair from her face. His thick thumb gently stroked the skin between her brows, and I knew he was using whatever abilities he could to ease her pain.

"You were always meant to do great things. I couldn't let him break you the way he broke me." Runa raised a shaky hand to Tyr's face. "I love you. Brother."

My heart cracked into a thousand pieces as the light faded from Runa's eyes. Her fingers wilted, then dropped to her chest as the life left her body.

"I love you too," Tyr whispered. A lone tear crept down his cheek as he brought his fingertips to Runa's eyes and pressed the lids closed. He slipped his hands beneath her knees and shoulders, lifting her easily in his arms. Then he turned a tight circle, surveying the scene.

Below him, two dwarves were bound in cuffs, Henrik on one side and Forse on the other. A sea of dead jotuns littered the far end of the dock, and near the hills lay a flock of smoking krugers. Odin and his guard moved unsteadily toward us, accompanied by Marshmallow, Hyro, and the rebel riders and feyndrals on the ground, and Sigrunn's pegasus team in the sky.

Brynn and I hovered just in front of the boat, our valkyries directly behind us. The battle was won.

All that was left was to sink the ship.

"Is Odin secure?" Tyr called to the guards.

"Yes, sir." The one with the most decorated uniform saluted. "We will escort him home via the Bifrost."

"And Thor?" Tyr pressed.

"He returned to Asgard to assist Sif."

"Good. Brynn," Tyr barked, "half of your team can escort the dwarf prisoners back to Asgard. I want them rotting for an eternity in the darkest of our cells."

"Got it." Brynn wiped her eyes with the back of her hand. She shot Mia a sympathetic look before directing three of her girls to take care of the war criminals.

"Forse and Henrik, sink this thing. I never want to see it again." Tyr jutted his chin at Naglfar, now covered in the blood of the last remaining members of his birth family.

"You and me both." Henrik grimaced.

"Brynn, I want you and Fang to take Mia straight to the valkyrie compound. And Freya." Tyr's eyes sought out mine. A thousand heartbreaks burst from their grey–blue depths. "Help me bring my sister home."

"Of course. She'll have a valkyrie funeral," I vowed. With a shaky breath, I nudged Starla forward. Brynn and Fang followed, and Naglfar bowed slightly as the two of us touched down on its toenail-crafted planks. Our mounts took a knee, allowing Mia and Tyr to climb up.

"Be safe, *prinsessa*," Tyr murmured.

"I love you," she replied. "I'm so sorry we lost your sister."

Tyr gave a tight nod and climbed on Starla's back. He settled in behind me, Runa still in his arms, and gripped my waist with one hand. "When you're ready," he said.

I glanced to my right to confirm Mia was secure atop Fang before clicking my tongue and urging Starla forward. My pegasus took to the air as a brilliant rainbow shot from the sky. The Bifrost was in place.

We could go home.

I held out my palm and called back the boar and the ship. Two capsules appeared instantly in my hand. I tucked them into my belt, where they would rejuvenate and be ready for use the next time they were needed.

Which, I hoped, was never.

"You ready?" I murmured over my shoulder. Brynn, Mia and the dragons had already entered the rainbow.

"Take us home, Freya." Tyr's voice cracked over the words.

With a nod, I lowered my head and tightened my grip on Starla's mane. She rode for the Bifrost; for security; for a land filled with hope in a cosmos ravaged by war. Gods willing, we'd return to Asgard to find the rest of our teams had won their battles—that Ragnarok had ended in victory for all who fought for the light. But the odds had been so stacked against us, the forces working to destroy Asgard so mighty, and their determination so strong. It would take a miracle to have thwarted the carefully devised plan Loki had set to end our world—all our worlds. And Runa's change of heart had been miracle enough for one day— I barely dared hope for another.

Instead, I gripped Starla's mane, entered the Bifrost, and prayed.

THE SECOND MY BOOTS touched down on Asgardian soil, I slouched off Fang's back, dropped to my knees, and thanked the gods I was out of that stupid Bifrost. Fang nudged her head against my shoulder, her anxious whinny harmonizing with Mia's gentle *tsks*, as I tried not to hurl my guts up. This transit had been particularly turbulent, as my party had borne the additional weight of the four feyndrals and their solidly built fire giant riders.

The smallest of those riders now leapt off her dragon and ran to my side, placing one hand to the small of my back in support.

"That rainbow sucks," Hyro sympathized.

"It sure does." I wiped my mouth with the back of my hand and stood up. The others would be right behind me, and I needed to look semi-professional when I dealt with the dwarves. Airsick valkyries did not exactly inspire fear, except in those within projectile range. *Blech.*

Hyro stepped back to pat Marshmallow, while Mia slid from Fang's back to give my elbow a gentle squeeze. "You okay?"

"I've been better," I admitted.

A flash of multi-hued light lit up the clearing behind the V.C., and the two most battle-seasoned members of my team emerged from the Bifrost, dwarf perps in hand.

"Take them to a holding cell," I ordered. "Activate a portal blocker in the room, and make sure you both remain stationed at the entrance—viewing screen *on*. Don't put anything past them."

"Yes, General." The girls saluted before marching their charges to the rear entrance of the valkyrie compound. Our holding area was subterranean—the only rooms in the compound lit not by natural light, but by torches mounted to the cells' exterior walls. This meant our prisoners were bathed in near-permanent darkness, a fact that drove them slightly mad and tended to encourage cooperation. They usually ratted out their accomplices within a day. We'd have Loki in custody by sundown tomorrow, latest.

I hoped.

"Poor Tyr," Mia murmured. "I can't believe Runa..." She shook her head. "I sent unifying energy at her pretty hard, but I had no idea she'd..."

"You couldn't have known." I shook my head. "You helped guide her to her most loving choice, and it turns out, she loved Tyr even more than she cared about self-preservation. If Hymir wasn't such a monster, she'd still be alive. Helheim, maybe she'd even be one of us. I always thought she'd make a killer valkyrie."

"I hope Tyr doesn't blame me for her choice," Mia whispered.

"Never," I said adamantly. "You may have teed her up, but that boar pushed her off the selfless cliff. You and Freya *both* helped her do what was in her soul's best interest…in *all* of our best interest. She killed Hymir, Mia. Don't forget her choice stopped that ship from sailing—and may well have turned Ragnarok in our favor."

"Maybe." Mia wrung her fingers together.

I slung my arm around her shoulders. "Hey, I get it. Our life is *really* hard. It's filled with difficult choices, with devastating consequences on both sides. If you ever want to talk about it…"

Mia rested her head lightly on my shoulder. Her chestnut waves tumbled over the blue and silver of my battle suit. "Thanks, Brynn."

"Come on." I nudged her. "The others will be here any minute, and I need to prep the V.C. Hyro, your feyndrals will probably spook the pegasuses, so I'll call over and have one of the stable hands meet you guys in that field." I gestured to the fenced pasture. "We can keep the dragons there until we figure out something more permanent for them."

"Sounds good," Hyro agreed. She led the dragons and the rebel fire giants toward the pasture. Meanwhile, I used my com to share my plan with the stable valkyries, pointed Fang toward her stall for a well-deserved treat, and set off for the V.C., my hand wrapped firmly around Mia's slightly trembling one. Poor thing. If she still wanted to be with us after all this was over, Tyr was one *exceptionally* lucky Asgardian.

We all were.

Inside, the V.C. was every bit as busy as it had been when I'd left. A team of valkyries jogged across the vast entry, making their way toward the back door where, hopefully, they'd be helping with the feyndral situation. Caring for fire breathers would be new for us, but we'd definitely handled weirder. Meanwhile, two of our contemplatives emerged from the children's room. Their smiles suggested the little ones weren't in imme-diate distress. *Thank gods.* Upstairs, Svetana peered over the balcony with a relieved wave.

"General Aksel!" she called. "It's over. Asgard has been victorious on all fronts!"

My torso wilted in relief. Mia staggered beneath my weight, and I quickly regained muscle control. "Excel-lent. Have the chapel prepped to receive a body. One of the hostiles died an honorable death. She's going to receive a valkyrie funeral, and we need to prepare her for send-off."

Svetana's eyes widened, but she didn't otherwise react—just spoke quietly into her com, and turned toward the rear of the V.C., where the chapel was located.

Two more contemplatives emerged from the children's room. I raised my voice to catch their attention. "How are they in there?"

"The young are well." One of the contemplatives folded her hands together, as if in prayer. "Their parents have been contacted, and they will be picked up as soon as the Alfödr greenlights intra-realm travel."

"Good." I nodded.

"Is Elsa still upstairs?" Mia asked.

"She is," the second girl confirmed. "Since open hostilities have ended, her work may be complete. Would you like me to retrieve her for you?"

"No. Tell her to go to the chapel when she's finished. Her brother will be here shortly." I turned back to the first girl. "I need you to wait here in the entry. Direct War and Love to join us in the chapel when they arrive."

"As you wish, General." Both girls bowed before setting off to perform their tasks.

"Mia, come with me. It's going to get real intense in here, real soon." I jogged up the stairs, Mia on my heels.

"More intense than psychotic giants and fire-breathing dragons?"

Point, mortal.

I ushered Mia into the chapel—a pristine, glass wall-and-ceilinged extension off the upper level of the V.C. It jutted into the forest that backed up to one corner of our compound, so all but the chapel's entry was completely encased in rich evergreens. Greenery burst from planter boxes stationed around the space, and a flower-rich altar stood at the front of the room.

It would be here that Tyr laid his sister's body—here that she rested for nine days, tended to by the most senior contemplatives, whose prayers would prepare her soul to ascend to Valhalla. I dropped to my knees before the altar, resting my hands atop its white-linened surface, and silently thanked Runa for her sacrifice—for all she had given for her brother, for Mia, for our world. Mia fell to her knees beside me, and bowed her head.

Before long, footsteps from behind let me know we had company. I glanced over my shoulder to see our friends entering the chapel. Freya came in first, followed by Henrik, Forse, Elsa, and finally, Tyr. War carried Runa in his arms, her crimson locks hanging listlessly over Tyr's elbow.

At the final click of the door, I pushed myself to my feet. "Lay her atop the altar." I smoothed the linen and stepped to the side. Mia mirrored my movement. "It's the most sacred spot in our compound. Runa will be honored here."

Tyr said nothing; he just marched up the short aisle. He lowered his sister onto the altar, carefully folded her hands over her waist, and smoothed her hair from her face. When he stepped back, tears coated his cheeks.

Mia moved to his side and took his hand in hers. They'd long passed the point where they needed words to communicate.

The next moment, Henrik and Freya stepped forward to flank me. As Henrik's fingers laced through my own, I leaned over to whisper in Freya's ear, "Svetana says fighting ceased, but one of us should make sure our services aren't needed."

"Already done," Freya whispered. She discreetly tapped her com and swiped up, eliciting the holoscreen. "Each of our missions was successful." She swiped left, showing victorious scenes in Nidavellir, Muspelheim, and Svartalfheim. "And those we weren't privy to have ended successfully, as well. Although *this* may need addressing." She swiped again, revealing the carcass of Loki's serpentine offspring, Jormundagr, and the massive, lifeless form of his canine son, Fenrir... Tyr's onetime pet.

"Gods," I whispered. Fenrir's death had been a necessity; we'd all known he and Jormundagr were out for Asgardian blood, and served as key elements in Loki's Ragnarok plan. But Tyr had already lost one family member today. Losing Fenrir might push him right over the edge. "Can we wait until tomorrow to tell him?" *Or never?*

"I'll tell him soon enough." Freya closed down the holo, folded her hands in front of her, and raised her voice. "Ragnarok has ended. All Asgardian teams were successful in their missions. I just learned that Loki and his surviving accomplices have been apprehended. They will be transported to the primary prison chamber, where they will await trial and, likely, be sentenced to death."

"Good," Henrik growled. My eyes sought out his, and the sadness that sparked in them tugged at my heart. We'd been through so much together—too much for any one lifetime, even an immortal one. I knew his heart broke for Tyr, for all he'd been through...for all he still had to endure.

"We'll arrange the finest funeral for Runa," I vowed. "One worthy of a valkyrie. She died an honorable death, and her soul will serve valiantly in Valhalla."

"*Ja.*" Tyr's voice cracked, taking my heart along with it. "I just wish...I wish things had been different. Runa deserved better. I lived in the same darkness that she did; her path easily could have been mine."

"I know." Freya stepped forward to wrap Tyr in a gentle hug. His stubbled jaw rested lightly atop her strawberry strands.

"I'm so sorry, Tyr." Elsa moved closer and wrapped her arms around them both. Forse did the same, pulling Mia in with them. Henrik and I followed, so the seven of us stood holding on to each other. I was humbled by the sacrifice of the least likely of allies.

After a short eternity, Mia pulled slightly back. "Should somebody check on my brother?"

Oh, my gods. I'd completely forgotten about Jason. The poor thing was probably still in the contemplative wing.

"I'll get him," Freya spoke up. "We have some things to cover. Tyr, will you be okay?"

"Yes," he said gruffly. Then, possibly because we were all still wrapped in a great big ball of love, he added, "Thank you all. For everything."

"You'd do the same for us," I said honestly. He had—

dozens of times. As he'd continue to do in the future. We were a family—not one related by blood, but one bound by love and choice. And in our world, that meant absolutely everything.

We dispersed shortly after that; Freya to the contemplative wing to retrieve Jason, Forse and Elsa to the gardens to decompress, and Henrik and I to the stables, to check on the fire giants and the feyndrals. Mia stayed in the chapel with Tyr. No doubt they had much to discuss. A Ragnarok-free reality changed the landscape of our worlds. With the threat of annihilation no longer looming, Mia and Tyr could finally figure out what shape their relationship would take— both now, and in the possibly eternal future.

Gods, I hoped Mia wanted to stick it out with us. And I hoped Tyr could find a way to make good on his long-ago promise that, should she want to, she could stay with us as long as she wanted.

Possibly forever.

Much to my surprise, the feyndrals were perfectly content in the pasture. Our pegasuses had adjusted to the dragons' presence, and now grazed happily beside them. The rebel fire giants were lounging comfortably in the barn, regaling our stable valkyries with tales from the fiery realm. The entire situation was one big happy, so Henrik and I were able to take a long overdue walk around the outskirts of the V.C. He laced his fingers through mine and rubbed his thumb lightly at the back of my hand. We strolled in silence, words unnecessary as our hearts decompressed in tandem.

"What a week," Henrik finally said.

"What a life," I muttered. A familiar voice from the nearby forest pulled me to a stop. I tugged Henrik behind a tree with a fierce, "Shh!"

"Shh, what?" Henrik asked thickly.

"I heard someone," I mouthed.

"A hostile?" Henrik's hand reached for his sheathed broadsword, but I batted it away.

"No," I whispered. "Freya."

Henrik's eyebrows shot up. We crept closer to the voice, now joined by a second, deeper one. I peeked around the thick, white trunk of a silver-leaved tree, to find Freya and Jason, heads bent together in quiet conversation. I wasn't eavesdropping, Odin's honor. But now that I was this close, I couldn't *not* keep listening.

Right?

"Jason." Freya sounded exhausted, as if she'd been over this countless times. "I just don't see any way this is going to work. My contract binds me to the Norns. They decide when my life is my own, and until they do…my heart's not mine to give. I'm sorry."

"I don't care," Jason said fiercely. "They have to release you some day, and I'll wait as long as I have to."

"That's sweet." Freya cupped Jason's cheek in her hand. "But I'm immortal—I'm going to be around for a really long time. The Norns might not release me for decades…or centuries. And you deserve a partner who can give you *everything*—while you're still alive to enjoy it! A family and a *life* and…"

Jason pulled Freya to him in a rough kiss. Her lips were swollen when he pulled away. *Way to go, Jason!*

"I'm not going anywhere," he vowed. "I'll take you however I can get you. Even if it's only a part of you. And even if it remains that way for the duration of my lifetime. Love, you're a girl worth fighting for."

By the time I tugged a gawking Henrik away, silent tears were streaming down Freya's face.

The. Poor. Thing.

"So obviously, you know what we have to do," I whispered as we neared the back corner of the V.C.

Henrik *tsked*. "You're not thinking of interfering, are you?"

"Duh." I threw a hand to my waist and jutted out my hip. "And you're going to help me. Ragnarok's over. We saved the worlds. You know we suck at idle time—what else are we going to do?"

"Idle time? I have a *skit*-ton of post-battle reports to draft. We both do. Plus, we'll need to debrief our subordinates and get Tyr and Freya whatever statistics they need to deliver to Odin so he and Forse can sentence the perps." Henrik wrapped one hand around my lower back and pulled my hips to his. He bent low to whisper in my ear, "And after that, I thought maybe we could celebrate. Just the two of us."

My lips parted in a sigh as Henrik's tongue traced a line from my ear to the hollow of my neck. I threw my head back as he moved lower, tugging the fabric of my battle suit down, and making my knees weak.

No, Aksel. Focus now. Play later.

With a groan, I pushed Henrik back. "First of all, thanks for the reminder about the busy work. And second, I am all for that celebration. In a few days."

"A few days?" Henrik's frustration came out on a whine.

I bit back my giggle. "Maybe sooner. Depends on how long it takes us to convince the Norns to release Freya."

Henrik's lips pursed in a low whistle. "That's a tall order, *sötnos*."

"I know." My brows knitted together. "They're so stubborn. If only we knew someone who had an in with them.

One corner of Henrik's mouth tugged up. "Well, call me your hero, Brynnie. My brother lives near one on Midgard. From what I understand, she was pretty closely involved in the Ragnarok efforts. Maybe she'd help us out."

"Gunnar's living with a Norn?" I gawked.

"She's got a place near his village—and from what I hear, she's a bit of a rebel."

"Ooh! Maybe Gunnar and Inga can come with us to try to talk the Norns into letting Freya out of her contract!" I bounced on my toes. "Gods, they're *amazing* at convincing creatures they actually *want* to do what we want them to do."

Henrik chuckled. "Gunnar sent me a message that he'll be around later, so I'll ask."

"Excellent." I rubbed my hands together with glee. "Let's do what we do best."

"Would that be designing realm-saving technology? Finding a place where we can be alone and—"

I cut him off with a kiss. "It's helping our friends." I laughed before adding, "And then the other stuff. Come on, Andersson. We've got work to do."

CHAPTER 14

"**Y**OU ARE NEVER GONNA believe this." Henrik returned from Odin's address the next day positively jubilant.

Freya and I had skipped out—we'd split duties on the mountain of post-war administrative tasks, and had only just finished the most pressing phase of our work. Mia and Elsa had been taking turns working with the contemplatives to spread peace through the realms, with Elsa ducking out as needed to oversee higher level healings. Now that Freya was done with our demanding high commander tasks she could join them, channeling love so that the new incarnation of the cosmos would be primed for as positive a rebirth as possible. We'd all worked around the clock to get to this point, and each of us was beyond exhausted. But with the valkyrie compound mostly back to business as usual, and with Freya taking a brief rest, I could kick back in the war room, and enjoy Henrik's recap.

"Do tell, boyfriend. What's the latest from our fearless leader?"

Henrik's lips brushed my ear as he bent low to whisper the impossible.

"Shut up." I balked. "Odin did not do that."

"He did."

"Oh, my gods! That's incredible! Do you realize what this means?"

"Shh," Henrik admonished. "There were extenuating circumstances, and I don't want to get Mia's hopes up."

"Does Tyr know?"

"Yes. But what he relays to Mia is *their* business. Not yours." Henrik softened his words by pressing his lips to the delicate spot where my ear met my neck.

Gods, he was good at that.

No. Wait. Don't let him distract you.

"Uh, *hei*." I pushed him away. "Mia's *my* best friend. It's *totally* my business."

Henrik's teeth grazed my lobe. "One meddle at a time, *sötnos*. Now that our work's done, I thought you wanted to help Freya."

"I do." I sighed as Henrik's mouth returned to my neck. "What did your brother say? Is he in?"

"Mmm-hmm." The vibrations sent a tremor through me. *Oh, gods.* Maybe helping Freya could wait an hour. Or six.

"And is…is Inga going to…uh…" The tremor hit between my thighs, and I groaned in frustration. "Seriously, you *have* to stop doing that. I can't think."

"Good. Stop thinking. Gunnar and Inga can't leave until morning, anyway."

The tremor shifted into a pulse. My resolve weakened. "Are you telling the truth?"

"Assassin's honor." Henrik held up two fingers in a salute. "You still have your private quarters here?"

"Yes." The word came on a breath. "Gunnar and Inga *really* can't leave until tomorrow?"

"They're meeting us in main hall of the V.C. at sunrise." Henrik raised an eyebrow. "*Now* do I get you to myself for the rest of the evening?"

I pretended to consider his offer. "After we pack, and go over the travel plans, and talk to Elsa about the best way to get the Norns on our side, *and* eat again, because all this world saving makes me hungry, *then* I'm all yours."

"Mmm...nope." Henrik tapped the back of my knees with one arm, catching me with the other as I went down. "We do my thing first, then all of yours."

"Henrik!" I swatted him through my laughter.

"They haven't moved your room, have they?" He took long strides across the war room.

"No, but—"

"Awesome." Henrik pushed through the doors and blurred up two flights of stairs before I could utter another protest. In seconds, he had us inside the room I'd rarely set foot in since joining Tyr's team. Thankfully, the domestic valkyries maintained even unused sleeping quarters, so it was impeccably cared for right down to the downy comforter and plethora of pillows atop.

Not that we actually cared.

"Henrik, we have work to do." I offered one last, half-hearted protest as Henrik flung the pillows to the ground with one arm and deposited me on the bed with the other.

"Oh, we'll get to it." He positioned himself beside me. "I just need a few minutes alone with my girl. Look, I know you can take care of yourself. But it still scares the *skit* out of me every time I see you in battle. I love you way too much to lose you, *sötnos*."

My heart swelled and I rolled on top of Henrik, framing his massive shoulders with my forearms. "You'll never lose me," I vowed. "You're stuck with me forever."

"I'd better be. Freya made me work really hard to get you. *Really* hard."

Laughter bubbled from my throat. "Good thing I was worth it."

Henrik snagged my hair between his fingers and pulled my face down to his. Laughter gave way to a contented growl as he brushed his lips across mine. "Good thing. But we're taking a road trip with my brother in the morning, and we both know he'll talk our ears off. So, I'm thinking…how about we spend the next hour or so in silence?"

"Silence?" I ran a hand down the rigid muscles of Henrik's chest. He stilled.

"Or not," he agreed.

And with a fierce twist, he pinned me on my back and made me forget all about Ragnarok, my to-do list, and the enormity of the task that lay ahead of us.

I didn't mind one bit.

"Well, well, well. Look who *finally* made Captain. About bloody time. My brother would not shut up about how *miserable* that no-dating-the-junior-valkyrie rule made him." Gunnar Andersson crossed the empty expanse of the V.C. entry with open arms. I ran into them with a squeal, flinging my arms around my former classmate.

With their dark hair, twinkling eyes, and tanned, muscular bodies, the Andersson brothers had broken plenty of hearts in school. But it was their sense of humor and innate kindness that had drawn me to the boys next door.

Well, that and their mom's Swedish pancakes. Good thing Mrs. Andersson taught Henrik how to make them.

"Gunnar!" I squeezed my friend before pulling back to study his cheerful face. It bore more stress lines than usual. "You look...amazing," I hastened. "But tired. Super tired."

"I *told* him to go to bed early last night, but apparently, some Midgardian sports match was being played. And *somebody*"—Inga raised an eyebrow to Henrik

—"delivered an inter-realm streaming device he'd developed as a birthday gift."

Henrik shrugged. "Sorry your present was late, bro. It's been one Helheim of a year."

Gunnar grimaced. "I'll say."

"Get in here, Inga." Henrik opened his arms and enveloped Inga within them. Her white-blond hair disappeared into the thick folds of his biceps. "How are you?"

"Thankful to be alive," she mumbled into his chest. "If we never have another situation like that, it'll be too soon."

I shot Inga a grin as the Anderssons released us. We'd always had an easy friendship, except for that time in high school when she'd called Gunnar a dumb jock and broke his heart. Naturally, I'd iced her out for hurting my friend…and then had to apologize when she *finally* came to her senses and gave Gunnar the happily-ever-after he so very much deserved. Now they were the picture of butt-kicking, sword-wielding marital bliss.

They were pretty much my life goal.

"I hear Ull's been keeping you guys busy." I tilted my head up to smile at Inga. "Winter fell for a mortal, huh? Who'd have thought?"

"And War, too." Inga laughed. "Those Norns have a wicked sense of humor."

Right. The Norns. I quickly sobered at the thought of the three immortal sisters who lived at the base of the world tree, Yggdrasil, wove the threads of fate, and *never* received uninvited visitors. We needed a miracle to get an audience with them...or a miracle worker. And somehow, Henrik's mischievous, sweet-talking brother, had managed to procure us an invite.

"Okay, Gunnar. Spill. How are we getting our audience?"

Gunnar shrugged. "Our norn friend called in a favor—Urd, Verdandi, and Skuld owed her one. She got us the appointment, and now we've got to make the most of it. According to her, Verdandi's the softest of the Norns—she has a fondness for the mortal realm her sisters don't share. We isolate her, convince her the mortals will suffer if Freya can't reach her full potential, and boom. Contract released. Love gets her man."

Inga glanced at me. "Gunnar told me that Freya fell for a mortal, too. What is it, contagious?"

"She likes Tyr's girlfriend's brother," I explained. "Jason and Mia are pretty much two peas in a pod— kind of like Tyr and Freya."

Inga pursed her lips. "Love and War *are* two sides of one coin. I'm sure there's something to their falling for siblings—hopefully, whatever it is, it's enough to make our case." She adjusted the straps on her backpack, then palmed the hilt of her sheathed rapier. "The trip should be fairly non-eventful, since any hostiles that survived Ragnarok will still be in recovery. But our norn friend told us to look out for Ratatosk once we hit the tree."

"What's Ratatosk?" It sounded *way* too much like Ragnarok for my taste. *Yikes.*

"Not what—who," Gunnar corrected. "Lots of creatures live around Yggdrasil, but the worst one is an evil squirrel. Little jerk's constantly gnawing on the world tree and stirring *skit* up. Apparently, there's a cloister of secondary norns whose full-time job is to keep him under control."

"Seriously?" My jaw unhinged. "After everything we just went through, now we have to fight an *evil squirrel?*"

"He might be hibernating." Gunnar shrugged. "Our norn wasn't too clear on his schedule, and it's been real cold what with Ragnarok and all. Maybe he thinks it's winter."

"Squirrels don't hibernate." Henrik rolled his eyes. "Honestly, if you'd paid the slightest bit of attention in science class—"

"I was distracted by something much more interesting. And hard to pin down." Gunnar's gaze roamed up and down Inga's body. "I needed all my energy focused on the most important subject."

"Right." Inga laughed. "But did you learn any better once I finally stopped rejecting you?"

"I am a god of action." Gunnar shrugged. "Not books. All righty then, are we Bifrosting out?"

"Yes. Heimdall loaned us his horse—it should be waiting at the transport site." Henrik pointed to the front door of the V.C. "The horse is familiar with Yggdrasil, so it can carry us in—and evacuate us, if need be—without getting deterred by the tree's...residents." He was totally talking about the evil squirrel. *Shudder.* "Okay, weapon check."

"Rapier, dagger, nunchucks, and throwing stars in my belt," Inga recited.

"Crossbow, blade, and these bad boys." Gunnar flexed his biceps.

I giggled at Henrik's eye roll. Two in two minutes—it was definitely family time. "Rapier and dagger on the belt, batons on the back, and my biggest weapon right here." I pointed to my head, mouthing the words, *genius brain* to the god of action. What I didn't mention was the secret weapon I'd tucked inside my jacket—an ace in the hole I planned to use if Gunnar's impressive powers of female persuasion somehow failed us.

Please, don't fail us.

"Awesome. And I've got the chemical tech in my backpack with our rations, plus my broadsword, and two ankle blades." Henrik adjusted the straps on his bag. "We're set."

"We're packing an awful lot for a pleasure cruise." Inga frowned. "It's better to be safe than sorry, but... don't you think coming in armed this heavily might hurt our chances of reaching an agreement?"

"We can always check some of the blades at the door—if this place even has a door. But I'm not going anywhere near that squirrel unarmed. Weapon up, doll. It's time to roll out." And with a confident wink, Gunnar led his wife across the marble floor of the V.C. Two sets of combat boots thudded softly against the shiny surface, the sound jarring me from my vision of some pointy-fanged rodent villain. Ratatosk. *Yikes.*

"You okay?" Henrik's hand on my lower back made me jump.

"*Ja.* Just not excited about the squirrel."

"Nobody is." Henrik shuddered. "It's okay. I brought one of the sleepers—we explode that bad boy, and it's lights out, vermin. And anything else in the vicinity."

"And then, we what? Put on our diplomacy hats and beg for Freya's freedom? Gods, Henrik. She can't continue living under this restriction. It's going to destroy her. Do you really think we can pull this off?"

"We'll do our best. Freya's a good egg. She deserves to have what we do." Henrik's palm shifted to squeeze my butt.

"Thanks for going with me," I whispered.

"I would follow you anywhere," Henrik vowed. "Even to the rodent-infested world tree."

Sometimes he said the sweetest things.

"Bifrost's here! Are you coming?" Inga's invitation from the front door ended our love fest.

"That's what she said." Gunnar snickered.

Inga swatted his shoulder. "Behave."

Henrik heaved his third eye roll in as many minutes, then turned to me with a shrug. "You sure you want him coming along?"

"Absolutely." Taking Henrik's hand in mine, I tugged him toward the door. "Come on. Let's unleash your brother on the Norns."

"And hope for the best," Henrik muttered. "In all things."

"Fingers crossed." I squeezed Henrik's hand and stepped out of the V.C.

It was time for the mother of all road trips.

"Get. Me. Off. This. Horse." My hand flew to my mouth. "Now," I mumbled through my fingertips.

Henrik gently hooked one arm around my ribs and slid me off Heimdall's enormous mount, Gulltopp. The equine shook his golden mane, likely in disgust, as my feet hit the ground and I bent over to empty my stomach on the ashy dirt. Poor horse. It was probably the first time this had happened to him. Heimdall didn't seem the type to get Bifrost sickness.

"Sorry," I muttered. Henrik rubbed lightly at the small of my back. "That was just…"

"It was rough," Inga agreed. She leapt gracefully off Gulltopp's back, the faint sheen on her porcelain face a near-perfect match to the sea of white-trunked trees in the forest.

"The worst." Gunnar grimaced. He landed beside me, resting his forearms on his knees. After a slow eternity, he raised his head just enough to scan the preternaturally still lake beside our drop spot.

"You gonna make it, princeess?" Henrik reached over to ruffle his brother's hair.

Gunnar lifted one hand in a vulgar gesture. "Don't touch the hair."

"Gentlemen. We have work to do." Inga's stern tone made both Anderssons snap to attention.

"Sorry, Inga," they muttered. Henrik rubbed my back again, then hastened to help Gunnar secure Gulltopp to a nearby stump.

I stared at Inga in awe. "Someday, you're going to have to teach me how you get them to do that."

"When Henrik pops the question, that will be my wedding gift to you."

"He's not—I mean, we're—it's only been—"

Inga's gentle laughter cut me off. "Someday."

"Right. So. Uh. Oh, *skit.*"

Henrik's sword was drawn before I'd finished the word. He blurred to my side with a whispered, "Where's the threat?"

"Up there." I slowly drew my own weapon, pointing it in front of me. There, in the limbs of a massive ash tree, sat a dog-sized squirrel. It's red, beady eyes narrowed as it tilted its head to the side. Thick whiskers brushed against muted, grey–green leaves, and the creature released an aggressive hiss before scurrying up. And up. And up.

Good gods, how big was Yggdrasil? The world tree absolutely *towered* over the rest of the forest. And Ratatosk was scaling it as if it were nothing more than a pile of acorns.

Show-off.

"Where's the access point?" Gunnar stepped forward, his loaded crossbow raised to eye level. His muscles flexed beneath his thin, black jacket, and I had no doubt he planned to tackle the squirrel and beat it into submission if his arrow missed its mark. Gunnar had a strike-first-ask-later approach to combat. Whereas Henrik…

"Weapons down," Henrik murmured. "There are too many of them."

"I only see one evil squirrel, mate." Gunnar tipped his crossbow higher.

"*Ja.* But there's a quartet of harts over there." Henrik tilted his head to the far side of the tree, where four huge, heavily antlered deer chewed on Yggdrasil's lower branches. "And the oversized eagle up there." He jutted his chin to the top of the tree, where Ratatosk had joined a truck-sized bird of prey. "Plus, the snakes."

"The snakes?" Gunnar's voice cracked. "What snakes?"

"Babe," Inga warned. "Stay calm."

Oh, gods. I'd forgotten how much Gunnar hated snakes.

"The snakes who live beneath the ash of the tree. Góinn, Móinn, Grábak, Grafvöllud, Ofnir, and Sváfnir." Henrik slipped one hand into his backpack. I swear, if he pulled out a rubber snake to torment his brother…"Don't you remember Mom's bedtime stories about them?"

"Of course I remember her bedtime stories," Gunnar hissed. "I had nightmares *for years.*"

"I know." Henrik kept his voice level. "And since I'm

actually going to need you conscious for this mission, I'll repeat myself. Put your weapon down. We're using a sleeper."

Henrik withdrew his hand from the backpack. In his palm was a small, silver ball.

"Oh, that's *perfekt!*" I slipped my rapier into its holster, smiling fondly at the tiny orb with the power to knock out every air-breathing lifeform in the vicinity. "Wait, did you bring the—"

"Masks for everybody." Henrik shot me a wink as he brandished four compacted gas masks and distributed them. "Once they're in place, we'll—"

"Traitors." An icy hiss pierced the crisp forest air.

The squirrel covered a third of the tree in one feral leap. It leveled its livid stare directly at Henrik, who drew his weapon. The rest of us quickly followed suit.

"Destroyers," the squirrel seethed.

"No destroyers here, mate." Gunnar raised the hand not holding his crossbow. "Just four friendlies, out for a walk."

"Liar," the squirrel snapped. "We three existed for millennia—creatures of above, surface, and below. Each in balance—each keeping to his part. Until *you* ruined everything."

My heart stilled. "Excuse me?"

"You," Ratatosk screeched at Henrik. "You destroyed the sentry. You unhinged our balance. And *they* are left to gnaw, to maim, to decimate."

"You're going to have to be more specific." Gunnar's bow was once again at eye level.

"The snakes," Ratatosk hissed. "Look."

My gaze dropped to the ground. *Oh, gods.* The earth closely surrounding Yggdrasil was transparent, providing a clear view to the three roots beneath. One led to Jotunheim. Another to Midgard. And the third, the one farthest from the ash altar where I'd heard senior members of the Æsir came to mete judgments, led to Helheim. It was *that* root the six snakes entombed; that root into which they'd sunk their fangs; and that root through which venom seeped, the blood-red puss slowly ebbing through Yggdrasil's veins.

"Oh." Gunnar's shiver was almost imperceptible. Almost.

"You said I destroyed the sentry? What sentry?" Henrik palmed the tiny orb. He'd already slipped his mask in place. He gave a subtle wave at Inga, Gunnar, and me, and we did the same.

"Nidhogg," Ratatosk spat.

"You killed the dragon king?" I gawked at Henrik. "First Garm, then *her father*? You have *got* to be kidding me."

"One, Garm was going to kill you back at the north-west compound. So again, you're welcome. And two, I didn't kill Nidhogg. We left him with Hel after we destroyed their crystal. You were with me. I sure as *skit* didn't go back." Henrik faced the squirrel. "I don't know where your dragon friend is, but I swear I didn't kill him."

"I did not say *kill*, Asgardian fool." Ratatosk's voice carried all the warmth of nails on a chalkboard.

"*Destroy.* You destroyed him the day you killed his daughter. He has not returned to Yggdrasil since Garm's spirit left the realms."

"Hey, Garm tried to kill my girl, so *flicka* had to go. No apologies there." Henrik's thumb clicked the lock on the edge of the sleeper. I double checked my mask was in place.

"I held the balance between Nidhogg and the eagle and carried their words back and forth, holding air and earth in harmony. And now our great tree rots. Because of *you.*" Ratatosk severed the branch above him with those yellowed razor-sharp teeth, aimed the pointed spear at Henrik, and wrenched his head down. The branch shot from his mouth to the ground, landing in the exact spot my boyfriend stood. Thankfully, Henrik had blurred in front of me a split second before impact. But even so…

The harts looked up from the other side of the tree. Anger flickered in their eyes as they angled their bodies toward the spot where the branch had impaled the dirt. They lowered their antlers to charge at the same moment the eagle took flight. If those massive talons so much as touched us, we'd be seconds away from *hei hei, Valhalla.*

No, thanks.

"Do it," I whispered.

"*Do it,*" Gunnar reiterated, his gaze darting to the now writhing snakes at the base of Yggdrasil.

"Nighty night," Henrik said calmly. And as Ratatosk launched himself from the tree, his furry squirrel body lining up neatly with the descending eagle, Henrik clicked the trigger on the sleeper. Both animals went instantly limp before floating gently to the ground and tucking into a deep, motionless sleep. On the other side of the tree, the harts halted their charge, folded their legs gracefully beneath them, and dropped into a resting stance. Even the snakes stopped moving, the pop of fangs releasing from the tree punctuated by the ebbing of the red puss from Yggdasil's veins.

Everything was still. Calm.

And then the Norns showed up.

CHAPTER 15

"WHO DISTURBS OUR BALANCE?"

"Who silences the sentinels?"

"Who halts the blight upon our tree?"

The voices came from a void—three tinkling bells echoing across the breeze. The wind shifted as if on a breath, swirling golden dust along the pristine lake. The dust rose, converging in the center of the water. It formed a translucent doorway through which stepped three divinely beautiful sisters. Each possessed hair of golden silk, a dress of teal chiffon, and eyes emblazoned with such clarity, I had no doubt they could see straight to my soul. They were Skuld, Verdandi, and Urd.

They were the Norns.

Before agreeing to loan us his horse, Heimdall had thoroughly briefed us on protocol. On seeing the Norns, Henrik, Inga, Gunnar, and I each dropped to a knee, our fisted hands atop our hearts. We kept our heads bowed until the sisters stood directly in front of us, their silver-painted toenails stepping into the top of my frame of vision.

Since Gunnar had a special way of connecting with other beings—particularly female beings—we'd all agreed he would open for us. I waited for him to recite the speech Henrik had prepared, and crossed my fingers he wouldn't deviate from the script.

"Your Graces," Gunnar offered in his almost too-suave tenor. "We come in peace and, more importantly, in love. We beg you to help our goddess, Freya—one of Asgard's most faithful servants. She has served as high commander of our valkyries, defending our realm—and all within our protection—from the darkness that threatens *all* lands. She has served as Goddess of Love, filling the cosmos with hope and light. She has performed her duties with the grace and goodness you instilled in her, and maintained her vow to you from the day you gifted her to us. Pursuant to your terms, Freya has never fully given her heart away. And in accordance with her promise, she remains neutral in all things."

"She *remained* neutral. But now," the tallest of the sisters breathed, "we see her with the human."

"Even now she maintains her vow," Henrik chimed in. "She cares for the human a great deal, and knows that choosing him over you could cost not only herself, but her realm. And Freya has always—*always*—put duty to realm over duty to self. But denying her heart for so many decades has drained her. Possibly beyond repair."

"What do your words mean?" The Norn on the left tilted her head. The three sisters looked so similar, save for a few inches in height, I had no way of knowing which Norn was which.

"They mean Freya's hurting," I blurted. "Hel poisoned her heart, and it took us more than a year to figure out how to fix it. And now the poison is gone, but her heart still isn't free. It's bound to her contract with you. She acts strong, but it crushes her to have to keep up her walls when she just wants to be free to have what she cultivates for everybody else. Being a channel of love but never being able to give herself over to it...nobody can live like that forever. But Jason, the human...when Freya's with him, she radiates love, and joy, and life. We can all feel it. That desolation, that pain...it leaves her. She's our Freya again...until she has to throw her walls back up so she doesn't break her vow to you."

"We know all of this." The shortest Norn steepled her fingertips together. "What we do not know is why she has not made a formal request to have her restriction lifted. Freya is well aware of the terms—before we can consider a contractual amendment, a formal request must be made."

Is she kidding me right now?

"Because of what happened the last time." I held the Norn's gaze. "Freya's the toughest *flicka* I know. But she loved Rhylark with as much of her heart as she was allowed to share. And when she asked you to release her from her vow—to free *all* of her heart to love, as she so freely gifted love to others—you told her no. You said that loving Rhylark would put her realm at risk, and you would lift her restriction when *you* decided the time was right. So, Freya turned away from Rhylark—she turned away from love. She sank into a depression so dark, the worlds went dark along with her. Freya was abducted. Midgard fell. Rhylark was killed protecting the innocents, and my sister—"

I choked on a sob. Henrik's palm settled lightly atop my lower back.

"My sister died in the fallout." I blinked back tears. "It was her choice to stay on Midgard—she knew the risks of remaining in the absence of Love, but she loved being a Norn, loved serving the three of you. And she willingly gave her life to ensure the worlds remained full of light. And hope. And someday, love. Freya learned her lesson after that—she never gave her heart away—never dared ask again if she even could. And now…I'm going to lose her too. She'll die of a broken heart, like Nanna, if she has to continue in this limbo state."

"My child." The shortest Norn stepped forward. She placed her palm to my cheek. My entire body filled instantly with warmth, and peace, and…

"Love," I whispered. "You're the giver of love. Anja worked under *you*. And you gifted Freya her title."

The Norn nodded. "I am Verdandi, the fullest embodiment of the present. Of what *is*. Of Love."

"You knew my sister."

"I know all," Verdandi corrected. "Including your sister. Anja's corporeal form was a bright light in a world of fog, though her soul shines even brighter now. She continues her work in Valhalla."

"Then here." I reached into my jacket pocket and withdrew a folded piece of paper. "My sister wrote this —her supervising norn sent it to me along with her things after she…after. You need to read it."

Verdandi's blue eyes clouded over. The taller of her sisters stepped forward.

"That which has past cannot affect eternal prophesy. Freya's fate was cast long ago, and set into motion the day she accepted her post."

"Please." I held out the letter. "Just read it. And if you still don't think Freya deserves to share in the love she gives…" I couldn't finish the sentence. Anja's letter would make them see reason.

It has to.

The third Norn gently pried the letter from my fingertips, and handed it to Verdandi. The three sisters stood together, reading in silence while I bit down on my bottom lip. I winced at the taste of blood, and Henrik reached over to take my hand in his.

"You okay, *sötnos*?"

I barely managed my nod.

After an eternity, the Norns raised their heads in one synchronized movement. When Verdandi handed me Anja's letter, I folded it up and shoved it into my pocket. And I waited.

And waited.

And waited.

My heart sank. The Norns' silence was their answer. They weren't going to release Freya. Her heart still wasn't hers to give. The worlds would again crumble in darkness. And I was going to lose a goddess who'd come to mean everything to me.

Again.

"Please," I whispered. Henrik tightened his grip around my hand.

"Ladies." Gunnar lowered his head to the Norns conspiratorially. "Isn't there *anything* we can do to get Freya out of this deal? I am *very* open to negotiation."

Inga elbowed her husband in the side.

"You told me to help," he hissed.

"That's not helping," she hissed back.

Verdandi met my gaze. "You love your love goddess."

"With all that I am," I said fiercely. "She's the family I choose—and every bit as much my sister as Anja."

"And you desire her happiness not out of self-preservation, but because you see that which your sister saw—that darkness stems from fear; that fear is the absence of presence; and that no being can ever be out of present time so long as they are completely filled with love. Love is the antidote to darkness." Verdandi drew a soft breath. "Before Ragnarok, there was too much of that darkness in the worlds to allow Love's focus to be split in any way—no matter how noble. But with Ragnarok behind us, my gift to Freya, and her gift to the realms, must be the foundation that rebuilds the worlds. The foundation on which each realm can draw, providing sufficient strength for self-governance. Self-sustenance."

I blinked against the tears flowing freely from my lids, and said simply, "Please."

Verdandi stepped back so she stood between her sisters. She clasped each of their hands in hers, and raised her arms to the sky. The three Norns closed their eyes, blond hair lifting in the gentle breeze, as they murmured a chant in a tongue so ancient, I wondered if Odin himself would recognize it. After a beat, they opened their eyes and spoke in one voice.

"It is done."

"What's done?" Gunnar asked thickly.

"That which you have asked of us," the tallest Norn said.

I dropped to my knees in gratitude. "Freya is free?"

Verdandi's gaze softened. "With so much of the realms' darkness finally vanquished, the time has come for your love goddess to love as she wishes."

My shoulders trembled. Henrik knelt beside me with worry. "*Sötnos?*"

"Thank you," I sobbed. "I…she means so much to…I can't…thank you."

Through my tears, I barely made out Verdandi's gentle smile.

"What about your tree?" Inga asked softly. "The

snakes...the balance...can anyone stop what's happening to Yggdrasil?"

"Balance will return," the tallest Norn promised. "Another will rise from Yggdrasil's roots, bringing an element of earth to mingle with the air."

"Though this time," her sister chimed in, "let us bring forth a being from the Midgard root." She leaned forward to whisper conspiratorially, "Much less drama than that which comes from Helheim."

If she only knew the half of it.

"How can we help?" Inga pressed. "The red rot the snakes created can't be good for the tree."

"No," Verdandi agreed. "It is not. Though of course, our position forbids us from interfering with such matters."

"Seriously?" Gunnar balked. "You gals decide our fates—I mean, *all* our fates. And you can't get rid of some snakes in your backyard?"

Inga's elbow was swift.

"Ow!" Gunnar hissed.

"Perhaps *you* would be so kind as to dispose of the reptiles for us." The tallest Norn smiled sweetly at Gunnar.

Her sister clasped her hands together. "Is it not your calling to assist ladies in distress?"

Beside me, Henrik choked on a laugh. "Well, that's settled. Gunnar, you're on snake duty."

"Uh..." Gunnar's skin whitened. "Ull's gonna need me back on Midgard in one piece soon enough to help look after the new—" He winced as Inga's elbow struck true again. "Ouch! Well, he needs me in working order, okay? And Inga's got this new position there she might need backup for, so if anything were to happen to me she'd be—"

"I won't need backup," Inga said sweetly. "And nothing's going to happen to you. They're just snakes."

"I have every confidence in your ability to handle this, princess." Henrik ruffled Gunnar's hair again. He was rewarded with a severe scowl. "And I have just the place to send our little reptile friends."

"Really? Where?" I cocked my head.

"One of Yggdrasil's roots leads directly to Jotunheim. And one of those icy demons nicked my favorite broadsword. Payback's a *tik*."

A bubble of laughter ripped from my throat. "By all means. Lead the way."

"Go in peace, Asgardians." The three sisters raised clasped hands. As they stepped backward, the shimmering doorway appeared behind them. "And go in love."

"Always," I promised.

With a breath of wind, the Norns swept through the doorway. They vanished in a whirl of golden dust. The powder kissed the lake before disappearing into the trees.

And after a considerably less easy sweeping of Gunnar toward the pit of snakes, we made good on our promise to restore health to the world tree. Then we awoke the four deer, one eagle, and a highly irritated squirrel, before riding Gulltopp along the still nausea-inducing Bifrost back to Asgard.

Where, by the grace of the Norns, we were able to give Freya the news she'd waited an immortal lifetime to hear.

CHAPTER 16

FREYA

THREE WEEKS HAD PASSED since my friends won me the right to my heart. As much as I'd wanted to revel in their gift, the end of Ragnarok created a litany of to-dos that kept me from fully appreciating my newfound freedom. My responsibilities had kept me running every day from dawn until midnight.

Elsa took the lead on organizing Balder and Nanna's joint funeral, and the rest of us filled in wherever we were asked. Our High Healer worked tirelessly to arrange for the *perfekt* vessel to carry her future in-laws to Valhalla, where they'd no doubt continue their purpose of bringing Light and Warmth to the realms. We had complete faith they'd be every bit as effective in fulfilling their callings from the other side as they had been in life.

Forse and his brother Nils broke down as the funeral ship sailed away, carrying the most loving parents the realms had ever known. Nanna and Balder had blessed each of us with their light, kindness, and purity of love. And while I knew the Styrke brothers would have difficult days ahead of them, I also knew they had all the support they could possibly need in their friend-families—and that they had the presence of mind to lean on us when shouldering their grief grew too wearisome.

Sure enough, in the days that followed their parents' funeral, Forse retreated to the warmth of Elsa's love, and Nils set about wrapping up loose ends so he could join us for an extended visit. Something told me we'd be seeing a lot more of the other Styrke sibling in the near future. I looked forward to bringing him into our fold.

While Elsa handled Nanna and Balder's funeral arrangements, I focused on finding a more permanent home for Hyro and her own friend-family—the rebel fire giants who'd aided us at Ragnarok. Hyro had forged a connection with the meadow elves during their brief time together, and the elves were more than happy to offer a parcel of their property to Hyro's compatriots in exchange for help with their land. As it turned out, this particular cell of fire giants happened to be highly gifted farmers; they owed their self-suffi-ciency to their time in hiding on a barren Muspelheim. The meadow elves were thrilled to have such compe-tent help, and the rebel giants were over the moon to have a place they could finally call home. The feyn-drals, having developed a fondness for the giants, opted to stay nearby. Hyro and her friends built a stable in the woods behind their settlement, and assured the meadow elves that their new dragon neighbors would not accidentally burn down the forest.

They hoped.

Once Hyro was settled, I devoted myself to overseeing Runa's funeral. As promised, Tyr's sister lay in the valkyrie chapel for nine days, during which time she received wreaths from my sisters in arms. In her final moments, Runa had demonstrated a strength of character that shone as a testament to the twin powers of love and *ære*—the very virtues my valkyries, and all Asgardians, fought for.

On the day of her funeral, Tyr led Runa's candlelit procession from the chapel through the forest, the hand not clutching his candle wrapped tightly around Mia's. Once the processional reached the sea, we sent Runa to Valhalla in proper valkyrie fashion, complete with a flaming arrow salute fired from our pegasus-riding ceremonial team. As the ritual wound down, Tyr's pain drove him to his knees. I wiped away my tears at the sight of my dear friend, his body broken in grief, releasing the sister who'd given her life so that he could live his to its fullest. Had it not been for Mia at his side, her steady hand on his arm, I doubted Tyr would have made it through the ceremony. Henrik and Forse rallied behind him as Runa's ship sailed into the horizon. They lent not only emotional, but also physical support as we guided Tyr back to the V.C., where he promptly fell into an exhausted, sorrow-stricken sleep. It took him almost a full day to emerge, but when he did he was resolved to live each day to the utmost, ensuring his sister's sacrifice not be in vain. Word around the V.C. was that before he left the compound, he and Mia had a *very* serious discussion about the future of their relationship—the outcome of which I couldn't wait to be privy to.

In light of this, I'd had a very serious discussion of my own with Asgard's ruler. The worlds were changing, I'd argued, Asgard along with them. Despite Odin's lifelong resistance to admitting mortals to the realm of the gods, he had conceded my point that Asgard would have fared far worse at Ragnarok had it not been for a certain mortal's assistance. And he'd agreed said mortal's willingness to sacrifice her own life to dispel the darkness was the very definition of *ære*—and the very heart of what it meant to be an Asgardian. He'd further agreed that he was likely to lose a key member of his council if he remained unwilling to amend his admittedly restrictive position. So it was with Odin's unexpected blessing that I'd been able to present Tyr with an additional option for his future—one none of us had truly dared hope for.

Now I hoped Mia would accept Tyr's offer. Almost as much as I hoped Tyr would manage to put it to her in a way that wouldn't scare our sweet, analytical mortal out of her logic-loving mind.

With my work nearly complete, I couldn't wait to join my team at our temporary Asgardian residence. But before I could take a break and push my nose further into my friends' personal business, I had to attend to one final piece of valkyrie business. Brynn had been hesitant to accept my promotion, claiming our organization had only ever had the one leader, and that if we were to take on a second, she was hardly the most qualified to accept the post. It had taken a solid day's argument from me, and another day's persuasion from Henrik, but she had *finally* signed the paperwork reassigning her as co-high commander of the valkyries. She and I would govern our brethren as equals, providing the realms with the additional support they needed during this post-Ragnarok transition, and allowing me to devote more time to my duties as Goddess of Love. Now that I had access to *all* of my heart, I was more determined than ever to gift the fullness of personal power that came from embodying love to every being who was willing to accept it.

Including myself.

Our team had temporarily relocated to the Fredriksens' Asgardian residence—the family home Elsa and Tyr had shared with their parents, once upon a time. It was there that I retreated after relocating the fire giants, restructuring the valkyrie administration, securing Mia's position, and sending Forse's parents and Tyr's sister off to Valhalla. And it was there that I *finally* let myself settle in—for the first time in a *very* long time—to the possibility of sharing my life with someone else.

Even though that someone wasn't *at all* what I'd imagined.

"There she is. Love herself. I was starting to worry you might not make it." Jason stood in front of the mirror in one of the Fredriksens' guest rooms, his muscular arms tensing as he buttoned his dress shirt. When he finished, he held out his arms. I quickly strode from the hallway and stepped into them, letting Jason's hands rub the tension from my back.

"Sorry, another batch of paperwork at the V.C. But that's the last of it. I am officially on vacation." I rolled my head to one side, then the other. Jason's hands changed course, pressing gently against the newly cracked vertebrae in my neck. "Gods, you have no idea how much I need this."

"Mmm. Need anything else?" Jason moved his hands back down to tug my hips into his.

I laughed. "I can tell that you do."

"You've had a hell of a couple of weeks. I'd be more than happy to help you…relax." Jason lowered his head to nip at my ear. I angled my chin so he could kiss lower. And lower. And lower. When he reached the deep *V* of my dress's plunging neckline, I strongly considered dragging him to the bed and *finally* taking the much needed alone time we'd been waiting for since the Norns released my heart. But I only had minutes before I needed to be downstairs to officiate Elsa and Forse's wedding…and what I intended to do to Jason Ahlström would require *much* longer than that.

I'd waited an eternity to be with my *perfekt* match—a few more hours weren't going to kill me.

Though they might kill poor Jason.

"Freya." Jason groaned as I pushed him away.

"Shh." I stepped backward so my calf rested against the bed. The lure of the downy surface was too tempting, and I sat, permitting myself a few seconds of doing nothing. "Sit with me for a minute?"

Jason crossed to the dresser. When he returned to my side, he carried a cup in his hand. "I had a feeling you'd be home soon, so I made you tea."

My fingers wrapped around the warm mug as gratitude filled my heart. "Thanks. I needed this."

"You're *sure* tea's all you need?" Jason waggled his brows.

"At this moment, yes." I nestled my head on his shoulder. We sat together in silence, Jason's comforting presence filling my entire being with peace. The feeling was new. And more than a bit overwhelming. "I haven't done this in a long time—let myself be..."

Jason wrapped an arm around my shoulders, tugging me to him so he could rub his thumb across my tricep. "Mmm?"

"Be still. And vulnerable," I whispered. "It's scary."

"You're high commander of the valkyries. You have nothing to be scared of." Jason's lips brushed my hair.

"It's a big deal for me, letting myself fall for you. But I know things will be different this time—that you're not going to go off to battle and...and die." I spoke the last two words on a whisper.

"Freya," Jason whispered.

I drew a deep breath. "I glossed over some... some

details when I told you about how my falling in love nearly broke the worlds. See, when the Norns told me I couldn't be with my first love…that they wouldn't release my heart…when everything inside me went black, and I couldn't do my jobs, and Midgard fell into darkness…"

Jason gently squeezed my hands. His unconditional acceptance radiated like a beacon within my heart, giving me the strength I needed to share this final piece of my journey.

"Rhylark was one of Asgard's finest warriors, and the light realms were his to protect. He vowed to save Midgard, to keep its people from killing each other long enough for me to pull myself out of my darkness —to save us all from a world without Love. But I couldn't do it—I wasn't strong enough then. Rhylark was slain while I mourned a heart that dwelled within my chest but contractually belonged to the Norns. If I had been able to see beyond myself, he would have had a long, fulfilling existence. Possibly with another goddess, but even so—his life wouldn't have been taken from him."

Jason reached up to stroke my cheek. "I'm so sorry you had to experience that loss."

"It's taken me a long time to release my guilt, and I'll probably never stop wishing I'd handled things differently. But I made it through that darkness, and I made it through this one. And I will never, *never* take for granted the incredible gift that is being in full possession of *all* of my power. Especially my heart." I shifted my mug to one hand, and placed the other atop Jason's chest. "We're a lot, Jason—me and my team are *a lot*. We are devastation, and loss, and pain, and sorrow. But we're also joy, and laughter, and learning, and love. We're a family. And if you're really going to be my partner, then we're your family too. For better, or worse, you're one of us."

"Good." Jason leaned forward to press his lips against mine. "I wouldn't have it any other way."

My heart swelled, the fullness of emotion igniting a warmth I hadn't known for decades.

I let myself linger in Jason's kiss until Henrik shouted from downstairs that the wedding cake was set up and everybody had *better be getting into place right now.* A fresh burst of happiness sparked in my heart.

"We'd better get downst—Jason!" I squealed as Jason set my mug on the nightstand, framed my waist with his hands, and lifted me onto his thighs. My heart quickened as I straddled his lap. Thank gods I'd selected a dress with a billowy skirt.

"Just getting one more kiss," Jason explained.

My laughter gave way to a blissful sigh as he pressed himself against me. "Okay. *One* more kiss. Then I have to go officiate a very important wedding."

"Mmm-hmm." Jason lazed his tongue along my bottom lip, eliciting a whimper. "That you do."

The pressure against my hips began to build, and as Jason's hands slipped lower to palm my butt, I melted into the mortal who, against all odds, the Norns had chosen to be mine.

I had no idea how our story would play out, or how this human was going to fit into our unbelievably crazy Asgardian existence. No doubt he, like his sister, possessed some to-be-discovered gift that would bring *ære* to both of our realms. But with the darkness of Ragnarok behind and a future of light ahead, there could be no doubt that the worlds were growing—and Asgard right along with them. All realms wishing to thrive would have no choice but to evolve. Despite all the uncertainties, I knew that no matter what the future threw at us, Jason and I would find our way through the challenges along our path. And we'd come out the other side all the stronger. How could it be any other way? After all, this smart, fearless, sexy mortal was my match.

And he was absolutely *perfekt* for me.

CHAPTER 17

"OH, ELSA. YOU LOOK...you're just..." A single tear spilled over the dam of Tyr's eyelid. It blazed a trail down his freshly shaven cheek as he gazed at his sister's classic white gown, simple tulle veil, and the delicate silver crown she wore atop her blond curls. In one hand she clutched pale pink peonies wrapped in strips of lace form Forse's mother's wedding gown—Nanna had gifted them to Elsa on her engagement. And on her wrist, she wore the strand of pearls her own mother and grandmother had worn on their wedding days.

Elsa was the quintessential blushing Asgardian bride. And she was *finally* going to marry Forse.

About bloody time.

"You're not so bad-looking yourself, big brother." Elsa reached up to wipe away Tyr's tear. She smiled fondly as he tugged at his bunad—our traditional formal wear that consisted of a multi-buttoned coat, embroidered vest, calf-length pants, and knee-high socks. The outfit had once belonged to the Fredriksens' dad, Ragnar—the original God of War. And I knew Tyr wore it out of love for his sister, as a means of bringing their father into this day. Tyr hated formal *everything* ten times more than the rest of us. But for Elsa…for Elsa, Tyr would move mountains.

And also, wear knee-high socks.

"You're sure you want to do this?" he quipped. "Say the word and I'll blur you straight out of here."

"I'm sure." Elsa patted Tyr's cheek. "There's nowhere I'd rather be. Thanks for walking me down the aisle."

A second tear snuck past the gates. Tyr hastily wiped it away. "Wish it could have been Dad."

"He's here, you know. And Mom. And Nanna and Balder, too. They wouldn't have missed this for the world." Elsa smiled up at her brother. The two of them shared a silent moment in the living room of their childhood home. Their connection was so palpable, their gratitude at marking this milestone in the place they'd grown up so strong, I quickly found myself blinking back my own waterworks.

To distract myself from the threatening tear-flood, I hastily looked around the room. Mia hovered before the L-shaped sofa, tinkering with the pink and green bouquets that rested atop the coffee table. She'd borrowed one of Elsa's bunads for the occasion, and the pale blue and silver fabric lent an extra sparkle to her eyes.

The fireplace stood to her right, lit with softly illuminated candles. Its mantle was swathed in equal parts ivory flowers and cream-colored votives, so that entire area appeared to be aglow. In front of her, the all-glass wall looked onto the tree-lined backyard. The Fredriksens' Asgardian property was situated at the edge of a forest, and Mia, Freya, Lornara, Inga, and I had spent the better part of the past two days layering the towering sequoias and white-barked birches with strings of fairy lights and orchids. Odin only knew how Lornara had managed to infuse the flowers with glitter, but they sparkled over the makeshift aisle we'd lined with sparkling petals, guiding the way to the wedding arch that Tyr, Gunnar, Jason, and Nils had built. Henrik's contribution to the arch had been limited, as he'd sequestered himself in the kitchen to create the mother of all wedding cakes.

It had been two of the most intense days of my life, but it had been (a) totally worth it, and (b) totally necessary. Elsa and Forse hadn't given us much notice when they'd announced their decision to eschew tradition and elope. Since letting them sneak away was *so* not an option for the rest of us, we'd convinced them to let us put together a small, intimate, *local* wedding. Which, of course, meant we went *all out* for the entirety of the forty-eight hours we had to prepare. Because that was what Asgardians did.

And also, because Mia made us.

Our self-appointed wedding coordinator looked up as the gentle sounds of the bridal march floated through the open window. The notes were barely a whisper as the small chamber orchestra Mia had somehow commandeered from Odin's palace began to play. She quickly gathered up the tabletop bouquets, handing one to me, and clutching one herself. "Okay. Everybody into position. I'll go first, then Brynn. Then Tyr will lead Elsa. Ready?"

I moved over to squeeze Elsa's hand. Then I angled my head at Mia and raised an eyebrow at Tyr. "You're going to have your hands full with that one. She's not going to stand for any of this 'small wedding' business when her day comes. You know that."

"I know." One corner of Tyr's mouth tugged up in a half smile.

"I heard that." Mia scurried behind Elsa, bending down to fluff out our friend's train. "And I don't recall being proposed to. Only asked if I wanted to join the 'immortal ranks of a benevolent fraternal organization.'"

"That's how you pitched joining Asgard?" Elsa elbowed her brother in the ribs. "Where's the romance? The virtue? The *ære*?"

"Do you know how many notebooks she would have filled with pros and cons if I'd said it *any other way*?"

"He's not wrong." Mia ducked her head. "I've already filled two."

Bless her sweet, analytical mind. Also, her note-booking.

"Well?" I waved my friends closer to the open glass doors. "What did you decide? And seriously, Tyr? No proposal?"

"She asked for one change at a time."

"I would have gone for the other thing first," I muttered. "Just saying."

"Me too," Elsa chimed in.

"Tyr knows my admirably malleable five-year plan does not currently include getting married before graduation. And as for the other thing, I decided..." Mia made one final adjustment to Elsa's train before taking her place in front of us.

"Yes?" I tapped my foot.

"I decided..." Mia bit down on her bottom lip. Behind me, Tyr's torso positively oozed tension.

I sucked in a breath as the realization hit me. Tyr didn't know. Mia hadn't given him her decision yet. Oh, gods, she wasn't going to break his heart the day of his sister's wedding, was she? This was so my fault—I totally triggered this whole conversation. *Stupid, Aksel. Abort. Abort!*

I blurted. "We can talk about this la—"

"I decided that there's no place I'd rather be than right here with all of you. Forever." Mia's ruby-glossed lips parted in a positively brilliant smile. The room filled to bursting with the relieved exhales of three breath-bated gods. *Whew! My BFF said yes to forever with us!*

"Right after I finish college," Mia tacked on.

Details. I subtly fist-pumped the air.

Tyr sprung to Mia's side and swept her into his arms in a *totally* swoon-worthy hug. "Thank gods. I couldn't imagine a life without you."

"Neither could I." Mia stood on her tiptoes to plant a soft kiss on his jaw.

Tyr's eyes clouded over as he pulled Mia closer. "Now, about that second question. Mia Ahlström, will you—"

Mia silenced him with another kiss. "I believe we have somewhere to be. We can't have Forse thinking Elsa stood him up."

Right. Elsa's wedding. This was happening. *So many good things!*

"Five-year plan be *fördömd,*" Tyr murmured. "We're talking about this later."

With one lingering kiss, Mia shooed Tyr back toward the bride. He shot his girlfriend a wink, and crooked his arm for Elsa to tuck hers through. "You ready, sis?"

Elsa beamed. "Absolutely."

It was true. Elsa couldn't have possibly been more ready to marry Forse. And we couldn't have been more ready to witness their union. At last.

The swell of violins urged Mia through the glass doors. Her borrowed bunad swished at her ankles as she made her way across the deck and onto the grass. I waited five counts before shooting Elsa a smile and positioning my bouquet in front of my hips. Sunlight kissed my face as I followed Mia's path along the petal-strewn aisle, and to the semi-circle our friends had formed around the altar. Gunnar and Inga stood on my left, joyful grins lighting their faces. They'd delayed their return to Midgard to celebrate the union we'd all been waiting for since high school. Nils stood beside them, alternating brilliant smiles between the groom and the bride. The pride in his eyes made it clear that he adored his brother and new sister-in-law beyond measure, and I was thrilled to see him genuinely happy for the first time since his parents' passing. Love truly was the balm to all wounds.

Henrik held the position beside the altar, and I had to force myself not to drool at the way his muscular chest and thick thighs filled out his bunad. We were *so* having alone time later. Or sooner. *Definitely sooner.*

Lornara and Jason stood to my right, the latter alternating curious glances at the fairy's shimmering wings with longing looks aimed at the goddess in front of the altar, resplendent in her rose-hued gown. The Goddess of Love stood ready to bind Justice and Inner Peace in eternal matrimony. And if the glow emanating from her pinked cheeks was any indication, she was nearly the happiest being in the forest.

But Freya's joy couldn't hold a candle to Forse's. Elsa's groom stood proudly at the end of the aisle, blinking back tears as he watched his best friend—now his bride—glide blissfully toward him. Elsa tugged at Tyr's arm as she practically skipped to her future, her radiant face matched in jubilance only by her groom's.

When she reached the wedding arch, Tyr unhooked her arm with a sentimental smile.

I could only imagine the silent conversation they now shared.

Freya drew her shoulders back, and opened her mouth to address the gathering. It took everything I had in me to hold my happy tears at bay. We were *finally* doing this!

"Who gives this goddess," Freya began, "Elsa Fredriksen, so that she may be joined in holiest of matrimonies with Forse Styrke?"

"Nobody gives her. She is her own spirit, gifted to us by Odin's blessing and her own volition, so that she may share her light with the realms." Tyr's jaw quivered. "But I, Tyr Fredriksen, sanction this union. As do our families, both those we were born into, and those we created of our own free will."

My eyes spilled over as a blubbering bleat escaped my lips. I was *so* not getting through this day with a shred of dignity intact.

Henrik stepped across the aisle to hand me a handkerchief. "I re-engineered it so it's hyper-absorbent. Should get you through the ceremony, at least."

Gods, I loved that god. "Thanks, babe."

Henrik stepped back with a wink.

Tyr placed his sister's hand into his best friend's palm. He took his place in the circle beside Mia, who slipped a comforting arm around his bicep. She nestled her cheek against his shoulder, and he lowered his chin atop her head. They really were the *perfekt* fit.

Henrik raised an eyebrow, and mouthed his question at me. *"Did she give him an answer?"*

As Freya began her blessing I snuck a peek at the bride and groom. They were completely immersed in one another. *Good.*

"She said yes," I mouthed at Henrik. *"After college."* Odin bless Mia and that ever-evolving five-year plan.

Henrik subtly pumped his fist, and I beamed in agreement. A yes was a yes. Our family was growing. Life was beautiful.

Elsa and Forse pledged to love one another for all eternity, and each of my friends stepped forward to make our own vow to love and support them, in good times and in bad. With each declaration, my heart filled with a level of joy even more overwhelming than the one I'd felt the day Freya gifted me with my own *perfekt* match. And as the newlyweds marched back down the aisle toward the table where my boyfriend's masterpiece of a cake awaited, I snuggled into Henrik's side with a blissed-out sigh.

He wrapped one arm around my waist, bending low so his breath tickled my ear. "What do you say, *sötnos*? Think we should do this someday?"

My breath stilled in my throat. Was that a hypothetical or a legit question?

"Um…"

Henrik's eyes gave away nothing. "Oh, look. Elsa's going to toss the bouquet."

Gods, he was the worst tease.

I forced my eyes from Henrik's unreadable face to

where Elsa now stood beside the monster of a wedding cake. It was four tiers of buttercream goodness—way too extravagant for our tiny gathering, and definitely Henrik's most opulent culinary confection to date. The top layer was a work of art, with layers upon layers of meticulously crafted sugar paste. I'd have to get closer to see what it was—Henrik hadn't let anyone in the kitchen once he began decorating.

"Unmarried ladies, get in here!" Elsa waved us forward, Forse beaming at her side. With a shrug, I followed Mia, Freya, and Lornara up the aisle. Only Inga hung back, holding Gunnar's hand and shooting me a wink.

"I'm going to throw it now!" Elsa turned around, pumping her bouquet over her shoulder. "One. Two. Three!"

But instead of Elsa's peonies launching through the air, the top layer of the cake rose to hover in their place. *What the Helheim?* It lifted from atop the tiered confection, soaring neatly through the air. My head whipped around to where Henrik stood with a tiny remote in his hands.

"You droned Elsa's wedding cake?" I squeaked.

Gunnar chuckled. "Wait for it."

The cake continued on its trajectory, stopping directly in front of me so it hovered at chest level. As I took in its spectacular design, my jaw dropped. The cake was decorated with miniature sugar-spun versions of every piece of tech that Henrik and I had ever developed. From the closer to the vacuum to Mia's aptly renamed space gun, it was an edible testimony to years of collaborations. And there, written in Henrik's tidy script, were the words I'd dreamed about from the minute I realized I was head over heels for the boy next door.

Marry me, Brynn?

The world became a tear-filled blur as I whirled around to find Henrik on one knee. He held the drone remote in one hand and a diamond ring in the other. He raised the ring, and spoke from his heart. "I love you, *sötnos*. You've been my partner in every epic adventure I've ever had. Will you do me the tremendous honor of collaborating with me on the greatest adventure of our lifetime?"

Henrik had barely handed the remote to his brother before I launched myself into his arms. Air *whooshed* from his lungs as I wrapped my legs around his waist, clinging to him as I kissed every inch of his face.

"I take it that's a yes." Henrik laughed. He lowered me to my feet and slipped the ring onto my finger.

"Yes. Yes! Oh, my gods, it is *so* a yes."

"Finally!" Freya tipped her face to the sky. "Thank gods for peace. And patience. And love."

"And Love." Jason clasped Freya's hand. She leaned over to kiss his cheek.

"Congratulations." Elsa beamed at me. "That was the *hardest* secret to keep!"

"Tell me about it." Forse grinned.

"You both knew?" I squeaked.

"We all did," Mia chimed in. She lifted my left hand

so my ring sparkled in the sunlight. "I'm so happy for you guys."

"Blessings to you both," Lornara said.

"About bloody time," Gunnar added.

"Congratulations," Nils chimed in.

"Remember, I've got an engagement present for you." Inga mimed tying something around her little finger. I barely contained my giggles. "Ull's going to be so sad he missed out on this."

"I haven't seen him in ages." I knew the God of Winter had been present during Fenrir's final battle, and that he'd had some bigtime life changes since the last time we'd seen each other, but we hadn't actually caught up in forever. A visit was long overdue. "Maybe we should come visit you guys after you get settled back on Midgard."

Inga smiled. "We'd love it."

Tyr bumped Henrik's fist, and treated me to a wry smile. "Congrats to you both. Just so you know, he's your problem, now."

"Hey," Henrik protested. But he grinned back at his friend and tucked me tightly into his side. "He's not wrong, *sötnos.* You sure you know what you've just agreed to?"

I stood on my tiptoes and planted a lingering kiss on my...my fiancé's lips. *Fiancé! Eep!* "I know *exactly* what I'm in for. And there is nobody I'd rather spend an eternity...how did you put it? Collaborating with."

Henrik's cheeks flushed. "I just meant that—"

"I know what you meant. I love you, Henrik Andersson."

"*Jeg elsker deg,* Brynn Aksel."

Tyr cleared his throat as Henrik lowered his head to mine. "So…is the rest of the cake a drone, too, or do we actually get to eat it?"

"Tyr!" Mia admonished. "Sorry about him."

Tyr shrugged. "We were all thinking it."

"I was kind of thinking it." Jason shot Freya a rueful grin.

"I was definitely thinking it," she admitted.

"Me too," I piped up. Henrik raised an eyebrow. "What? You make really good cake!"

"Who am I to interfere with mass love for my truly remarkable baking? Elsa? Forse?" Henrik gestured to the table. "Blade's to the right. Carve it up."

With a private smile, the bride and groom clasped hands, lowering the knife to slice their wedding cake. As they doled out pieces of confectionary awesome, I took in the sea of happy faces, letting myself absorb every ounce of the joy with which the cosmos had blessed us. There would be a lifetime for teasing. And laughing. And living. But for the rest of *that* day, we simply ate, danced, and celebrated the freedom each of us had to love and be loved. There truly was no greater gift in all the realms.

Elsa once said that families came in all shapes and sizes, each as unique as the multitude of beings that comprised them. As I celebrated with the beings I loved more than anyone in all the worlds, I knew beyond a doubt that I'd lucked into the family that was my absolute, hands down, unconditional *perfekt* match. Whatever adventure awaited us next, we'd step into it as we had everything else in our crazy, messy, amazingly beautiful lives.

With love.

Together.

ACKNOWLEDGMENTS

To my handsome husband and beautiful boys—I'm so grateful God gave me you. *Jeg elsker deg.* Forever.

To my friend-family—thank you for filling my life with love.

To Lauren (McKellar) Clarke, whose sharp eye and gentle wit always brings out the best in our Norse crews. To Mariana, whose infinite kindness keeps everyone grounded. To my beta readers, technical advisors, and production team, who keep me on track. And to Alison, whose kitchen table pep talk made sure Freya *finally* got her happily-ever-after. Bless you.

To the readers who embraced War's crew from day one—I'm humbled and thankful for all of your support through this series. Thank you for dreaming across the realms with me.

To everyone who strives to bring love and *ære* to our world—thank you for making Midgard a better place. Never, *ever*, give up.

And to MorMorMa. I love you to the moon and back. Always.

Before finding domestic bliss in suburbia, internationally bestselling author S.T. Bende lived in Manhattan Beach (became overly fond of Peet's Coffee) and Europe…where she became overly fond of McVitie's cookies. Her love of Scandinavian culture and a very patient Norwegian teacher inspired her YA Norse fantasy books. And her love of a galaxy far, far away inspired her to write children's books for Star Wars. She hopes her characters make you smile, and she dreams of skiing on Jotunheim and Hoth.

Learn more about the world of S.T. Bende at www.stbende.com.

Meet the Vikings (including Henrik's Midgardian relative) in VIKING ACADEMY!

When seventeen-year-old Saga Skånstad discovers an antique dagger, she's sucked into a world where Vikings rule the seas and dragons roam the skies, and the only thing more dangerous than the chief who takes her captive is the rival who steals her away.

Learn more at www.stbende.com.

And now, a sneak peek at VIKING ACADEMY . . .

ET OVER IT, SAGA. Cold water never hurt anybody.

Maybe not. But as I stood at the edge of Norway's North Sea, dead tired and shivering in the early morning breeze, I wanted nothing more than to climb back into bed and sleep off my late night. As we always did on the last evening of summer, my cousins and I had hung out by the campfire until well past midnight. And, in typical Skånstad family fashion, I was the only one of us who'd dragged her butt out of bed for a morning swim.

Routines died hard with me.

Just get it over with already. You're making it worse by putting it off.

Icy water lapped my goose-pimpled legs as I held my breath and waded into the frosty cove. With a nod at Steinar, the only other nutjob crazy enough to swim at six a.m. on a perfectly good Friday, I pulled my goggles over my eyes and dove in.

I was immediately filled with regret.

It took a solid fifty strokes before my skin acclimated to the cold, and another fifty before I could breathe without wincing. But eventually I fell into a rhythm, making my way toward the little island just offshore, one stroke at a time. By the time I reached my marker and doubled back, my breathing was steady, my body temperature was several degrees above miserable, and my thoughts had shifted from *good God, it's freaking cold!* to *I wish it wasn't my last day here.*

I cherished my summers at the cabin—the early morning swims, the afternoon lefse baking with my grandmother/guardian, Mormor, and the late-night deck-side Monopoly matches with my cousins. Our trips had been a family tradition long before my parents died, but this one was special—it was my last before starting college. My flight home departed in twenty-six hours, and by next week, I'd be rooming with my cousin Olivia, studying international relations and earning out my archery scholarship at Northern Minnesota University. For a school that was just a few hours' drive from our hometown, it felt like it was worlds away. Everything about my life was about to change.

As a girl who appreciated predictability, I had mixed feelings about this.

I turned my head to the side, drawing a breath as I neared the shore. Mormor always made a huge breakfast on the last day of our trips—Norsk waffles, bacon, fruit, eggs. And coffee.

God willing, she'd made *all* the coffee.

With a final stroke, I lifted my head and lowered my feet. My toes dug into coarse sand as I waded to shore. When the sand gave way to rocks, I stepped more cautiously . . . and yelped when I jammed my toe into an unexpected protrusion.

"*Skit*," I swore, reaching down to rub my foot. My fingers brushed against a smooth, sharp surface, and I stilled.

That was no rock.

Wrenching my goggles off my head, I bent down to study the crystal-clear water. Air whistled through my teeth as I sucked in a breath.

Holy. Freaking. Mother.

I bent lower and placed my hand around the thick, leather hilt of what appeared to be a dagger—a dirty, age-worn dagger, that was wedged firmly between two surprisingly immobile rocks. When my tugging proved futile, I wrapped my goggles around my wrist and used both hands to pry the blade free. It took a solid minute, during which my body temperature dropped back down to miserable, but with one fierce yank, I landed on my butt in the ocean, stubborn dagger firmly in hand.

All the coffee, Mormor. Please.

I scanned the area for additional weapons because apparently, ocean weapons were a thing now. Finding none, I made my way to the shore, rested the dagger across my palms, and took in every detail. It looked really old—the handle was well worn, and though the blade was badly tarnished, it bore a few dirty gems, and what looked like runic etchings. Runic etchings? How old was this thing? And moreover, who threw a dagger into the ocean? Kids swam here. I swam here! Sure, beach people were all kinds of laid-back, but seriously. *Who threw a dagger in the ocean?*

I glanced up toward my grandmother's cabin. The light was on in the little kitchen, which meant Mormor was likely puttering around, manifesting my coffee dreams into reality. She lived for history—she'd worked our family tree all the way back to one thousand A.D., and she had a basement filled with family heirlooms that went as far back as the 1800s. She would be all over this dagger . . . after she and my eco-warrior cousin ripped into the perp who'd littered in their precious ocean. Olivia and I were born three days apart, and she'd been my closest friend since the day I moved in with my grandmother—just two doors down from my cousin's house. We'd been looking forward to rooming together since we'd gotten our acceptance letters to NMU. Just one more week . . .

I transferred the dagger to one hand and held it overhead, hoping to catch Mormor's attention. Or Olivia's, if she'd dragged her butt out of bed yet. But the moment I raised the blade, my knuckles tightened around the hilt and my elbow locked at my ear. The cabin wavered in and out of focus as the beach spun in a dizzying circle that left my stomach churning.

What the hell was happening? And, more importantly, how did I make it stop?

My knees buckled and I took a step back. As the beach spun faster, I stepped again. And again. I was calf-deep in the sea when dizziness finally won. My knees hit the water, then crashed hard on the rocks in a moment of bone-searing agony. I started to double over, whether to throw up or pass out I hadn't determined, but my arm may as well have been soldered to my ear. Now the dagger was vibrating, its intense pulses making my arms shake to the point of exhaustion.

The dagger had to go.

I flexed my hand, willing my fingers to release the wretched relic, but its will was stronger than mine. Switching tactics, I used my free hand to pry my fingers from the hilt, and begged. *Please, please let me go.*

My request was denied.

I wrapped my hand around my wrist in a pointless effort to push the dagger back into the ocean. But its vibrations increased until my entire body trembled. The world gave one final, violent wrench before it shattered. The shoreline literally peeled away, pieces floating upward until I was left in a pure, white void.

Panic seized my throat, making breathing impossible. My lips parted and my chest heaved as I tried to forcibly inhale, but the air simply would not flow. I tried again, and again, but either I'd lost the ability to breathe, or there was no air in this void.

Was this how I was going to die?

Suddenly, the void was replaced by a familiar, *non-spinning* shore. The ocean stretched behind me, the rocky shoreline ahead, and the thick, deciduous forest that had stood behind my grandmother's cabin for at least a thousand years was exactly where it had always been.

But the trees looked different. Shorter.

Shorter? That was impossible. Trees didn't shrink. And daggers didn't have wills of their own. Clearly, I'd over-exerted myself swimming, and was now suffering from hallucinations.

Clearly.

But it wasn't just the trees that were different. The cabin was . . . well, it wasn't. My grandmother's redwood-decked beach house had been replaced with a cluster of huts built from thick logs and covered in grass roofs. The ornately carved front door of one opened to reveal a long-haired man wearing muddy, leather pants. He held his free hand to his eyes as he studied the ocean. The thick muscles of his chest tensed as he let out a fierce cry that sent chills racing up my spine.

"*Inntrengere!*"

I didn't know that word, but it didn't sound good.

"*Inntrengere,*" he shouted again, louder this time.

"Um, *hei!* It's just me! Saga Skånstad, Bertha's granddaughter!" I held my hands in front of my face, but with the dagger still in hand, I failed to neutralize the threat. "I live, uh, right there. Where you are, actually. Only not. So that makes us, kind of neighbors in a—"

"*Inntrengere!*" Leather Pants bellowed again. A dozen new leather-clad longhairs emerged from their huts, each more muscular than the last.

Why aren't they understanding me?

The second I thought it, a ripple passed from the dagger up my arm, rocking my body with a series of jolts. The mumbles of the leather-pantsers were suddenly intelligible; it was as if an invisible translator had slipped into my brain. I hoped it worked on both ends, and they'd be able to understand me, too. I needed them to stop staring at me like they wanted my blood, already.

"Intruders!" the men bellowed, a chorus of doom-sayers banging on their chests and reaching for their swords. These guys kept swords hanging by their front doors?

"I'm not an intruder!" I raised my hands again, then quickly lowered them. *Stupid dagger.* "I'm Saga, and I'm hallucinating, so if you could kindly—"

"Defend the shoreline against the boats!" The first leather-pants shouted.

Boats?

Maybe Steinar's grandsons were out in their kayak, or a fellow early riser was heading out to fish? I glanced over my shoulder, expecting to see one of our neighbors. My heart clenched at the sight of three Viking warships, red and white sails raised, streaming straight for the shore.

Oh. My. God.

"Defend!" The leather-clad chorus chimed. They raced from their huts, swords in hand as they made their way to a building at the edge of the settlement. They emerged bearing *even more weapons*—bows and arrows and shields and axes.

And they charged straight for me.

My options were slim. I could swim for the little island offshore—and risk being scooped up by what I seriously doubted were friendly Viking fisher-folk. Or I could run for the forest—and risk being axed by one of the leather-pantsers.

I opted for the latter.

But when I lifted my foot, my legs got tangled in something thick and heavy. I face-planted on the beach with a pain-wracked, "Oomph!" Spitting rocky sand from my mouth, I pushed myself up and tried to run again. This time, I discovered my movement was hindered by a dense, damp fabric.

What the hell am I wearing?

I didn't stop to freak out about whatever quick change had occurred while I'd been sizing up the leather-pantsers. I just hiked up the ridiculously dense skirts of whatever absurd dress I was stuck in, tucked the dagger into the fortuitously placed loop at my belt, and ran like my life depended on it.

In all likelihood, it probably did.

The leather-pantsers charged the shore, hitting the beach as I neared the northern edge of their village. When I reached the tree line, I hid myself behind a trunk and chanced a look back. My breaths came in shallow gasps as the Viking ships struck the ocean floor. Their riders leapt into the shallows, swords drawn, and shields raised. They ran for the beach, water flying as they neared their foes. Swords clashed, arrows flew, and the water ran thick with red. The two clans furiously massacred one another while I stood helpless, clinging to a birch tree.

I'd just escaped my first Viking raid.

And I hadn't even had my coffee yet.

If you like the gods of *THE ÆRE SAGA*, you'll love meeting S.T.'s *other* Norse crew. Get to know Henrik's brother Gunnar, along with Inga, Kristia and Ull, in the completed series,
THE ELSKER SAGA.

Kristia is stunned to discover that her boyfriend, Ull Myhr, isn't even human. He's a Norse god, forbidden to love and destined to die in a battle that will destroy Earth. But these two just might break all the rules — and save the world while they're at it…

Learn more at www.stbende.com.